Here With You

Marianne Rice

Published by Marianne Rice, 2019.

HERE WITH YOU

Editor: Silla Webb

Cover Artist: Just Write Creations

Publisher: Star Hill Press

Copyright © 2019 by Marianne Rice

DEDICATION

To my FILWNE girls, Bobbi and Brenda. You two are hilarious, sweet, adorable, and have the BEST Halloween costumes EVER. Hands down. Keep rocking your sister relationship.

Hugs and laughter.

M-

CHAPTER ONE

IT WAS ONLY HER SECOND trip carrying boxes into her new shop, and she'd already broken a nail. Grace set the box of lingerie on the temporary counter of her new boutique and held out her hand, inspecting her French manicure.

Thankfully the Sea Salt Spa was next door, and she could slip in for a manicure during her lunch break. Or would she even have one? Opening her business was the first step toward adulting. At thirty-one, her family, especially her older sister Alexis, was relieved to hear Grace would be settling down.

Finally.

And who would have thought she'd come back to Crystal Cove, Maine after living in Europe for more than ten years? After high school, she needed to get away or she'd get stuck working and living on her family's winery for the rest of her life.

While the vineyard work and wine making was right up her sister's alley, Grace wanted nothing to do with it. Sipping wine while wearing designer shoes and dating glamorous men was more her style.

And yet, here she was, schlepping boxes, shopping for paint instead of Louboutins, designing her new boutique instead of her next wardrobe.

She missed the constant hustle in Paris. The cheese and chocolate. The accents. She missed the elaborate fashion statements. The romantic men.

She plopped herself down on the burgundy chaise and sighed. Yes, the men were amazing. Her dating life had been a constant flurry of fancy candlelit dinners, concerts in the park, gala openings, charity events, and even quick getaways to Greece or Italy.

The men knew how to romance her with words of endearment. God love those European men. Even the scandalous ones excited her. Which was the main reason she'd come back home.

The front door opened, and the cool fall air swept across the room before Mia Parker called out, "Sitting down on the job already? Love what you've done with the place." The piles of boxes sat between plywood and cans of paint, and a splattered drop cloth took up most of the open space by the front window.

She hobbled across the obstacle course of boxes in her walking cast. Even a hit and run accident couldn't keep her still.

Mia was feisty, and Grace had liked her immediately. Grace hadn't known how the town would treat her, especially the girls she went to high school with, after being gone so long. Times had changed. Her sister, Alexis, had been the social introvert all her life and now had a sexy husband and kid, and a group of girlfriends Grace had squeezed her way into.

They'd all been accepting. Inviting her to book group, to girls' night out, and family cookouts. Lately they'd been at Ty and Lily's.

"Your brother said he'd be done sometime next week. I figured I'd get a head start bringing in some of my inventory." Ty owned the most reputable construction company in the area. That he was Mia's brother and dating one of their friends made him the go-to person for her renovation project.

Mia opened a box and pulled out an eggplant silk negligee`. "You think people around here are gonna wear this stuff? You remember how cold it gets in winter, don't you?"

"And if you paid any attention in science class, you'd remember body heat is more effective at warming than clothing." Grace got up and swiped the Charlotte Freya original from Mia.

Charlotte, along with four other designers Grace had connected with while in Europe, had recently graduated from fashion school and needed a place to showcase their work. Grace came up with the idea to open a boutique to help new artists share their styles, as well as bring a little culture to small town America. She figured most of her sales would be online, but maybe she could help put Crystal Cove on the map.

Thanks to her brother-in-law, Ben, she'd come up with a decent marketing plan. She hoped to get her life together enough to open start-up boutiques like this one in cities across the country within a year. Two tops. Not everyone could jet away to New York or Paris or Milan for the hottest fashions.

And she realized most people didn't have an extra five grand to drop on a pair of designer shoes. While her new merchandise would support the up-and-coming fashion industry, she would also have a gently used section of well-known brands.

While she'd been blackballed by many, she still had a few connections from working retail in Europe. She may not know how to sew a button on a blouse or how to sketch a ball gown, but she had a good eye.

"I paid attention to Mr. Brownstone. Remember him? He was the new health teacher my junior year in high school. You would have been a sophomore. Tall, dark, and sexy."

"Yeah. I remember him. I also remember Stacey Perelli spreading rumors that they'd had sex in the locker room."

"She was such a bitch. I still don't believe it. Too bad she ruined Mr. Brownstone's career. It was the first time I actually paid attention in class."

Mia and Grace may not have traveled in the same circles in high school, but at least they were never friends with Stacey. Grace stuck with the cheerleaders—which was odd cheering for her sister who played football up until her senior year in high school—and preferred dating boys from nearby towns.

The boys in her school stopped holding her interest by the end of seventh grade. Many thought her to be a snob, which she probably was. The boys didn't have high aspirations and were content working on their farms or working at their family's small business.

Not this girl. Grace had hightailed it out of this little town the second she crossed the stage and grabbed her high school diploma. Coming back and renting the former insurance company's office space next to Lily's spa was only temporary.

Maine wasn't exactly known for its fashion. The way she saw it, if she could make it in Maine, she could make it anywhere.

"So what brings you by? I'm guessing it's not to help me move. You look like an ogre hobbling around in that thing."

The geriatric man who had a stroke behind the wheel left Mia with a broken leg that had only recently begun to heal. She wasn't hobbling along on her crutches anymore, but Grace didn't think Mia should be doing anything as physical as lifting either.

"Ty says when he's done in here he's going to build an outside stairwell to the apartment above the spa. He said something about you moving in."

"Yeah. I've been at my parents' house now for almost a year. I need my space."

"I can't even imagine." Mia plopped down on the chaise Grace had recently vacated. Her small, rugged figure looked incongruous to the feminine couch.

"Now that Lily's moved into your brother's house, has he talked about popping the question?" With Lily's tall, modelesque figure and Ty's rugged looks, they'd make a stunning couple. Heck, they were gorgeous. And perfect. And Grace didn't like Lily any less because of it.

Was it only a few months ago when she'd learned of Lily's past? It seemed like so much more time had passed. Their random connection had brought Grace closer into their close-knit circle of friends, and she was forever grateful.

She admired Lily for coming out on top. From life as a bazillionaire to discovering her husband was a murderer, and then barely escaping her own father's attempt on her life,

Lily's new life—thanks to the FBI and the witness protection plan—suited her well.

While Grace had secretly envied Lily's heritage, small town living actually looked good on her. Funny how Grace was hoping for the role reversal—small town girl turns into millionaire.

"You're going to Ben's surprise party at Ty's tonight, right?"

"Since he's my brother-in-law there's no escaping it."

"Yeah, well, even if he wasn't you'd still go. It'll be fun. Now that Ty's come out of his shell and is all ga-ga over Lily, he's invited the entire town. My brother's been in desperate need of friends, so this is good."

It was nice to be included, to be part of a group. She'd had plenty of *friends* in Europe, but most of the men and women were more focused on their careers or making connections than building relationships. Business acquaintances she'd call them now, even though she'd thought of them as friends before.

"I told Lily I'd be over early to set up." Grace slipped her cell phone out of her Michael Kors bag. "Which is about now." Too bad she wouldn't have time to get her nails fixed before the party.

"Cool beans." Mia got up and met Grace at the front door. "The place is looking good. It's been Bergeron Insurance for as long as I can remember. I don't think I ever stepped foot in here until Ruth and Herb retired and moved south. I've caught a glimpse or two of their grandson. Ryan is it? From the back, he seems like a hottie."

"Yes." Grace would keep his identity a secret as long as Lily needed her to. The FBI agent was critical in keeping Lily safe from her imprisoned ex-husband and his criminal connections. Agent Thorne didn't want the town knowing about him, and Grace would follow his wishes. The fewer people who knew who he was the better.

People in town knew of the Bergeron's grandson who used to visit them when he was younger but other than that, Ryan Thorne was just a name. When he sat Grace down and interrogated her after she'd admitted to inadvertently exposing Lily's identity, she'd promised to keep his identity and presence in town between them.

He'd set up Lily in what was now the Sea Salt Spa and gave her a new identity. Who knew she'd find her true love and happily ever after. Grace would find hers one day as well.

Just not here.

"Do you know if your new landlord is coming to the party?" Mia wiggled her brows and quickly turned her grin into a frown when Grace didn't return the smile. "Don't tell me... you have your eyes on your landlord. I won't take him from you if that's what you're worried about."

"Ag—Ryan? No. I'm not interested in him. It's just business between us."

"You sure?"

"Totally."

"Okay. Well, I should probably tell you who *will* be at the party."

There was only one person in Crystal Cove she didn't want to run into. One person she'd managed to avoid for years, even living across the road from him.

"I'm going to celebrate Ben's birthday. I don't care who else shows up," she lied.

"Then it shouldn't bother you that Carter and Brady Marshall will be there."

"Good for them. Since they're neighbors with Ben, I figured as much." No. She hadn't. Instead, she'd busied herself with the opening of her new shop and pretended the boy she'd been caught naked with in the middle of a row of blueberry bushes on prom night and his older, brooding brother didn't exist.

The most embarrassing night of her life had been caught on camera and spread all over the Internet by bitchy Stacey. It shouldn't still bother her over a decade later, but the disapproving looks she'd gotten from Brady Marshall for months after were embarrassing, especially since their families were so close.

Carter, she didn't care as much about. He had just as much a flighty reputation as Grace, but since he was a guy it didn't seem to matter as much.

Hypocrites. Everyone was a hypocrite. Another reason she fled from Europe so quickly. She just didn't expect the same here in Maine.

• • • •

BRADY HAD NINE HUNDRED things to do, which included him getting up at five in the morning, but he'd put in an appearance at Ben Martelli's birthday party and pay the price in the morning. The man had been a good neighbor. A friend, Brady supposed.

Running a farm in Maine was a twenty-four seven job. With blueberry season over and apples in full swing, Brady didn't have much time to spare. The last of the apple pickers had cashed out, and Brady drove his side-by-side through the orchard, cleaning up trash and making sure there weren't any apple picks left in the rows.

His younger brother, Carter, took the golf cart to the back end of the field, loading it with the bushels of drops their weekend workers had filled throughout the day. Normally, Brady would spend his Saturday night pressing cider, but duty called. Being neighborly was just as important as cider pressing. Maybe.

Making nice with the locals was good for business. Not that Brady had any problems with Ben. He was a good guy. He even convinced Alexis and her winery to form a partnership with Marshall Farm. He wasn't much of a wine drinker, but the blueberry wines and raspberry wines had sold well, bringing him more business and a few extra bucks on the side.

His father would've been proud. He'd been close with the Le Blancs and respected their winery, Coastal Vines. Before he died, he made Brady promise to finish his senior year at high school and to make a career doing what he loved. At seventeen, Brady didn't have a clue what that would be but knew it would be something involved with the land.

School didn't come easy for him, but farming did. He loved driving the tractor in between the apple trees and along the blueberry trails. Planting, growing, pruning, and seeing the fruits of his labor had been more satisfying than anything else.

Even the soft curves of a woman. He didn't have much time for dating or being picky. He'd been on a handful of dates with farm girls from neighboring towns, but other than his on again off again dates with Julie Tufts from Lincolnville, he didn't have much of a social life.

If he were to settle down—which he hoped to someday—it would be with a woman who enjoyed farming and appreciated the land as much as he did. His mother had her eye set on Alexis Le Blanc for the longest time. She hadn't been subtle with Alexis or her mother in her desire for them to get married, pump out a dozen babies, and live happily ever after.

He and Alexis had humored his mother a few times by going out to Fish on the Wharf and having Billie fry them up some haddock and sea scallops. They enjoyed a few laughs and a bottle of wine, but there was no spark. They'd both been too in love with their land to want to waste any time on a relationship.

He respected Alexis and really liked her husband, Ben. Which was why Brady found himself parking his side-by-side in the barn.

The low rumble of the golf cart told him Carter was done as well.

Carter hopped out of the cart and began stacking the bushels of apples against the barn wall. "Got some nice looking drops. It's ridiculous how many perfectly good apples people toss to the ground. They should realize what they buy in the grocery store eleven months of the year isn't better than these drops." He tossed an apple in the air, then took a bite out of it the second it reached his hand. "Nothing beats our Cortlands."

"No way, man. Macs are the best." Brady picked through the bushels for a Macintosh and took a bite of his apple. It was his fourth of the day and he'd never tire of the crisp, sweet juice from the fruit.

"Want to ride out to Ty's together?" Carter asked.

"I'm not planning on staying long."

"Party pooper."

"Some people have to work in the morning." Carter did too, but he was the type to roll out of bed and straight on to the field while Brady preferred enjoying his cup of coffee and big breakfast while watching the news online, scouting the weather. He could go a solid seven hours before coming in to eat while Carter tended to stop every few hours for a snack. The kid was always eating.

Three square meals, that's all Brady needed. He was disciplined and scheduled. Since he couldn't schedule the weather and had limited control on the growth of their fruit, the one thing he could control he did so with precision.

"You haven't been out in a while. Think folks will recognize you?"

"Why? Who all is going? I thought it was just Ben and Alexis' friends."

"Ben's done a lot for the community. Sounds like it's going to be a rager. The Petersons brought over their spit for a pig roast. Guess Ben's helped them get a lot of business too. Bacon, it's all the rage."

The Petersons' pig farm had done well with more people buying fresh instead of the grocery store specials. Anyone who's had fresh sausage, bacon, or pork chops from a farm-raised pig would never buy from a grocery store again.

According to Bill Peterson, his pig sales had doubled since Ben came to town. Brady could say the same about the blueberry farm. Not that his family had doubled its income, but they were in the black for the first time in nearly five years.

"Just don't do anything dumb. I don't feel like bailing out your ass tonight." Brady followed his brother outside and locked up the barn behind them.

Carter tossed his apple core in the compost pile. "Kinda hard to stir up trouble in our sleepy little town, big bro. But don't you worry your pretty little face. I'll be home before my Harley turns into a pumpkin."

"Whatever." Brady held the door to the kitchen open for his brother. "Tomorrow's going to be a long day." Apple season was nearing its end, making way for pumpkins and snow. Not necessarily in that order.

Fishing season never ended, but the farmers had a short window, needing to get the biggest bang for their buck. Once his bushes and trees were prepped for winter and snow fell, Brady would put the plow on the truck and spend his winters plowing the roads of Crystal Cove. That too was a twenty-four hour job. Especially the past few winters.

"Something smells good." Brady picked up the lid to the crockpot and was rewarded with a smack to the back of his hand.

"How many times have I told you to never lift a lid without knowing what's inside."

He winked before kissing his mother's cheek. "Sorry, Ma."

"It's a good thing it's done cooking. Don't forget to bring the pulled pork with you to Ben's party."

"Aw. Ain't you going to be adorable skipping down Ty's driveway with a crockpot in hand?" Carter snickered from the other side of the counter where he guzzled down a bottle of water.

"And I have a tray of brownies for you to bring," their mother added.

Carter's laughter came to a screeching halt, his hand frozen in midair.

"Want to borrow Mom's apron?" Brady snagged the bottle from his brother's hand and finished it off. "I'm taking the first shower. I can't guarantee there'll be any hot water left."

Their farmhouse hadn't been updated since his father inherited it from his father some forty years ago. The floor in the kitchen slanted toward the back door. The sink in the downstairs powder room had rust stains around the drain, and the upstairs toilet ran. Ben swore he fixed the damn thing at least once a month.

The upstairs wasn't much better. The ceilings in the hundred-fifty year old farmhouse were low. So low Brady had to duck when entering his bedroom and the bathroom.

He stripped down in the small bath, ignoring the faded floral wallpaper—which he and his brother had complained about since they were boys—and turned on the water, not bothering to wait for it to heat before stepping in.

He had to crouch to rinse his hair. Since the faucet only reached his neck, he didn't spend much time in the bathroom. One of these days, when he wasn't working seven days a week, and his mother would allow him to spend money on her and the house, he was going to remodel the place.

Maybe he'd talk to Ty about it tonight. While Brady was handy with a tractor and shovel, anything that needed fixing often got put on to Carter, who wasn't much handier than Brady.

Their mother never complained. She was the type of woman who would have loved growing up in the eighteen hundreds. Farm life was good for her, which was why she was never leaving Marshall Farm.

That and because it was the only piece of their father she had left. Brady admired the love his parents had for each other. He was too young to appreciate it when his father was still alive, but looking back at the photos and listening to the stories his mother shared, he wished someday he'd find a sweet farm girl who loved the land as much as his mother had.

Turning off the water, he made quick work toweling off and running a razor through his thick layer of shaving cream. Shaving was another one of those time-sucks he didn't care for. In the winter he let his facial hair grow out a bit. Not too long. He wasn't the bearded type, but typically only shaved a few times a month. The little extra layer of hair was just enough protection to keep the biting wind off his skin.

Opening the bathroom door, he called down to his brother to let him know he was done, jiggled the toilet handle one more time, and padded to his bedroom down the hall. The same bedroom he'd had for the past thirty-six years.

When he'd turned thirty he'd stripped the blue striped wallpaper and slapped on a coat of white paint. Other than that, nothing much had changed. He opened the top drawer to his heavy oak dresser and pulled out a pair of boxer briefs, then opened the second drawer for a clean shirt.

He wasn't one for name brands or fancy sayings on his clothes. Simple and functional was all he required. He chose a plain black t-shirt and opened the next drawer that housed his jeans. Seven pair of work jeans and one pair of not-work jeans. He saved those for the few times he went out, which wasn't often.

Carter liked to remind him on a weekly basis how much of a hermit he'd become. There was no major reason. Brady simply liked to work. He enjoyed being outside. Sure, he liked socializing, that was a big part of running a farm.

In the early summer, they'd have people come from all over to pick strawberries. Toward the end of July and straight through to Labor day the blueberry pickers would come. That was definitely his favorite season of all.

His mother would run the store, frying up blueberry donuts, popping the kettle corn, and weighing the hundreds and hundreds of pounds of blueberries people picked every day.

Brady and Carter had built a trellis a few years back and brought in picnic tables for families to enjoy their snacks. Ben had talked them into offering weekend entertainment. Local musicians to play country music on a guitar. This year they featured a family day, hiring a children's musician, a balloon artist, and offered face painting.

Students from the high school volunteered to help out with the kids. It was the farm's most successful weekend to date.

This year for apple picking season he did more of the same, but with hay mazes, hayrides, and pumpkin picking. His mother had been busy in the kitchen making pumpkin whoopee pies and apple pies to sell, while Carter ran the cider press and answered questions about which types of apples to pick for different eating and recipes.

Brady liked driving the tractor that pulled the hayride. It was a short, slow ride, but the kids loved it. He enjoyed interacting with the families and answering questions about farming as well.

This was the life. It was so much better than being cooped up in an office all day or sitting behind a computer screen. This was why he'd connected with Ben and Alexis so well. They valued the land and all it had to offer.

Ty was a good guy as well. They went to the same high school back in the day. Ty was a hotshot soccer player while Brady skipped the sports, needing to rush home after school to work on the farm.

They were friendly as most townsfolk were, but it would be the first time Brady had been to his house. The only other social events he'd attended were the town dances and events at Coastal Vines, which were still fairly new.

Marshall Farm and Coastal Vines had formed a new partnership since Ben moved to town and married Alexis. It was great for cross-promotion. Not normally much of a wine drinker, he appreciated it more now after having a tour of the vineyards and tasting his own fruit in some of the wine blends.

Which was why Brady found himself tugging on his "going out" jeans. It would mean a late night and an earlier morning, but he owed it to Ben for doing so much for their community.

"'Bout damn time." Carter stuck his head in Brady's room. "Wow. Really spiffing it up tonight. Those your 'I need to get laid' jeans?"

"You talk about it so much, I'm beginning to think your sex life is duller than mine. Trying to live vicariously through me, little bro?"

"God help me if I ever go through a dry spell as long as you. When was your last time? Prom night with Anna Levers? She was a hottie back in the day. I hear she's down in Florida dancing around poles and shit."

Yeah, Brady had heard the same thing. Too bad. He hadn't seen that coming. Anna was a nice girl in high school. Top of her class. Went to school down in Tennessee to study agriculture and never came back. Never earned her degree either.

"Sounds like the kind of establishment you like to visit."

"If only we had something like that around here. I'd be there every night." Carter liked to make himself sound more irresponsible than he really was. He worked hard and played harder. Brady just stuck with working.

"Yeah, well, we've got the fall festival in a few weeks. Once the crops are bunkered down for the winter you can visit all the strip clubs you want."

Brady knew even if there were some in the area Carter wouldn't have time to go. While he took up plowing in the winter, Carter spent his time behind his laptop. He'd taken some graphic design courses and had a real knack for it. Every now and then he'd get a job that would take him off the field, but he'd been pretty good about scheduling them around their busy season.

"Like I'd forget. That's the best time to pick up women." Carter saluted him and left. A moment later Brady heard the groaning of the pipes in the wall.

As if he'd be picking up women. Most of the women who came by were with their families or boyfriends. Still, Carter was always on the prowl. Brady had begun to think about his future a little more lately. Especially since Ben and Alexis married.

Not that he'd ever had his eye set on Alexis, she'd been a friend only—a friend his mother had always hoped would turn into something more—but she was the last person on earth he'd ever expect to settle down. Maybe he should work on getting out more. Or at least talk to people about something other than agriculture.

Yeah. Not likely.

Brady would make an appearance, chat a little with some of the other business owners he hadn't seen in a while, then come back home and send some emails. Snow would be on the ground before anyone was ready, and he needed to check in with his customers to make sure they still wanted him to plow.

And if time, he'd watch some YouTube videos on how to fix a dang toilet.

CHAPTER TWO

THIS WAS NICE, BEING part of something. Having friends. Lily had outdone herself decorating the back of Ty's yard. Granted, now that Lily had moved in with Ty it was her yard as well.

Twinkling lights wrapped around the railing of the deck and outlined the shed over by the fire pit. Three long tables covered in red and blue plastic tablecloths and more food than the entire town could eat made the gathering seem like it was for a fourth of July celebration instead of a thirty-fifth birthday party.

The host and hostess were adorable with their matching smiles. There were those who were personally invited, but Grace heard talk from many others who planned on showing up out of gratitude of Ben's business savvy, and because of the free food.

Not one to cook, Grace brought a veggie tray and placed it on the table.

"Thanks so much, Grace. I'm glad you're here." Lily hugged her. These hugs. They were kind of nice as well. The hugs she'd given and received from her *friends* while traveling and working in Europe were superficial. Quick hugs and air kisses so not to rumple any clothing or smudge makeup.

The hug Lily gave her was tight and warm as if she really was glad to see Grace.

"Everything looks great." She hitched a thumb toward the group of men playing beer pong. "And I see my brother-

in-law is ignoring the big three and five balloon and pretending he's twenty-two."

"Ty's no better." A loud cheer and some friendly swearing erupted from behind. "And it sounds like they're having
a blast. It's nice to see the guys being... guys."

Grace understood. While she'd only been back in town
for less than a year, she knew about Ty. How private and reserved he was before he fell in love with Lily. Heck, Lily was
the same way. Granted, now Grace and a few others knew
why.

Ben, on the other hand, had a big personality. It was easy
to see how he drew Alexis out of her shell.

"Thanks for coming," her sister said, sidling up next to
her.

"Of course I'd come."

"Backyard barbecues aren't exactly your thing." Alexis
probably didn't mean to sound snotty, that wasn't her way.
It was fact. Yeah, these ho-down things weren't something
Grace looked forward to. Ever.

The few nights out Mia had organized in Rockland were
more Grace's style. Those were fun nights.

"This is nice."

"You're not exactly dressed for the occasion," Alexis
pointed out, as she liked to do.

"I think you look fabulous," Lily interjected, seeming to
pick up on the hostility in the air.

Grace looked down at her coral peep-toe wedges. She'd
known better than to wear heels unless she wanted to aggra-
vate the lawn. Or aerate. Whatever it was called. She worked

damn hard to take the country girl out of her. City style was more her pace.

"White pants? A thin blouse. Really?" In her sweatshirt and jeans, Alexis fit in better with the crowd than Grace did.

"They're capris. I have a sweater in the car figuring it would cool down once the sun set."

"You're staying that long? Sorry." Alexis punched her knuckles into her palm. "I didn't mean to sound so—"

"Bitchy?"

"Yeah. I know you're trying. I appreciate that especially since this isn't your scene. I'm sure it means a lot to Ben that you're here. For some reason, he really likes you." Her words weren't as sharp this time.

"And for some reason he really likes you too."

"He *loves* me." Alexis beamed. Really beamed. Grace had never seen her like this before. Her sister was a happy kid in high school playing sports, hanging with the guys. She never had girlfriends, just lots of guy friends. Where Grace had a different boyfriend every week and a variety of *girlfriends* at her beck and call. Had being the operative word.

Funny how irony worked. Now, Grace found herself with no friends of her own and borrowing her sister's. And boyfriends? Marcus Dubois, the ass wipe who spent more time in front of the mirror than Grace?

He'd used Grace to get in with her connections, then dumped her for George. Apparently, she didn't have the right parts to keep him entertained for more than a few months. And then there was Robert Powers.

Her cheek warmed with embarrassment and shame. No, better not to think about that mistake.

"Ladies! Care to take on the losers?" Ben strolled over and snaked his arm around Alexis' shoulders. "They're having a pity party over there because we keep kicking their asses. Seems like they could use some more practice."

Grace hadn't paid attention to his opponents but didn't think they'd have much of a challenge playing her. Beer pong wasn't something she worked on in France.

"Since I'm on responsible parent duty tonight, I'm out. Lily and Grace, you should play."

"Now this I'd like to see." Ty gently gripped their shoulders and turned them around, steering them toward the beer pong table.

"I've never played before. Have you?" Lily asked.

"Not once."

"It's easy." Ty dropped his hands and picked up a ping pong ball from the grass. "You toss the ball in your opponents' cups. Like this." He flicked his wrist and the ball went into the first cup.

"And then what?" Grace counted the ten red cups at the vacant side of the table.

"Then they take the cup away. You win when all their cups are gone."

"What happens if we lose?"

Ty chuckled. "You look like those two."

Grace followed the direction of his laughter and almost threw up.

Brady and Carter Marshall emerged from the house. Carter laughing—as always—and Brady wearing an annoyed look on his face.

"They're the Marshall brothers, right? I know you introduced me to them when they got here, but there are so many new faces and names," Lily said.

"Yeah. Their farm is across from Coastal Vines. I'll take you apple picking tomorrow." Ty rubbed his hand down Lily's back, and she leaned into him. They were sweet, those two.

"You must know them if they live across from your family's vineyard."

"Yup. Grew up with Carter. Brady's a few years older than me."

The last time she'd seen the older, brooding brother she'd been stark naked in the middle of his blueberry bushes. Mortified wasn't strong enough of a word to describe that encounter.

Brady had looked her up and down with disgust instead of interest, then he'd grabbed the collar of his shirt behind his neck and tugged it over his head. He'd tossed her his shirt with a gruff, "Hell. Put this on." After she was semi-dressed he'd asked her if she was okay or if she needed a lift. She'd told him she was fine and ran all the way home. The half-mile had seemed like ten, but she'd made it home and up to her room before her parents had come up to wake her for the day.

Grace had been proud of her body back in high school. Most of the guys had drooled over her, and she'd loved showing off her flat stomach and long legs. The shorter the shorts and tighter the top the better.

She'd filled out some since high school. While she wasn't anywhere close to being overweight, she didn't have the muscle definition as in her youth. Too many nights drinking wine and too many days dining on coffee and croissants, and not enough time taking care of her body.

Although, she felt better about her self-image in Maine than she did in Paris. There, in the fashion industry, if you weren't five-ten and less than one hundred ten pounds you were overweight.

She was three inches too short and twenty-five pounds heavier than her colleagues, which was why working behind the counter instead of in front of it had worked out so well for her.

The *clunk* of a ping pong ball in the red cup at her end of the table brought her back to her current situation. Facing the Marshall brothers.

"Hey, Gracie. Haven't seen you since you've been back. You look good." This from Carter, the flirt. The man who thought anyone with boobs looked good.

"Thanks, Carter. Nice to see you again. Brady. You too."

"Yeah. Welcome home." His eyes didn't reach hers. He was older than her, and they never interacted much growing up. Other than the time he tossed her his shirt. If the situation had been different, and she hadn't been buck ass naked in the grass, she would have appreciated his bare chest.

Lean and sculpted from hard, physical labor.

Ben came sidling up to the long table, a beer in one hand, Alexis in the other. "You ladies go easy on these boys. Ty and I have skunked them two games in a row."

"I highly doubt Grace has ever played a game of beer pong. Lily either, for that matter." Alexis sipped her water with a smirk. "This should be fun."

"I'm glad I'm not playing against you, Alexis. You were prime back in the day." Carter chucked a ball at Alexis' water bottle.

Of course she was. Alexis was the athletic one who hung out with all the guys while Grace was only wanted for her body.

"I'll play one more and then I need to get going." Brady moved the cups in front of him until they formed a perfect pyramid.

"Don't be such an old fart. It's not even eight yet." Carter sipped from his bottle before setting it in the grass. "Besides, we're not even playing the right way. It's not like we're going to get shitfaced."

"What's the right way?" Lily had to ask.

"Normally." Ty placed a ball in Lily's hand. "Each cup has a beer in it. When the opponent gets a ball in the cup you have to chug it."

"But since Ben's married and old—"

"Easy," Alexis warned with a smile.

"Marriage looks good on you, Alex. I never thought I'd see the day." Carter pointed at Ben. "Back to the birthday boy. We're keeping things on the down low so the party doesn't get out of control. Not like the good ol' days, right, Grace?"

Her cheeks weren't used to warming in embarrassment. Grace loved being the center of attention at parties, only now the attention wasn't what she wanted.

"Are we going to stand around and talk all night or are we going to play?" She took the ball from Lily's hand and aimed at the cups across from her. The ball went wide and bounced off the side of the plywood table. Brady caught it and tossed it back, sinking it in the cup in front of Lily.

"Drink." Carter tipped his bottle at the girls.

"Oh. I don't have a drink yet."

"I'm sorry, Grace. I should be a better hostess. There's sangria in the pitchers on the table." Lily held up her full plastic cup. "It's one of the few recipes I can actually follow. Or there's wine in the buckets."

"I have some beers in the cooler if you want one of those. You used to shotgun a beer faster than any guy in school."

Thanks, Carter. He seemed to be stuck on bringing up Grace's high school years. The fewer reminders she had of them the better.

"I'm all set, thank you."

"Ty, can you get her a sangria?"

He took off and was back with a plastic cup before Grace had time to decline.

"We'll go easy on you ladies. No chugging required, but a good healthy swig every time we sink a ball."

"Well, since it's floating..." Grace pointed at the white ball bobbing in the cup full of water.

"Always was a wise ass." Carter smirked.

"And what do you and... Brady do when we *sink* a ball?" Grace didn't know why his name tingled on her lips."

"I'll pay up and drink half a beer each time. Workaholic over here is girly-sipping his beer."

"Someone's got to be the responsible one in the family."

Brady had the reputation of being a hard worker. Grace remembered when his father died. The whole town came out for the funeral and pitched in at the farm during blueberry season. Grace was only in sixth grade but remembered having fun eating more berries than she picked and playing manhunt in the bushes with her friends.

Even back then the oldest Marshall brother scowled at her for being an immature frolicker. He'd grown up and out over the years. Always tall, his frame didn't appear so gangly like it had before she took off for Italy. His shoulders were wide, his arms strong from hours and hours on the farm.

If he ever smiled, he'd pass as attractive. He wasn't heart-stopping but wasn't ugly either. Not that Grace had ever given him much thought other than to hide her face from him and his judgment.

While he never said more than five or six words to her over the years, she could read his dislike for her in his stoic face. Most people smiled around her. Not Mr. Grumpy. Not wanting him to ruin her evening, she pushed thoughts from the past aside and sipped her sangria.

Fresh berries and sweet red wine coated her tongue. "This is delicious."

"Thanks. One thing I can whip up in the kitchen is a good drink. Let's see if I'm any better at beer pong than you." Lily tossed the ball and missed.

They both took a drink.

It didn't take long for the Marshall boys to get them down to two cups, and Grace and Lily had still to make a shot.

"This time. I can feel it." The competitiveness she must have recently inherited from Alexis drummed through her veins. "I'm not going down without a fight."

Grace focused in on the closest of the red cups, took a breath, and let the ball fly through the air. It bounced off the rim of one cup, then another before finally splashing in one of the cups in front of Brady.

"I did it!" She jumped up and down and clapped her hands. "You guys are going down now." She gave Lily a high five and wiggled her hips, and stared at Brady's hand that held the ball.

When he went to toss it she waved her hands in hopes of distraction, which worked like a charm.

"What the hell was that?" The ball missed the cup by a good six inches.

"Don't be a sore loser now."

"Sore loser? You guys have made one shot to our eight." Brady crossed his arms, and his shirt tugged tight over a chest Grace hadn't realized was so chiseled.

"Yeah. Well. It's our first time. You've had more practice." Lily tossed the ball in return and squealed when it landed in a cup. "We're getting the hang of this, Grace. Drink up, boys."

Two shots later they lost the game and were feeling pretty buzzed.

"I declare a rematch before the end of the night," Grace said with liquid confidence.

"Ben and Ty are back at it now. How about horseshoes? You ladies up for a game?" Carter asked.

"I'm all set but you can play, Grace."

Her confidence wasn't so high without Lily by her side. Spotting Hope across the lawn they thanked Carter and went to visit with their newlywed friend.

"Having fun?" Hope had a smile that hadn't left her face since Cameron came into town last winter. Another perfectly adorable couple that made Grace feel like she was missing out on something.

At least she still had Mia and Jenna as her single friends. With Mia's quirky personality and love for going out, Grace couldn't see her settling down anytime soon. And Jenna was so reserved, so aloof when it came to discussing men. She didn't mind hearing about other people's stories but kept her past love life a secret.

The same could be said for Grace. Although she did tell the girls one night at book club about Marcus, and her random bad dates, and a handful of fun one-nighters.

Robert, however, she wouldn't be mentioning. If she never saw him again it would be too soon.

"Lily and I got our butts handed to us in beer pong."

"I can't believe you got her to actually play that game." Hope laughed.

She tried not to be offended. She knew Hope didn't mean it as an insult. Grace worked hard to get away from this small town and her party animal reputation. Sure, she was a partygoer in Europe, but that sounded much more classy than chugging beers and doing keg stands at parties in the woods.

Maybe coming back to Maine was a mistake. But she had nowhere else to go and needed to get out of France as quickly as possible. Thankfully news of her scandal hadn't made its way to the dead-end town of Crystal Cove. The off the grid town was the perfect place for her to escape while still moving forward with her career in fashion.

"It was fun. I'm more in shock that Brady Marshall is here. He must have changed a lot while I was away. Rumor has it he never left his land."

"You knew him back in the day, I only know of him now. Mostly it's hair salon gossip." Lily refilled their sangrias and smiled out across the lawn at the dozens of people. "I suppose small towns run on gossip? It's still pretty new to me. You grew up here though. The old biddies who come in to get their hair set every ten days absolutely adore Brady. They say he's Daddy material. I can't tell you how many have argued that their granddaughter is the better woman for him."

"I can only imagine." And she could. He still lived at home with his mother and worked like a horse seven days a week. Grace had heard her mother swoon over him too many times during her teen years and even now a dozen years later.

A family guy with solid family values. Loyal. Honest. Hardworking. Geesh. If he was so perfect, why was he still single and living at home?

Yeah. She was single and living in her childhood bedroom as well, but she'd also spent a third of her life far, far away finding her independence while Brady had yet to cut the umbilical cord. Or maybe that was his mom's job.

Grace didn't know too much about Mrs. Marshall other than she always wore jeans and flannel and an oversized sunhat. She was friends with Grace's parents and they went out occasionally when their farms didn't need tending, which happened almost never.

Although her parents were going out more now that Ben was around to help run the winery. Good for them. They were getting older and shouldn't be doing hard physical labor every day.

"You and Carter must have gone to school together."

"Yup." She sipped her sangria and debated how much to tell Lily. If she wanted to have girlfriends, she'd need to learn to open up. But talking about the old days when she was a Crystal Cove rebel wasn't the impression she wanted to give Lily.

"Alexis says you were quite the wild child."

And once again Grace's temper flared. "Not everyone is as perfect as Alexis. Or Hope. Or hell, even you. Some of us have skeletons in their closet they don't want to be revealed. You of all people should know that."

Grace gasped and sucked in her lips, ashamed at what just came out of her mouth. Afraid to look at Lily, she closed her eyes and swallowed hard.

"That was a super bitchy thing to say. I'm sorry."

When she peeked through her lashes she was surprised Lily was still there with a full cup of sangria. If the roles were reversed, Grace would have tossed it in her face.

"I'm sorry for being insensitive. There's an obvious tension between you and Alexis. And to be honest, I have no idea what it's all about. I'm not one to pry. As you noted and know so well, I have skeletons." Lily's voice was kind and understanding. "I'll respect your privacy, but if you ever want to talk, I'm here. I don't know the old you and the old Alexis. I'm totally unbiased and nonjudgmental. And I want to be your friend. I'm here if you need an ear. Or a shoulder."

Grace watched Lily's retreating back and chugged the rest of her drink.

"There's the Gracie we know and love."

She spun around and tossed her empty cup at Carter's chest. "Go to hell. And while you're there, grow up."

CHAPTER THREE

BRADY WATCHED CARTER chuckle as Grace stormed away. He'd said something to piss her off something fierce, and he didn't appear to give a rat's ass about hurting her feelings.

Not that he cared about her feelings either. Grace Le Blanc meant nothing to him. She was a flighty girl back in high school with a loose reputation. Hell, the last time he'd seen her she was buck ass naked running through his blueberry bushes.

He hadn't asked what the hell she was doing or who she was doing it with. All he wanted was to get her off his land. It was bad enough every time he walked down the path between the Duke and Blue Crops he could picture her tall, lithe, naked body. She'd had curves a young girl shouldn't have had at that age.

She may have been eighteen at the time, but to his twenty-three-year-old self, she was one hundred percent off limits. Not that he'd ever been tempted to cross the line. She'd been with his brother that night, who'd passed out from too much Jack Daniels in the apple orchard with three of his other numbnut friends.

Brady had no intentions of cleaning up after his brother's mess, but he didn't have to stand around and watch. Again.

"You done causing a ruckus around here? I'm heading home."

"Ruckus?" Carter laughed. "You sound older than you are, Brady. Why can't you ever learn to chill a little? Have some fun?"

"I'm not twenty-one anymore, and neither are you." Cleaning up after Carter's thirtieth birthday this past spring was about as fun as mucking stalls. Which was pretty much what Brady found himself doing.

"You can leave if you want. I'll catch a ride with Ben and Alexis later."

At least Brady knew Alexis wasn't drinking and would get his brother home safely. Brady made the obligatory rounds, thanking Ty and Lily for hosting the party, and then saying goodnight to Ben.

"Happy birthday, Ben. Thanks for inviting me."

"Hey, anytime." They shook hands and did the guy pat-on-the-back thing. "I normally like something a little more low-key, but coming from a large Italian-French family, this sort of thing doesn't phase me much. Alexis says your big three-six is the day after Halloween. How about we celebrate with a couple bottles of wine around the fire pit at my place."

"I'm not one for celebrating birthdays, but I'll take you up on a few drinks around the fire pit."

Ben had been a nice addition to the Le Blanc family. He was the only guy Brady really talked to, besides his knuckle-head brother.

He pulled his keys from his pocket and twirled them around his finger on his way down the driveway to his pick-up.

Bright lights from a tiny car blinded him. He held up his arm to shield his eyes as he saw the struggle. The car was blocked in between a Ford 250 and a Dodge Hemi. Big trucks. He had a hemi too but had parked it down the road so he wouldn't get bottlenecked in.

Seeing the struggle the driver had, he made his way to the driver's window and hunched down, motioning him or her to roll it down.

"Need some help getting out?" The bright lights had blurred his vision, and large black dots filled the space where the driver's head was.

"I'm stuck," a familiar voice said as his eyes began to focus.

Grace.

Brady stood up and sighed, surveying the space between the vehicles. "I'm pretty sure the Ford is Cameron's. I have no idea who owns the Dodge. That thing is a beast."

"I don't care whose truck it is. I just need to get out."

He could go back to the party and ask around or he could try to finagle her car out himself. He took two steps toward the rear of the car and guessed there was about eighteen inches of space. Doable.

"Why don't you get out? I'll see what I can do."

"I know how to drive a car."

"I'm not questioning your ability to drive. The trucks have you penned in, and it's dark as night out here."

"It is night."

Leave it to Grace to point out what a dub he sounded like. He could only imagine what she thought of him. Alexis had complained often enough about Grace sowing her wild oats and hanging with fancy fashion designers and the snobby type in France. He didn't like her looking down her nose on him.

"Do you want me to try to get you out or not?"

His mother would skin him alive for talking so rudely to a woman. Thankfully he didn't see Dorothy and Grace sitting down for a friendly chat anytime soon.

"Fine." With a huff and an attitude the size of the Mount Katahdin, Grace flung those long legs that hadn't changed much since high school out of her car.

He had a hard time folding himself behind her wheel. He moved the seat back as far as it could go and adjusted the mirrors.

Going easy on the gas, he inched forward a smidge then put the car in reverse and guesstimated the eighteen inches he'd eyeballed before. Fourteen ten-point turns later, he had Grace's little toy car on the driveway, free from imprisonment.

"Thanks. I didn't think you'd get it out of there without denting my car."

"Me either."

"Now you tell me." Her laugh was like liquid sunshine after a long, cold winter. It warmed him in places he didn't want to think about.

"You sure you're okay to drive?"

"I had two sangrias in the past two hours and ate about a hundred meatballs to soak up whatever alcohol was in them. I'll manage."

"We're going in the same direction. I'll follow you to make sure you get home safely."

"I'm not drunk."

"I didn't say you were."

"You implied."

"No. It's late. It's dark. It's the gentlemanly thing to do. See a woman home."

Hell, Carter was right. He did sound like he came straight out of a Paul Newman movie.

"Oh. Well. Oh." Grace appeared as stunned at his words as he was. "Thanks. I guess. We are going the same way."

He'd never noticed her eyes before. Something between grass and a green berry still ripening in the sun.

With a quick jerk of his head, he jogged down the driveway and out on to the road to his truck. By the time he'd buckled up and started the engine, her little white car had pulled out in front of him.

Brady followed the red taillights all the way to Coastal Vines and was tempted to tap on his horn when she turned down her driveway. Instead, he waved, knowing she couldn't see him, and continued down the road to his farm.

Twenty minutes later he was stretched out in bed thinking things he shouldn't be thinking about.

No one could argue that Grace wasn't attractive. That didn't mean he was interested in her. She was a flight risk, not the kind of woman he was drawn to.

It was the party atmosphere, seeing friends he hadn't seen in a long time, maybe a slight buzz from his beer early on; although that had worn off as soon as he started playing beer pong with Lily and Grace. And it was because he'd seen her naked. Just once a long, long time ago.

Hell. Brady rolled over and punched his pillow. He hadn't been out on a date in months. And it had been even longer since he'd slept with a woman. Unlike his brother, he didn't let his lower head guide the head on his shoulders.

When the right woman came along he'd know it.

And Grace sure as hell wasn't her.

. . . .

MANUAL LABOR SO WASN'T her thing, but if she wanted her boutique done on time, she'd have to lend a helping hand.

"You don't have to worry too much about getting paint on the floor. I'm going to strip it and sand it when we're all done."

"Oh. Good." Grace dipped her roller in the burgundy paint and ran it across the pan.

"That doesn't mean you need to make a mess. Still, be careful. I'll cut in along the ceiling and then you can roll out the walls." Ty climbed up the ladder, a mini bucket and brush in hand, and slid his brush along the seam where the wall met the ceiling.

"You're good. I'd be getting red all over the ceiling if I was up there."

"That's why you're paying me the big bucks."

In actuality, she wasn't paying him a dime. In her rental agreement with the Bergerons, they gave her a set allowance to make some minor interior cosmetic changes. Ty had knocked down the back walls that used to house two small offices and a kitchen and made it into one large open space. She kept the bathroom and put in two changing rooms.

The space was small and perfect for her needs. Since her inventory was minimal, she didn't want a huge room. It would look barren.

Over by the front windows on the left she would showcase local designs and her designer friends, and used clothing on the right. The whole concept could be a bust in this rinky-dink town, which was why she wanted to ask Carter to help with her website.

While he appeared to be the total goofball, she'd checked out his online portfolio. He made stunning websites and graphics for companies across the world. According to his profile, he started playing around with his skills and offering services through Fiverr.

Not having much of a budget herself, Grace contemplated hiring someone through the cheap site as well, and then she'd learned about Carter. There wasn't much of an opportunity to talk to him last night as she'd hoped. After she finished painting she'd call him up and discuss her ideas.

Surprisingly, she and Ty made quick work of the painting. Since he couldn't do the finishing work until it dried, she called Carter once she got back to her parents. He didn't sound as surprised as she expected when she told him what she wanted.

"You want to hire me?"

"Maybe. I'll need to see your references and a possible mock-up first." No, she didn't, but she didn't want to come off too easy either.

"You wouldn't be calling me if you hadn't already looked at my online portfolio."

Damn cocky brat. "There aren't many people in Crystal Cove who can design a website. Your name popped up. Since I've known you since we were in preschool I thought I'd give you the opportunity to prove yourself."

Carter's chuckle on the other end told her she didn't fool him. "Sure thing, princess. Why don't you come over around seven? We should be cleared out by then."

"Or we could meet somewhere?" She really didn't want to sit in his family's kitchen with his mother and Brady looming over them. Dorothy always adored Alexis and never cared much for Grace. And Brady wasn't her biggest fan either.

"You asking me out on a date?"

"As if."

"I promised Brady I'd be around tonight to look over the books."

"Oh. Well, if you're busy we can do this another time."

"Nah. It won't take long. Mom's been making apple pies all week. We'll snag one and talk shop. See you in a few hours." He disconnected before Grace could decline his offer.

With nothing left to do but wait, she fiddled around on her laptop making lists of what she'd like to have on her website, and bookmarked links to sites she liked so Carter could model hers after them.

Dinner with her parents was as it had been for the past year since she'd been home. They talked about the winery, Ben and Alexis, and Sophie. Grace pretended to be interested and smiled at all the right places.

Her mother scraped the rest of the green beans in the bowl with the potatoes. "You must be getting closer to opening up. Will Ty have the work done by the end of the week?"

"He should." She picked up the dish with the meatloaf and consolidated the rest in with the beans and potatoes. "We painted the walls today. Tomorrow he'll put up the trim then finish the floors."

"I'd love to help you set up when you're ready."

"Thanks, Mom." She knew her mother offered out of obligation. Fashion, clothing, and shopping were not up her alley. Not up her sister's or father's either. The three of them were a lot alike, and Grace was always the odd man out.

Even with her father backing off of the winery business and getting back into woodworking, his true passion, he still had more in common with Alexis than Grace.

"I'm meeting Carter to work on my website tonight. I won't be gone long." She didn't need to check in with her parents, but knew they wanted her to as long as she was living under their roof.

As soon as Ty was finished with her shop, he and his crew were going to build an exterior set of steps to the third-floor apartment above the Sea Salt Spa. Since Lily had moved out it had been vacant. Only it wasn't really rentable since you had to walk through the two floors of the spa to get there.

The Bergerons owned that building too and were more than happy to have the outside stairs and landing built. Agent Thorne was their grandson and seemed to have a lot of say in who they rented to. For some reason, Grace wasn't on his shit list, even though she was the one who could have ruined Lily's identity when she posted a picture of her on Facebook and pointed out her resemblance to the jewelry heir Veronica Stewart Gervais.

"We're proud of you, honey." Her father kissed the top of her head and picked up the dirty plates from the kitchen table.

Her parents were good people. It wasn't their fault they had a daughter who wasn't happy with what they provided. However, Grace didn't know what it was that made her happy anymore.

For a while, it had been visiting the wineries in Italy. She thought if she learned from them, drawn in by the romance of elaborate villas and vineyards, that she could bring some class back to her family's little mom and pop winery.

Only she tired of the wine business—all but the tasting part—and fell in love with the fashions of the women who toured the expensive vineyards. She'd always been obsessed with clothes and fashion and found her calling.

From Italy she traveled to France, but couldn't afford to go to school and live in an apartment, so she worked retail, climbing her way from teenage outfitters to some of the high-end specialty stores.

It was fun and fast and frivolous until she pushed her luck too far and paid a high price for being careless. She couldn't outlive her reputation, not even in Europe, and with nowhere else to go, she landed back in nothingville.

Going over to the Marshall Farm brought back memories she'd rather forget. Unfortunately, it didn't seem like the Marshall brothers were ever going to let her live them down.

CHAPTER FOUR

THAT LAUGH. HE'D HEARD it two nights ago and it hadn't left his thoughts since. And he swore he heard it again, but this time coming from his den and not his memory.

Brady rounded the corner past the kitchen and stood in the doorway to the den. Carter and Grace sat huddled together on the couch as cozy as two lovebirds sitting on a perch laughing at something Carter had said.

"I can't believe you still remember that."

"We had too many good times to forget." Carter tipped his head back on the couch and closed his eyes, seemingly unaware of Brady's presence. "Remember prom night? We all—"

"Have you seen Mom?" Brady interrupted, not needing to relive that night again.

Grace startled and turned toward him. He did his best to ignore her, keeping his glare focused on his brother.

"She's probably in the store setting up the pies."

"And you're not helping her?" Their mother had been acting strange lately. Not her cheerful self and she'd been retreating to bed earlier than normal and waking later than usual. Of course, his selfish brother would rather flirt with a woman while his mother worked all night.

"I did. While you were cleaning out the wagon I made eight trips. She's organizing or something. Told me to get out of her way."

The wagon was a mess of straw after the weekend's rush. He'd fixed up the wagon ride and walked through the orchard as he did every night during apple season. Just as he did with his blueberry bushes in the summer.

He didn't notice the lights on in their little farm store or he would have stopped in to help his mom. It wasn't big. More like an oversized shed. A long counter to house his mother's baked goods, the cash register, and a cooler on the back wall for the cider.

There were small bins of tomatoes, potatoes, and corn, when in season, and a larger one for the mini pumpkins. Although most stayed in the field and were picked by customers.

They had a pretty good thing going. A nice variety for their small forty-five acre farm.

Like the Le Blancs across the road who'd cut back on hours because of their age, his mother was aging as well and needed to slow down to rest more frequently than in the past. With Carter taking more time off to pursue his web design business, Brady would need to hire more than his part-time help next spring.

It was spring that brought the longest days. The land needed to be tilled, seeds planted, young trees and bushes cared for. Not work he hired out to high school kids looking to make a few bucks.

Growing season was easier. He paid kids to pick berries and apples. Do some weeding. Even carry pumpkins to cars. His mother had been as strong and active as a teenager until lately. He'd noticed her slowing down with her baking as well.

"You think Mom's okay?" he asked, stepping into the den.

Grace dropped her feet to the floor and brought the laptop from the couch to her lap. Her feet were bare, but a pair of pink heels sat on the floor next to Carter's giant boots.

The matching pink bracelets on her wrist and in her ears jingled as she opened her computer and typed.

Carter shrugged. "Sure. She seems more tired lately, but it's been a long season. A profitable one, but long."

Nodding in passive agreement, Brady glanced at Grace, then back to Carter. "I'll leave you two be then."

He wasn't far down the hall when he heard Grace laugh again. "Stop it. Be nice." She giggled.

He had no doubt the two lovebirds were making fun of him. Brady trudged up the stairs to his room and closed the door behind him. Reaching behind his neck he tugged at his collar and pulled his gray Henley over his head.

The hole under his armpit had gotten bigger since last month when he first noticed it. Unbuttoning his jeans, he noticed the dark stains on his thighs and knees. No wonder Grace had been embarrassed to look at him and had laughed behind his back. She was always put together from her hair, makeup, and clothing. Hell, even her shoes and jewelry matched.

Here he was, a grown man of almost thirty-six, wearing stained and ripped clothing, living in his mother's house. He assumed he wasn't the kind of man she went around with in Paris.

Why he thought about her and his lack of love life he didn't know. No one had ever made him feel inferior before.

He had money in the bank, some decent investments making money in the stock market, and a successful farm.

The farm was technically his mother's, but she'd shown him and Carter the deed and her will. After their father died and the shock wore off, she wanted all the paperwork to be in order in case anything ever happened to her.

She even went as far as offering Marshall Farm to Brady and Carter a few years ago. All she asked in return was to live in the house until she died.

Carter had no interest in living on the farm for the rest of his life. Like the Le Blancs had done with their property, giving a piece to Alexis and Ben to build, Carter had asked for a few acres at the south end, away from the growing area, to one day build on. He preferred new and flashy while Brady had an appreciation for the old.

Yeah, the farmhouse needed some serious updating, but he'd never ruin the integrity of it. The wallpaper could go, and a lift in the ceilings would be nice. Maybe modernize the kitchen a smidge. Other than that, he wanted the character and the memories of his family home to stay intact.

Call him old fashioned, but it mattered to him.

He wouldn't judge his brother for wanting something different. Wanting something and someone more modern. More fun. More outgoing.

Brady may be an old stick in the mud, but he had a good life. He didn't need a sexy woman with a vibrant laugh and fancy clothes to make him think otherwise.

• • • •

CARTER'S PHONE RANG for the fourth time. "I'll let you take that. You've been really helpful. I'll be in touch with my decisions."

"Sounds good." He picked up his cell and greeted his caller.

Grace tucked her laptop into her Michael Kors bag and showed herself out. The kitchen door stuck and she had to give it a tug with two hands to get it open. Once she stepped outside on the back porch, she gripped the knob and closed it hard to keep the cold night air out of the house.

"That door's nearly a century old. I suppose it's time we replace it."

She jumped at the voice coming from the dark on the porch. "Oh. I didn't see you, Mrs. Marshall." She squinted and could barely make out her shadow in the rocking chair in the moonless night. "You must be cold out here."

"The cold tells me I'm still alive."

Mrs. Marshall rocked slowly, her arms cradled around her middle. Her voice sounded deeper and scratchier than Grace remembered. Granted, it had been forever since she'd seen her. And even then, they never interacted much.

"Would you like me to get you a blanket?"

"You and Carter chummy again, I see." Her tone was almost accusatory like Grace was the devil looking to poison her son.

Taken aback, Grace bit her tongue to her sarcasm and went with the facts. "He's helping me create a website for my store."

"That's right. Your mother told me you were opening some fancy shop in town for classy people."

"Actually, the clothes will look high-end but will be affordable and comfortable."

"The hardworking people in this town don't need fancy clothes. Work boots, jeans, and warm shirts for the winter is all. We've got L.L. Bean not too far from us. That store cares about the working class."

Wow. Grace hadn't expected dig after dig from Mrs. Marshall.

"You're right." Grace opted for the high road. It wasn't one she often visited. "My shop isn't meant to outfit those working in the fields—"

"And on boats. We've got our share of fisherman too."

"And boats," Grace added.

"I don't see your sister wearing anything from that kind of shop. She's the kind of woman who works hard all day and is loyal to her family. Such a nice girl. I'll admit I wasn't fond of her husband at first. But that's only because I wanted her as my daughter-in-law. That Ben is a worker as well. And a good daddy."

Grace didn't need Mrs. Marshall reminding her how she'd never measure up to Alexis. How she'd never measure up to be fit enough to date her sons. Grace knew that all on her own. And if the people in Crystal Cove didn't mention it over and over again, there were those in Paris who'd remind her. Not many, but a few who could do some serious damage to her already fragile reputation.

She'd have to work hard to earn the respect from people in this town. If that was even possible.

"My sister struck gold when she found Ben." That was no lie. He was the inspiration behind her opening her own business. Too bad her sister couldn't cheer her on as much as her husband did.

Mrs. Marshall stood too quickly and fell back into the rocking chair. Grace leaped forward and grabbed ahold of her arm before she fell to the floor.

"Are you okay?" She made sure Mrs. Marshall was steady on her feet before she let go of her arm.

"I'm fine." She shook her head and shoulders as if embarrassed at her almost fall.

Grace stepped back out of her way as she marched past her to the door.

"You should go home before people start talking about you sniffing around here so late at night." With a twist of her wrist and a bump with her hip, the door opened and quickly slammed behind her.

She didn't remember Mrs. Marshall being so old and crotchety. The way Carter painted her was always with admiration. His mother sat high up on a pedestal, especially after his father died. The few times Grace had seen them interact it was with Carter cracking jokes and making his mother laugh. She seemed to love her sons.

And she totally hated Grace. Why, she didn't know. She'd never done anything to any of the Marshalls.

It was her reputation. Party girl in high school and slut in Europe. Although she didn't think Mrs. Marshall was aware of that rumor, which wasn't quite a rumor.

Did a woman's past have to follow her around for the rest of her life? The only thing Dorothy Marshall knew about Grace was her seventeen and eighteen-year-old life. People grew up. Her twenties may have been pretty wild as well, but she needed to find herself. It was the time in her life when she could have a good time. No responsibilities. No pressure. No commitments.

Freedom.

Until it came crashing down on her.

There was nowhere else to go so Grace would have to suck it up. The town gossip in Crystal Cove wasn't as harsh as gossip in Paris, but it was more personal. There she was just a name and maybe a face. Here, she was a person. She had a perfect sister and parents whom everyone loved and admired.

Knowing she couldn't solve anything tonight, she fished her car keys from her bag and plodded down the steps to the dirt driveway. Her ankles gave way when her shoes hit a rock, but she caught herself, singing a string of curses the rest of the way to her car.

No one had a paved driveway in this redneck town. Who the hell would buy maxi skirts and off the shoulder blouses? Maybe Mrs. Marshall was right. She should open an L.L. Bean type of shop instead.

Needing a dose of perk-me-up, she turned left out of the driveway and headed up to see her brother-in-law. He was the one to blame for planting this hair-brained idea in her head, and he was the fancy marketing exec from San Francisco. So far his advice had brought tourism and money to the town.

Was he on to something about her store, or was he just trying to appease his sister-in-law?

The downstairs lights were on in their kitchen otherwise Grace would have turned back home. Not that she had a home. Yet.

Her headlights must have warned Alexis of her arrival for she was at the front door before Grace had a chance to knock.

"Sophie just went to bed, so I didn't want your knock waking her."

"She can hear the front door?" Grace stepped inside her sister's kitchen and closed the door behind her. It closed much easier than Mrs. Marshall's. Granted, the house was less than a year old so everything looked and operated perfectly.

"No. I didn't want Hemmy to bark though."

Hearing his name, the great Bernese Mountain Dog rounded the corner. Grace squatted and rubbed his ears. "Hey, Hemsworth. Did you miss your auntie?"

She never would've considered herself a dog lover before, not unless it was a tiny lap dog, or one that fit in her Valentino bag, until she met Hemmy. He may be the size of a small pony, but the dog was as gentle as a baby.

"What brings you by at nine at night?"

"I thought you guys would be in bed already. Early to bed, early to rise and stuff." Her sister had always been an early riser. Before the sun, or with it in the summer months.

"Then why did you come by?"

"I was hoping Ben was up. I have some... business stuff to talk to him about."

Alexis leaned against the kitchen wall and lifted an eyebrow. Skeptical was an understatement. Her sister was annoyed. On the verge of pissed.

"You have quite the infatuation with my husband."

"What?" If Alexis seriously thought—

"Hey, Grace. I thought I heard your voice." Ben stepped in between the sisters and stooped to give Grace a hug. "Glad you stopped by. Want a glass of wine? I was just about to make myself a midnight snack."

"I thought you were working," Alexis grumbled.

"I am." Ben kissed his wife with a smile and led her to the long country-style table in the open kitchen. "I'm taking a break and pouring you a glass as well."

He took a bottle from the fridge and poured three glasses. Grace didn't want to talk business in front of Alexis. She'd already expressed her opinions about the boutique, and Grace didn't feel like listening to her eye rolls—which were totally loud—or disapproving snorts.

And she really didn't want to admit her doubt in her ability to pull off a successful business in front of her sister either.

"Hungry?" Ben set a box of Wheat Thins on the table and took out a block of cheese from the fridge.

"Sure." Eating and sipping wine would help her stall and give her time to figure out how to bring up her insecurities without her sister giving her the *I told you so* smirk.

Alexis picked up her wine glass and snagged a handful of crackers from the box. "I'm assuming you're here to talk shop—pun intended—so I'll get out of your way."

"You're more than welcome to stay." Ben ran a hand up and down Alexis' leg in a sweet gesture Grace could only daydream about.

No man caressed her for the sake of caressing. It was always about getting something or somewhere.

Sex.

"No offense, but talking numbers and clothes is not my thing. I'll go play in the dirt." Ben patted her on the back of the leg before she walked away.

And this is what Mrs. Marshall was talking about. A woman who was one with the earth instead of searching for dollar signs.

Not that Grace cared one bit what Mrs. Marshall thought.

"You must be excited to open next week."

"I am."

"And nervous, I bet too."

"Definitely. It does seem silly to open a business during a time when most are closing up for the winter around here."

"It's actually perfect. We went over this already. The bulk of your sales will most likely be online. You'll establish yourself as a reputable seller, and slowly garner interest in your storefront. Your inventory is limited right now until you start bringing in income. Working online is the perfect way to get your feet wet."

"But having a storefront is attractive to repeat buyers. I know. You told me this already."

"So what's the problem?"

"I don't fit in with the Crystal Cove way."

"Which is?"

"Farming. Fishing. Lobstering."

"Do you think there are other people in the area who feel the same? If all we offer is more of the same, you're not unique. You won't stand out. You won't know anything until you try."

"I know." Grace crunched on a cracker and washed it down with a healthy gulp of wine.

"Rent is cheap, and your lease is only for six months. Worst-case scenario, you sell solely online. There's a huge market for that."

"I know," she said again.

"And your store idea is original and fresh. There are other women in central Maine looking for fashionable merchandise."

"But they don't live around here."

"Maybe not. But they'll come visit." Ben pushed his glass away and leaned in closer. "I'm pretty sure there are women in the cove who wouldn't mind getting dressed up every now and then. And husbands who would like their wives to wear something pretty to go out somewhere special."

Grace snorted. "Good luck getting Alexis to doll herself up."

"I wouldn't change a thing about your sister, but if she ever wanted to dress up, your shop wouldn't be too far away."

"I feel like this is some sort of challenge."

"Not at all. No pressure on you and none on my wife. I prefer her naked anyway."

"Gross. You didn't need to go there." Grace finished her wine and pushed back her chair. "Thanks for the pep talk.

Keep your shoulders handy. I'll need them to cry on when this thing busts."

Ben hugged her tight and pushed her slightly away, keeping his hands on her shoulders. "You've got this, kid. And if you need advice, help, a place to vent, and when you celebrate, Alexis and I are here for you."

Alexis probably not; Ben would be though.

"Thanks. Tell Alexis I said goodnight." Hemmy lifted his head from the dog bed in the corner and trotted over as if knowing she was leaving. "Bye, buddy." She gave him a quick pat and headed out the door.

This time next week she'd have her own apartment and her own shop. One step closer to freedom.

And to starting over.

CHAPTER FIVE

THE DAYS TURNED INTO nights as Grace moved her storage bins from Alexis' old room in their parents' home to The Closet. While she unpacked and steam ironed the clothes, Ty and his crew were finishing up the outside staircase to her new apartment.

She couldn't believe she'd be opening her store and moving into her apartment in the same week. In the whirlwind of packing, unpacking, organizing, and planning, she'd managed to squeeze in a few meetings with Carter to finish up the website.

He'd found a graphic designer to make her logo; it was perfect. A purse and clothes hanger all in one with *The Closet* written underneath. She'd research storefront awnings during the winter months. There was no rush in hanging one now with winter around the corner. In the meantime, her website and store had a brand.

It would be a few days before her shopping bags would arrive. The adorable black and white purse hanger stamped on the front of light gray bags. Simple and classy. Grace thought about going pink, but the community was not a *pink* one. There was nothing frilly and feminine about a coastal town in central Maine. Rugged, yes.

So she painted the walls a deep burgundy and kept her logo to a simple black and white color scheme. She could always add a new color accent with the new stores she hoped to open in other cities.

Close to five, Ty knocked on her front door and let himself in.

"We've lost the sun so we're packing up for the day. As long as the rain holds off tomorrow, we should be able to finish the railings. If you're not in a rush and can wait two more days, Cameron, Ben, and I can help you move in on Saturday."

"Actually." Grace hung up an asymmetrical navy dress on the rack and turned off the steamer. "I'm totally impatient. I'm thirty-one and have been living with my parents for over a year. It's time I move out."

"We're all working tomorrow though."

"That's okay. I don't have anything heavy to move. Just my suitcases. Maybe a small dresser from my bedroom."

He leaned his hip against the counter and squinted at her. "What about furniture?"

"I don't have a couch or much of anything, really. I highly doubt I'll be entertaining many people for a while. Is the bed still there?" Grace really didn't want to bring her thirty-year-old twin mattress from home.

"Yeah. Lily didn't need to move it into my—our house. I already had a decent one. Her couch is in the basement right now though. I can bring it over this weekend until you find something you like."

Why were all the sweet, hot men taken? "I should have moved back a few months earlier. Before Lily stole you."

Ty blushed and looked away, obviously uncomfortable with her compliment. "You sure you don't have a twin somewhere? Maybe Mia got mixed up at birth and you really have a long lost brother?"

"Not likely." Ty laughed.

"Damn. Guess I'll stick with fashion then."

"Better you than me. All I know is jeans and work boots. Lily's excited for you to open though. I have a feeling she'll be your best customer."

Even though Lily shopped at stores like Target and TJ Maxx, she always looked like she stepped out of a fashion magazine. With model long legs and stunning facial features, Grace was more than thrilled to dress her new friend.

"Works for me."

"Lily told me to give you the keys." He dug in his pocket and held out his hand. "The gold key opens the front door to the spa. She says to make sure you lock it behind you before going up to the apartment. The silver key is to the apartment doors, both the inside and the new outside one. You'll have access to it by dinner time tomorrow."

"Perfect." Grace folded her fingers over the cold metal. Her final step to total freedom. To starting over. Giddy with happiness, she tapped her toes and bit her lip, peering around Ty's tall frame to peek out the window.

"She said you'd want to get in as soon as possible. I won't keep you." He opened the front door and paused, turning back. "Don't forget to give us a call if you need a hand."

"Will do."

As soon as the door closed behind him, Grace ran around making sure everything was off, the back door locked, and the place didn't look like a complete shambles from the front window. Deeming it passable, she pushed the front door open and jogged the fourteen steps to the Sea Salt Spa.

Using the gold key, she let herself in and locked the door behind her. Grace was halfway up the first set of stairs when she remembered she forgot to lock up The Closet.

A few minutes later, both businesses were locked up and she finally reached the second set of stairs that led to the apartment. Having to walk through the spa every day to get to her apartment would have been a pain. It was awesome that the Bergerons had agreed to let Ty build her an outside staircase.

It obviously wasn't an issue when Lily lived up here. It was her spa. However, living where you worked probably had its downside. Grace took out the key and opened the door to her new home.

The living room was small and empty, except for a floor lamp in the corner. The windows looked out to her building, and beyond was the rest of Seaview Drive and then the ocean.

Grace peeked into the bedroom. It looked the same as it had last month when Lily showed her the place. She'd visited Lily a handful of times here over the months. They weren't best of friends, but slowly were becoming close. Especially with their somewhat connected pasts.

A cold chill crept up Grace's spine, and she shivered it away. No need to go down that road. This was about starting over. She followed the short hall to the kitchen and opened and closed the cabinets. Lily had said she would leave odds and ends for her. There were four plates and glasses. Plenty for her.

Underneath the silverware drawer, she found two pots and a strainer. Living on a tight budget would mean spaghetti and jarred sauce five nights a week. Maybe a frozen dinner on the other two nights.

She'd make it work.

With the fridge and food cabinets bare, a quick stop to the grocery store was in order. Boon's Variety wasn't very big, but it had the essentials. After locking up the spa, Grace hopped in her car and drove with a smile on her face.

She stopped at her parents' place first to grab her already packed suitcases, gave her parents a hug and a kiss, and skipped back to her car. The drive to Boons was short. The bigger grocery stores were a few towns over, but Boons served well in a pinch. Besides, she was supporting local businesses this way.

The lot was practically empty for seven o'clock on a Thursday night. Not that she knew when prime grocery shopping was. She tossed her keys in her purse and marched into Boon's excited to make her first meal in her new apartment.

While she wasn't the greatest cook, she could follow a recipe just fine. Not wanting to take the time to make anything too elaborate tonight, she opted for an omelet loaded with veggies.

The produce was scarce, but she found a decent red pepper and some mushrooms and added them to her basket. She tossed in a box of Special K for breakfast and some coffee grounds and headed to the dairy section.

She set the basket on the ground and reached in for a half gallon of milk and a dozen eggs. Remembering to check them, she opened the container and deemed the eggs satisfactory.

"Don't tell me you eat store-bought eggs," a deep voice scoffed behind her.

"Geesh!" Startled, she juggled the carton and one egg crashed to the floor.

Brady reached out and grabbed ahold of the carton, his large hands covering hers in the process.

"Just because store bought eggs are crap doesn't mean you should scramble them on Boon's floor."

"Funny. You shouldn't sneak up on people."

"That wasn't my intent." Brady walked off with the carton of eggs leaving Grace alone and confused. A moment later he returned with a roll of paper towels.

She moved her basket out of the way as he wiped up the floor, cleaning up her mess. Although if it wasn't for him startling her she wouldn't have dropped the egg.

He walked off with the wad of dirty paper towels, muttering under his breath. Assuming he left the eleven eggs at the counter, Grace weaved her way through the five aisles and set her basket by the register. Wanting to quickly pay for her groceries and leave before Brady came out from wherever he was hiding, she flipped through her wallet and pulled out a twenty.

"You only got eleven eggs here, Grace. Wanna pick a new carton?"

"I dropped one. Brady Marshall was here a minute ago and cleaned it up." She didn't want to look around for him and forced her eyes to stay focused on Albert Boon.

"That he did. Don't sell many eggs here when Dorothy sets her fresh ones out for folks to buy. To tell you the truth"—Boon leaned over the counter, at least as much as his protruding belly would allow, and scratched his bald head—"I don't eat them eggs either." He waved the carton in front of her. "Marshall eggs are the way to go."

"That's what I was trying to tell her."

Grace jumped. Again. "Good lord. What's it with you and sneaking up on people?" She turned her back to him and handed Boon her twenty.

"Your pa says you movin' into Lily Novak's apartment. Didn't take long for Ty to get his girl to move in with him, eh?" Boon said with a wink.

"I'm very happy for them. Ty's wonderful." Grace could've sworn she heard Brady grunt from behind her. Boon handed her the change, and she stuffed it in her wallet.

"I have a pound of butter. You can put it on my tab." Brady swept up her bag and brushed past her to the front door.

"Sure thing," Boon called from behind them.

She had to jog to keep up with him, even though the store wasn't that big and she'd parked close to the front door. When she got outside, Brady had her bag of groceries sitting on the hood of her car, and he was rifling through it.

"What the hell do you think you're doing?"

"You're not eating these eggs. Do you have any idea how long they've been in that store?" He jerked his thumb over his shoulder. "These big companies don't give a damn about the conditions of their farms and cram as many chickens they can into—"

"Seriously?" Grace snagged the eggs from his grasp. "I highly doubt it's as bad as you think it is. The government regulates everything these days. Now back off and leave me and my eggs alone."

"Why didn't Carter give you some of our farm eggs? You've been seeing a lot of him lately."

Where the hell did that come from? It sounded almost as if... as if Brady was jealous. "Maybe we were too busy doing other things to talk about *eggs*." She taunted.

Brady huffed and stomped off to his truck. He'd peeled out of the lot before Grace could register what had just happened. The last thing she wanted was for anyone to think she and Carter—heck, she and anyone—were having an affair. She wanted nothing to do with men or relationships. Or even quick hook-ups, which was what Mia had been pressuring her into. It would take time and patience to clean up her past, and messing around with men was one sure way to slow down the process.

Shoving the eggs in the bag, Grace noticed two packages of butter sitting on the hood of her car. She should drop them off at Brady's on her way home. Only his farm was no longer on her way home. He could come back and buy another package of butter.

Screw the arrogant odd farm boy.

Boy. Yeah. That word didn't apply to her old neighbor anymore. Brady Marshall had filled out in all the right places.

Which made him nothing but trouble.

• • • •

TY AND HIS CREW FINISHED ahead of schedule, which meant Grace could skip up the outside stairs to her apartment and not have to go through the spa. With all her belongings already moved in—which wasn't much—she had nothing to do but spin around in her new place.

After a few spins, which unfortunately didn't turn her into Wonder Woman, Grace poured herself a bowl of cereal and dined alone in her kitchenette.

No more checking in with Mom and Dad when she was coming and going. Not that they hounded her. Still, it was the polite thing to do.

No more having to make idle small talk in the morning before her cup of coffee, or at night before bed. Grace loved her parents, she really did, but she didn't like the pressure of having to always be... *on*. Sometimes vegging out was all she wanted to do. Yet she felt guilty doing so after her parents worked all day and she, well, didn't.

Her father had taken up his carpentry work again and spent most of his days in the barn. Even though their mother was supposed to be cutting back hours at the vineyard, she still put in a full day's work.

Since she'd been home, Grace had helped out here and there. Pouring samples to visitors or selling wine from inside the tasting room. Working in the fields was not her thing. Dirty her hands? Risk breaking a nail? Never.

Even though her family thought she was a lazy, pampered princess, Grace had no problem putting in a fifteen hour day in a boutique, or behind her computer shopping for her store, and making lists and budgets. It was the manual labor gig that wasn't her style.

Starting her own business was a lot more work than people gave credit for. She'd invested nearly her entire savings in her belief in a handful of fashion designers. Thankfully they weren't the high maintenance divas she'd worked for in Paris.

Arianna grew up in Scotland and wanted to infiltrate more stylish dresses and skirts into her countryside towns. Kendall was from a family of five brothers. Her family owned a pub in Ireland, and she'd ventured on her own to follow her passion. Her focus had been on designing stylish pants and jeans that hid common troublesome areas but were cute and trendy.

Maria's Icelandic background had her gravitating toward winter gear, which was perfect for Mainers as well, while Lacey's rugged attitude reminded Grace of her sister. Lacey didn't have many friends in the fashion industry. Many balked at her attempt to make flannel fashionable. Grace had a feeling her designs would be more widely accepted in Maine than in France.

For months, Grace witnessed firsthand how women—and a handful of men—were scoffed at and laughed at not only behind their backs, but to their faces as well for their designs. At first, it hadn't bothered her. She, too, didn't know why people would spend so much money to study fashion in Paris when they clearly didn't fit in with the outlandish stereotypes.

It was after a year working retail, when she felt snickers behind her back, that she'd fallen for Robert Powers. He was her ticket to the top. Not in design, for she knew that ship had sailed, but in fashion merchandising. With his connections, anything was possible.

Only he'd never used his connections to help her. He used her for one thing, and it ended up ruining her career.

Now, here she was, sitting at the two-person rickety table in her new kitchenette with her bowl of cereal for dinner, and four hopefully up-and-coming fashion designers supplying her store with up-and-coming designs.

Four women who didn't fit in. Just like Grace. She respected their passion and determination to stay true to their styles. Paris may not have approved of them, but they were perfect for The Closet.

The five of them would come out on top. They had to.

Wanting to look at her storefront one more time, Grace rinsed her bowl and danced across her apartment to the new outside door. Lost in her own happiness, she nearly tripped over a basket of something and tumbled down the twenty-two stairs.

"What the—" She bent to pick it up and peeked inside. "Eggs." No doubt they were fresh farm eggs. Grace couldn't help the slight tug at her upper lip. The man had some odd obsession with his farm's eggs.

Leaving the eggs for a few minutes, she skipped down the stairs to admire her store. This end of Seaview Drive wasn't busy with foot traffic like the other end with the bookstore and The Happy Clam, which were closer to the water. That would change though.

The brick building was old but well cared for and looked charming on this end of the street. The windows weren't as big as she'd like, so she'd made sure to utilize the space well.

Ben had rigged mannequins out of PVC for her. So sweet, her brother-in-law. The one on the left donned a pair of practical olive khakis and a cranberry cotton and wool blend long-sleeve shirt. The top was loose, wide, and free in the arms, but the cut pulled in toward the waist and wrists, streamlining the body instead of making a woman look boxy. Kendall's designs were simple and flattering.

The mannequin on the right wore one of Arianna's skirts. Patterns were only a hit on skinny models and in flashy cities, yet this area of Maine needed some sprucing up other than the plain black skirt, so Grace showcased a burnt orange, auburn, and maroon swirled maxi skirt and paired it with an off white fitted shirt and auburn infinity scarf.

The windows looked good. Two more days and she'd be open. Just one more weekend to get it all ready, and Grace couldn't be more excited. She turned to her left and admired the Sea Salt Spa. The lower half of the building was brick as well, but somewhere along the way someone must have expanded, building up. The second and third floors were sided with sage colored wood shingles, and cream colored shutters hung next to each window.

Lily had cute flower boxes in front of her windows. In the summer she kept them filled with petunias, and in the fall she planted mums. That's what was missing in front of her store.

Tomorrow, she'd find some bales of hay, cornstalks, and mums. The fall festival was only one week away. Decorating for it should've been on the top of her list. Grace cursed herself for completely missing the obvious. She'd been so excited about her shop, and then her apartment, and worried she'd have enough inventory without ordering too much, that she'd spaced on decorating the outside of her store.

With a new mission for tomorrow, she took the steps two at a time until she reached the top. The basket of eggs still sat there. A reminder of the surly and unimpressed, cute yet not her type man who lived not too far away.

Picking up the basket, she let herself inside and got ready for bed.

CHAPTER SIX

"YOU'RE SERIOUSLY OUT of hay and cornstalks?" Grace couldn't believe her luck. The Robertsons had a billion horses. There was hay everywhere.

"We only have a few bales that we need to save for the horses. Nowadays we buy the big rounds of hay. That's not going to look so pretty in front of your new store. Try the Marshalls. They're busy this time of year so they could be out, but they sell all that kind of stuff. Mums too."

Figures. "What about the Petersons? They have a farm."

"Pig farm, honey. They're not going to have the stuff you're looking for."

"Okay. Thanks anyway."

Grace trudged back to her car and drove down the road to the Marshalls. Maybe Brady would be busy in the fields and not spot her. Why she was avoiding him, she didn't know. But it was never good when they ran into each other. He scowled too much. She didn't like it.

The dirt parking lot was crowded, even for a Saturday. Wanting to make her purchases and leave, she headed to the store and hoped a local teen was manning the cash register.

No such luck. Mrs. Marshall smiled as she talked with the customers. She looked up when the door opened, her smile faltering just a smidge. The sleeves of her green work shirt were rolled up to her elbows and her hair pulled back in a bun. She'd never worn makeup or jewelry, except for the plain gold band on her ring finger. Even some fifteen years after her husband's death, she never took it off.

"Grace. What brings you here? Carter's busy working."

"I'm not here to see him. I'd like to buy some mums and pumpkins. And a few bales of hay and corn stalks if you have any left."

"Slim pickings with it already being October. I can ring you up for most of it, but you buy the pumpkins by the pound. You'll need to get those yourself." There was an edge of challenge in her voice as if she didn't expect Grace to be able to pick out a few pumpkins.

"Sure. I'll be right back."

Grace went outside and picked up two decent sized pumpkins, impressed with herself for carrying one under each arm. It was a good thing she'd had the forethought to wear flats instead of heels today. Her light gray top would need to be washed, but that was what washing machines were for.

When the next customer opened the door, she asked him if he could hold it for her. Thanking him, she stepped inside and waited in line as Mrs. Marshall took care of the two customers in front of her.

They'd purchased some of the baked goods Mrs. Marshall was known for. Maybe Grace would buy a few treats as well. When it was her turn, she placed the pumpkins on the counter, grateful to have feeling in her hands again, and wiped her palms on her jeans.

"I'll take six mums, four bales of hay and... um... six corn stalks as well. Oh." She reached for a pumpkin whoopee pie and a blueberry donut. "And these."

With only the lift in her brow as communication, Mrs. Marshall tapped into her calculator and gave her the total.

Grace paid and thanked her with a polite smile. She managed to pick up the pumpkins, but the rest would be a challenge. Biting her lip, she looked at her treats, then the door, then Mrs. Marshall, who didn't appear to be in the giving mood.

"I'm going to make a few trips."

"You do that."

In all her years living across from the Marshalls, Grace never remembered the Mrs. being so... bitchy. After a few runs to the car, loading the pumpkins and mums in the trunk, she looked over at the bales of hay she stacked by her car and sighed.

"I'm so stupid." Once again, her brain had been in overdrive and didn't think things through. How the heck was she supposed to fit all this in her tiny sedan?

"How the hell are you going to fit all of that in your toy car?" Brady, reading her thoughts, mocked behind her.

Not wanting him to know what an idiot she was, she shrugged him off. "My back seat." She opened the backdoor and cringed. The straw would make a mess.

"That's the most ridiculous thing I've heard all day. All week." He stepped forward into her peripheral vision. He was a sight in his heavy work boots and jeans. A pair of gloves hung from his back pocket. The gray Henley with "Marshall Farm" etched over his heart pulled taut across his broad shoulders. Holy broad shoulders. Were they always that big?

He might be somewhat attractive, but she didn't like being treated like a fool. Not by his mom and not by him.

"I can manage."

"No, you can't. I'll load this stuff in my truck and bring it by on my way to the town meeting."

"Um. Sure. What time is that?" She wanted to be sure she was at the store when he got there.

"You're not going?"

"To a town meeting?" She nearly shuddered. Only old people went to those. She remembered her father and mother going when she was younger. "No thanks."

"Figured as much," he muttered.

"What's that supposed to mean?" She cocked her hip and gritted her jaw.

"Nothing."

"Bullshit."

Brady lifted an eyebrow and stared her down. "We're in the final stages of planning the fall festival. Since you haven't been part of it from the beginning, I didn't think you'd be there tonight. Shop owner or not."

Without asking her permission, he picked up a bale of hay in each hand, grabbing on to the twine that magically held it together, and strode across the parking lot. She watched him heave them into his truck. His stride was long and casual as if he wasn't in any rush, but not lazy and slow either.

Methodical, maybe. No words were spoken as he picked up the rest of the hay and did the same. Figuring she should help out at least a little, Grace managed the corn stalks and handed them to him at his truck. She had no comeback regarding the meeting.

He was right. She hadn't paid any attention to the meetings in the past. When Hope and Alexis talked about the festival during their book talks, Grace tuned them out, thinking about color swatches and patterns that would work well for the rural women.

Avoiding his revelation on her lack of commitment to the town, she attempted to save her dignity by acting as her name suggested. Gracefully. "I appreciate this. Oh. And the eggs. That was... nice of you."

"They're better than store bought," he stated as fact. Which was true.

"I had a lovely omelet this morning. So thank you." She wouldn't kiss his ass too much.

"Hmpf," he grunted before taking off.

Manners were not a specialty in the Marshall household.

True to his word, the headlights to Brady's truck shone in her storefront at ten minutes to seven. He'd already unloaded her hay and corn stalks by the time she locked the door behind her.

His gray eyes peered at her over the back of his truck.

"I appreciate the delivery."

"Sure."

"I guess I'll see you at the meeting."

His eyebrow quirked similarly to how it had this afternoon, as if she surprised him. There was no lift in his lip to say he was amused or furrow between his brow that indicated he was annoyed. Just the light brown caterpillar above his intense eyes bumping up in the middle.

"Guess so." He slammed the tailgate shut and stepped up into his truck, leaving her in a puff of exhaust and her hay dust.

So much for small talk.

She rifled through her small Coach clutch until she found her keys and jogged out back to her car. She'd tidy up the pile of hay when she came back. It was more important to make it to the meeting on time.

After returning from Marshall Farm this afternoon, she'd texted Hope and Alexis and asked about the meeting. Sure enough, they were thrilled she was coming. The fall festival wasn't a thing the last time she lived here. It was Ben's doing, drawing the community together and garnering one last surge of business before winter turned Crystal Cove into a cold, lonely town out of a Stephen King novel. At least, that was how she remembered it from her high school days.

Hope had encouraged her to offer incentives for shopping during the festival. Buy today and save twenty-five percent off your next purchase. Or something like that. If Grace had paid attention to this event earlier, she would have had cute cards and signs made up. Maybe there was time, though, if she could get Ben or Carter to design something simple, she could get them printed and ready for next weekend. She'd ask Ben tonight.

It took less than five minutes to drive to the town hall. The building hadn't changed at all over the years. An old farmhouse converted into a meeting center. The parking lot was full. Of course with only ten spots, that didn't mean the meeting was necessarily packed.

Grace drove down Maple Street, past eight more cars, and parked in front of Brady's truck on the side of the road. Running her hands down her skinny jeans, she took in a few deep breaths, dropped her keys in her clutch, and walked with purpose toward the front steps of the meeting hall with the poise of a woman who knew what she was doing.

"Hey, girl," Mia greeted her with a hip check. "Surprised to see you here."

Annoyed that it wasn't just Brady who had low expectations of her, Grace scowled. "I *do* own a business in this town, you know. I'm more surprised to see *you* here."

"*Rrrr*," Mia screeched like an annoyed cat, curling her fingers in a claw-like motion. "Someone's pissy tonight." She laughed.

At least she took Grace's sass in stride. "Sorry. I didn't mean to sound so..."

"Bitchy?" Mia said with a smile.

"Yeah. Sorry."

"Please. I'm the queen of bitchy. I'm only going to be mad at you if you start to take over my role." They strode side-by-side up the weathered steps of the meeting house. "Normally town meetings aren't my thing. But I had so much fun volunteering at last year's festival that I wanted to make sure I got the good jobs again this year."

"What exactly are the *good* jobs?"

"Face painting at Marshalls. Hey, speak of the devil—" Mia punched Carter in the shoulder.

"Ladies. You two are looking fine tonight." Carter winked and draped an arm around each of them. "Gonna volunteer at the farm again this year, Mia?"

"Damn straight. I'm not getting stuck in the welcome booth like Hope did last year. Although, it did force her and Cameron together. That was kinda cute."

"What are you signing up for, Grace?" Carter directed his attention toward her, squeezing her into his side with his arm.

"I hadn't really thought about it. I'll have my shop open, so I'm not sure how I'll be able to help out."

"That's true. You're coming to the dance Saturday night, right?"

"Dance?"

She could picture a honkytonk dorky dance right out of the black and white Nick at Night specials her parents used to watch. Really, really not her thing.

"It's so much fun. Of course you're going. Hey. Jenna's here." Mia ducked from under Carter's arm and strolled off to greet Jenna.

"Guess we'll see you then. Good luck at your opening this week. Let me know if you plan on modeling any of those sexy underwear things. I'll come by and give you my input."

"I'm sure you will." Grace laughed.

"I have a good eye for those things." He pinched her cheek before pulling out a chair and gesturing for her to sit.

● ● ● ●

THE CHAIRS IN THE MEETING hall hadn't been this filled since the ice storm four years ago wiped out power to everyone in the town for a solid ten days. Brady arrived early enough to talk with Jed Freeman about getting a building permit to add on to the farm store.

Over the years he'd been able to cultivate more of his parents' land, bringing in bigger and bigger crops. What started out as a farm stand shelter, had turned into a small addition when Brady was in high school, and could no longer hold all of his mother's baked goods as well as the fruits and vegetables for sale. It was a good problem to have.

Jed didn't see any problem in Brady obtaining a permit and told him to come by Tuesday morning when the town hall was open to fill out the paperwork. When he'd rounded the corner to the main room, he stopped in his tracks.

His brother sat snugly next to Grace in the back row, his arm draped casually behind her chair. It shouldn't bother him this much. Grace being here. Carter so close.

It was ridiculous how she'd tried to shove so much in her little car at his farm. What was she thinking? He'd watched her struggle for a few minutes and had chuckled to himself, enjoying the show. It was cute and pathetic.

And he hated having to come to her rescue. She wasn't a damsel in distress, and he wasn't a hero. Far from it. She needed him as much as he needed her. Yet he couldn't leave a paying customer with no way of getting their goods home. So he'd offered to help. He'd made plenty of home deliveries before. There wasn't anything special or unique about this one.

Brady scanned the crowded hall. He could name every person in there. Even knew what road they lived on. He was part of the community and would do anything for it and for everyone who lived there. His father instilled a sense of loyalty and pride in him years ago, and it was something he was proud of.

More laughter from the last row brought his attention back to Carter and Grace.

The stirring in his gut made no sense. It couldn't have been jealousy. It definitely wasn't lust. Heck, he didn't think he even liked the spoiled party girl. It didn't matter anyway. Tonight was about the town. About helping each other's businesses grow. Now that Grace was a business owner he'd be running into her more frequently, although not too often.

After all, what did a poor farmer and a snotty boutique owner have in common?

CHAPTER SEVEN

FOR THE SECOND YEAR in a row, the first day of the fall festival was a success. The apple cider and most of the good carving pumpkins were sold out, and they still had the Sunday rush to contend with. In the meantime, Brady had the Saturday night dance to attend.

He stepped out of the shower and wrapped a towel around his waist. He picked up his shaving cream and pressed down on the top, watching as the tiny ball of white foam grew in his hand. He patted the shaving cream on his cheeks and chin, spreading it evenly across his face.

Dances weren't Brady's thing. He never attended them in high school, not even his prom. Getting dressed up in a rented penguin suit and standing around a dance floor watching people make fools of themselves wasn't his idea of a good time.

He slid his razor through the thick foam and rinsed it off under in the stream of water running under the faucet, then swiped it across his cheek again in slow, methodic movements.

It was the right thing to do, attend the dance and represent Marshall Farm. His mother wasn't feeling well and went to bed already. Of course, Carter would be there, but Brady didn't necessarily consider him a representative of the farm.

Sure his brother worked hard, but once his jobs were done, Carter either buried his nose in his laptop and did his computer thing or partied like he was still in high school.

Similar to Grace, Brady supposed. Not much changed in his town. What you were like in high school pretty much represented the type of adult and career person you'd be.

Like him, Alexis had always been loyal to the family business, and like Carter, Grace had no interest in making it her life. At least his brother stuck around and stayed loyal to the family while he worked to find his true calling.

Grace, on the other hand, ditched her family to sow her wild oats. Or do whatever she did in Europe. Not that Brady cared. He didn't know why he was even thinking about her right now.

Making one last sweep across his chin, he tapped his razor under the water, washing off all the foam and whiskers, and placed it on its shelf in the medicine cabinet behind the mirror.

The latch didn't hold when he closed it. Just one more thing to replace in the old house. Padding across the hall to his bedroom, he made a quick mental note about what he had hanging in his closet.

A suit coat he hadn't worn since his father's funeral, two winter jackets, a raincoat, a handful of flannels, and three nice button-down shirts. One white, one light blue, and the third a green and blue plaid his mother got him for Christmas a few years back.

Brady had only worn it on Thanksgiving and Christmas, not having much need to dress up for any other occasion. In his line of work, a plaid shirt was dressing up.

Since he wore the light blue shirt to last year's Fall Festival, Brady took the plaid one off the hanger and tossed it on his bed. He found his nice pair of jeans in his bureau buried underneath piles of work jeans and pulled out a clean pair of boxers and a pair of socks.

"You walkin' or drivin' over?" Carter asked from behind him as Brady tugged on his jeans.

"I'll drive. That way if anyone needs a ride I'll have my truck handy."

"Always the boy scout."

He ignored the overused joke. If Carter hadn't been so unreliable over the years, Brady wouldn't have to always be on his A-game. Not that driving tonight had anything to do with his brother. Carter could walk the half-mile home if he drank too much. Brady and his truck would act more like a taxi service, making sure the rest of Crystal Cove made it home safe and sound.

Last year, he ended up driving the Patterson boys and Mary Lou Bullock home from the festival. The Patterson boys, he expected it from. Mrs. Bullock, however, had shocked him. The normally reserved seventy-five-year-old grandmother had too many beers and had partied it up on the dance floor like she was still in her twenties. He hadn't minded being her designated driver.

"Mom says she's sitting this one out. Wants to go to bed early."

She'd once been the go-go-go mom of the year, never accepting help when she could do something herself. This past summer and fall's harvest seemed to have put her over the edge. Brady feared there was something bigger going on with her. Since their father died, she'd been diligent with getting regular check-ups, and making Carter and Brady go as well.

Had their father's cancer been caught earlier, he'd still be with them today.

Maybe he should stay home to make sure she was okay. "Why don't you go on over to the party and give me a call when you want to come home?"

"No way, man. You've gotta get your pathetic ass off the farm. You need a social life." Carter dipped his head to the right.

He didn't *need* a social life, but his conversations with his fruit trees and seedlings did get pretty old. It would be nice to have someone reciprocate the words.

Brady tucked his wallet in his back pocket.

"You're worried about Mom." Despite his careless attitude, Carter was no dimwit.

"Yeah. I think we need to have a sit down with her. See what's going on."

"She got mad when I tried to help carry a crate of mini pumpkins across the parking lot."

"You know she doesn't like feeling helpless." Brady finished buttoning his shirt and nodded toward the door. Carter stepped back and headed down the stairs. "We'll need to be more tactful in suggesting she see a doctor," he said to Carter's back.

"You think it's something bad?"

"I don't know." It wasn't something he wanted to think about. To admit out loud.

They climbed into Brady's truck, dropping the subject of their mom. The drive only took a few minutes. Once he parked his truck, Carter hopped out and gave Brady a hard pat on the back.

"I'm gonna be the bigger man here and let you have your pick of the single ladies tonight."

"Thanks." He chuckled, knowing the dance wasn't an event that drew in the younger crowd. For the most part, it was locals and elderly tourists who attended small town events. Not exactly a singles hookup place.

The country band was well underway when they stepped inside. The barn had been decorated with tiny white lights, and bales of hay were strategically placed around the room with mums and other fall décor. Tables made from oak wine barrels were decorated with cornucopias filled with apples and oranges, and colored leaves spilled out onto the tables, while little white candles flickered as people walked by.

From what he'd heard at last week's town meeting, Lily, Jenna, and Grace had a hand in decorating the room.

"I'm getting a beer. You want anything?"

"Sure."

Carter gave him a two-finger salute and strode off toward the bar.

"In all the years I've known you," Mia said as she sidled up to him, looping her arm through his. "I think I've seen you more this past year than the past ten."

It wasn't like he and Mia were close friends. He went to school with her older brother Ty, and their parents had always been friendly with each other. Other than that, they weren't much more than mutual acquaintances.

"You're welcome," Ben said as he outstretched his hand toward Brady. "Glad you could stop by."

Ben deserved most of the credit for bringing the town together. Ironic since he'd never stepped foot in Maine until less than two years ago. The three-day trip intended to help Coastal Vines with its marketing and strategic planning turned into a marriage to Alexis and the businesses seeing a spike in sales.

It meant Brady was busier than normal, but he'd also spent more time at town meetings and paying it forward. Networking with not only the other farmers, but the restaurants and local shops were important as well.

"It always amazes me how nice this turned out." Sitting on top of the tasting room, the function hall had once been Alexis' apartment. It was Ben's idea to gut it out and turn the unused space into a town gathering place.

"Thanks. It was definitely a group effort. Ty and his crew do impeccable work. And Alexis has some great friends with an eye for this kind of thing." Ben picked up one of the mini pumpkins on the table and tossed it in the air.

"Easy on the decorations," Lily said, looking lovely as always in a girly but elegant brown top and long skirt. "Jenna, Grace, and I spent a lot of time making the hall look pretty."

"You girls did an amazing job," Ben said.

"Holy shit." Mia picked up Lily's left hand. A light pink stone sparkled in the candlelight. "What is this? Why didn't you tell us? My brother's an asshole for keeping it a secret." Mia wrenched her arm from Brady's and pulled Lily into a tight hug. "Congratulations, sister-in-law."

Lily bit her lip and held out her hand, glowing with newly engaged smiles at her ring. "Ty proposed tonight. In the gazebo. It was so romantic." She held her hands to her heart and closed her eyes.

"Congratulations, Lily." Ben hugged her as well. "Where's Ty at?"

"Grace, Cameron, and Hope drove in as we were leaving the gazebo. He's outside talking to them. I was too excited to keep it to myself so I ran in here to share with you guys."

"I'm going to have a sister." Mia tugged at Lily's long ponytail. "I'll probably be a pain in the ass."

"Don't we know it," Ty said from behind their growing crowd.

"Congratulations, both of you." Brady hugged Lily and shook Ty's hand. "I haven't seen you this happy since..."

"Game-winning goal in overtime my senior year."

"Hockey?" Ben asked.

"Soccer." Ty draped his arm around Lily's shoulder. "Now if you don't mind, I'm going to take my fiancée out on the dance floor."

Lily giggled as Ty looped his fingers through hers and tugged her on to the dance floor. Brady admired those two. From the little he knew, Lily didn't have any family around. She'd be marrying into a strong family unit though. The Parkers had a solid reputation in town. Mia may be a bit of a wild child—just like Carter—but she had a good heart.

"You guys hear the news?" With his back to the door, Brady hadn't seen Hope and Cameron come in. The music was loud enough to block out the squeaky barn door, but not so loud you had to scream so the person next to you could hear you.

"I can't believe my shit head brother didn't tell me he was going to propose. Jerkwad," Mia muttered and strode off toward the bar with a smile.

"He kept it from all of us. Said he told his parents, but don't tell Mia that." Hope rubbed Brady on his triceps in a friendly gesture. "Nice to see you, Brady."

He always liked Hope. It wasn't often Brady left his house to eat, but when he did, he went to Hope's restaurant, The Happy Clam. The Sunrise diner wasn't a bad little hole-in-the-wall place either, but he preferred to make his breakfasts at home. And his mother made amazing dinners, so why go to a diner?

Because of its reputation, Brady had gone to Willies BYO place a handful of times. When living in coastal Maine, fried fish was a staple, and making it at home just wasn't the same. Other than that, like Carter had accused him of over and over again, he didn't leave the property much and was a bit of a bore. He didn't mean to be, didn't want to be, but he had responsibilities.

"Looks like we'll be planning a bachelor party again. You in this time, Brady?"

He felt bad about bowing out of Cameron's earlier this spring. He had planting and pruning to do and couldn't get away. Carter managed to squeeze in a night of debauchery though.

According to Carter, the night was far too tame, too mellow to call it a bachelor party. Cards and beer at Ty's. It was more Brady's style, and he'd wished he'd gone.

"I'll do my best."

As more people streamed into the hall, it got harder and harder to hear each other. He noticed Carter across the room, double-fisted, and went over to snag his drink.

"Thanks for the beer." Brady took the bottle from his brother and brought it to his lips. The cold ale went down too easily, too fast. How long had it been since he'd been out with a guy to have a beer? Too long. And cracking open a cold one in his mother's kitchen didn't count.

"Just getting caught up with Steve."

Brady nodded to his seasonal worker. "How's the Achilles doing?" He'd tore it last week carting around a crate of pumpkins. He had three decades on Brady and could lift more than any man half his age.

"Doc says it's gonna be a while. Good thing the season is almost over. 'For you know it, we'll be cursing the snow and icy wind."

"Ain't that the truth." The three men held up their beer bottles and tipped the tops together.

The band changed its tempo from the slow ballad to an upbeat tune, and dozens flocked to the dance floor, including Grace.

He hadn't seen her until now, not that he was looking. He was actually intentionally *not* looking. It was hard not to notice her tonight in her teal dress. It hugged her in all the right places without being too revealing and left her long legs bare. Brady trailed his gaze up and down them, stopping at her toes. They peeped out from her white heels. Or were they beige? Maybe tan. He couldn't tell and it didn't matter, and he silently thanked God or whoever created those shoes for what they did to her calves.

Hell, her ankles. Even her kneecaps looked sexy.

He took a sip from his beer and turned his back on the dance floor. If he was thanking God for high heel shoes, he absolutely needed to get out more.

"You hear the news? I'm gaining another daughter." Wade Parker slid onto the stool next to him and asked the bartender for a draft beer.

"I did. Congrats. Lily's a nice lady."

"That she is." Wade sipped his beer and nudged his elbow against Brady's. "I didn't think I'd ever see the day when Ty would settle down, or be as happy as he is."

"He's definitely that."

"How about you, Brady? How are you doing?"

When Brady's father died, Wade and Celeste Parker were at their farm every day, helping his mother with chores, bringing by dinners for the boys. Wade had made it clear he wasn't trying to replace their father, but that he'd be there for them if they had questions, needed support, stuff they would need from their dad.

At first, Brady had resented his attempt to push himself in their lives, but that was a typical knee-jerk reaction. Wade and Celeste had always been friends with his parents. It was only natural—and kind—that they'd offer to help.

Even though Ty and Brady had grown up with each other, their parents forcing them together for play dates when they were toddlers, and hanging out during family get-togethers, they never had much in common other than age.

When Ty came back from the war he stayed to himself, as Brady had always done. And he didn't have any war stories to hide from. It was only the past year when they both came out of their hiding. Ty more than Brady.

There wasn't anything he didn't like about Ty. They were two socially quiet guys who kept to themselves. When they did see each other through their mutual friends—mostly Alexis and Ben—they got along just fine.

Wade cocked his head, waiting for a response. "I'm doing well. Season's about to come to a dead halt, so I'll find myself with a few extra minutes to spare. Once the snow flies, I'll be busy keeping up with the removal."

"That's good. That's good." Wade sipped his beer again. "Is there a special girl in your life?" He hadn't asked that question in over a year. Not since he went out on a date with Amber Bellows from Lincolnville. She worked on her father's lobster boat. Something Brady deeply respected.

Hard, physical labor, families working together, but other than common interests, he and Amber had nothing in common. Which sounded absurd. There wasn't a spark. Any interest other than work related and small town talk. The same went for his sporadic dates with Julie.

"No. I don't have a lot of time to date."

"When you find the right woman, you'll make time." Wade winked and clinked his glass with Brady's bottle.

As soon as Wade vacated the stool, Ty filled it. "My dad talk your ear off?"

"Not at all. He's happy for you."

"My parents didn't think they'd ever get grandchildren."

"Is Lily—"

"No." Ty chuckled. "I didn't mean it like that. She's not. I wouldn't mind if she was. Maybe in a year or so though."

"Ty." The furrow in Hope's brow was deep with concern. "There's a problem."

"Lily?" He shot out of his stool.

"No. Yes. Chill." She put a hand on his shoulder and pushed him back down. "The woman is so in love with you it's almost sickening." That earned a cheeky grin from Ty. "She's concerned though. About the ring."

All the excitement and adoration that had been on Ty's face a second ago dropped. Brady turned away from them not wanting to eavesdrop on their private conversation.

"She doesn't like it," Brady heard Ty's heavy sigh behind him.

"Are you kidding? She freaking loves it. That's the problem."

"Not following."

"She's worried you spent too much on her. She knows you've been saving to finish the house."

"I told her I'd been saving for her ring."

"Yeah. She said that. She also said that you totally blew that budget."

"Actually, the opposite. Grace helped me out."

"Grace loaned you money?" Hope's voice squeaked. "I thought she was barely making ends meet."

"I don't know anything about her financial status. She has connections though. Friends who are in the fashion and jewelry business. She helped me find an antique ring. Something unique and special for Lily. I knew I couldn't compete with Stewart Jewels."

Brady didn't know much about Lily and didn't get the jewels comment.

"Ty, you have to know Lily loves you for you."

"I do. Still, I needed to impress her with the ring. Grace is a miracle worker. Not only did she help me find the perfect ring, but she also wheeled and dealed for me. I only spent half my ring budget."

"Really? That's awesome." Brady got a little jab in the back when Hope leaned in to hug Ty. "Why didn't you tell me you and Grace were ring shopping?"

"I should have told you. I know." Ty and Hope had been best friends for years. For a while there, the entire town thought her daughter, Delaney, was his.

"Yeah. I'm totally jealous you didn't let me know you were planning on popping the question. It's cool about Grace though. That's sweet. Her helping you with the ring. She and Lily have become close too."

"I want Lily to have friends. To have the freedom she never had before."

"What are you two up to over here?" Another jolt to Brady's back and he swiveled in his seat, his back no longer to the growing group. "My fiancée may not like to dance, but I know you do." Lily kissed Ty on the lips and tugged at Hope's hand. "Let's dance."

Cameron filled the spot where Hope once was. "Hope reading you the riot act over here? She told me to play interference with Lily while she talked with you."

"We're good." Ty sipped his beer with a smug smile.

"Tell me I never looked this whipped when Hope and I first got together."

Ty spit his beer out and bent over laughing. "Dude, you still have it bad."

"You can be objective, right?" Cameron pointed at Brady with his water bottle.

"I can try."

"Who's more whipped? Ty or me?"

Knowing either way he answered wouldn't earn him any brownie points, Brady scanned the dance floor and the tables, filled with families, couples, young and old, and jerked his head toward the back left corner.

"Ben."

Both men followed his gaze and bust out laughing.

"I like this guy. Bartender, get this man another beer." Cameron slapped a bill on the counter and covered it with his empty water bottle. "And another water for me."

"You driving?"

"Yeah. Figured Hope would want to celebrate with Lily."

"What about you celebrating with me?" Ty pouted.

"That's what bachelor parties are for."

The three men tipped up their bottles in a cheer.

Even though Brady wasn't part of the conversation, he felt a familiar connection with these men.

Friends. He was quickly gaining them.

As well as a new admiration for the not-so-selfish fashion boutique owner who flowed like a turquoise Caribbean wave out on the dance floor.

CHAPTER EIGHT

EVEN THOUGH HER DRESS was light and flowy, Grace felt like she was wearing a heavy sweatshirt. She loved dancing. And dancing with girlfriends was even better. Girlfriends who wouldn't judge her for her looks, her clothing, her upbringing.

Straight-up real people. This was kind of cool. Of course, they didn't know about her secret. Once they did, once the rumor mill—which was based on truth in her case—made its way across the pond, she'd be ostracized by the women who had higher morals and values than her.

In Lily's case, it hadn't been rumors that spread across the pond; it had been a case of being in the know. It took a few months for Grace to realize why Lily had looked so familiar. Once she did, not knowing about Lily being in the witness protection plan, she'd posted a picture of them together, unbeknownst to her, revealing Lily's whereabouts.

Even with her alias, Lily could've been detected by her ex-husband's criminal connections. Grace would never forgive herself for potentially putting Lily's life in jeopardy. Thankfully Lily had a huge, forgiving heart and had befriended Grace. Grace would do anything to try to right her wrong, including helping Ty find the perfect engagement ring.

During one of their monthly book club meetings, Lily had talked to the girls about Ty's insecurity about her past wealth. Lily, or rather her given name, Veronica Stewart, was heir to a billion dollar jewel industry. Stewart jewels were right up there with Tiffany.

Lily had given it all up in order to protect her identity and had told them how little she cared about money. Grace couldn't imagine trying to compete with that. The least she could do was help the guy out. It would make Lily happy, which in turn, eased Grace's guilt. A little.

The "Cotton Eye Joe" ended and Grace let out a loud *woot!* "I need some water. Lily, what can I get you?"

"Oh. Water sounds good." Lily wiped the back of her hand across her forehead.

"Wine it is. You're celebrating."

"I knew you two were destined to be with each other," Priscilla, the eccentric waitress from the Sunrise Diner said as she traipsed across the dance floor to give Lily a warm, motherly hug. "I hear Ty has finally asked you to marry him."

"Finally." Lily beamed. "It took him long enough."

Their friendship hadn't turned into anything romantic until this summer, but, according to Lily, when you knew, you knew. And, yeah, their love was pretty freaking evident.

"I'm happy for you, sweetie. You two come to breakfast tomorrow. My treat."

"Aw, thanks, Priscilla."

The band asked for requests, and Mia yelled out a song by Sugarland.

"Oh, good call." Lily moved with the music and sang along with the band. The woman was a perpetual ball of positive energy.

"I'm too old for this, but you girls keep at it." Priscilla turned to Grace. "I haven't seen you since puberty first introduced itself to you. And look at you, lit up like a Christmas tree."

"Excuse me?" The music got louder, making it hard to hear Priscilla very well.

"Red. Full of adventure. Travel. Food." Priscilla smirked. "Your love life."

A lump formed in Grace's throat, making it difficult to swallow. No. There was no way she could know about...

Priscilla stroked Grace's arm. "There's a layer of green underneath, trying to work its way out. Let it, dear. Good things will happen. Very, *very* good things. " She sashayed off the dance floor with a knowing smile on her face. What she actually knew, Grace hadn't a clue.

Maybe Priscilla was on to something. She claimed to read people's auras and Lily's, she'd said, was purple. Full of life, love, spunk, and secrets. When Grace got home tonight she'd Google the crap out of green and see what the hell the crazy lady was talking about.

Grace had stayed clear of the diner. It wasn't her... cup of tea. Breakfast consisted of copious amounts of coffee. She didn't need food until lunch. And greasy food was not her idea of a good meal.

Besides, she'd been living at home, and her mother was an excellent cook. The only times Grace went out was with the girls, and The Sunrise Diner was not on their list of girls' night out hot spots.

So either wacko lady was full of crap or she knew her shit. Needing a drink now more than ever, she weaved her way through the dancers and found her way to the bar.

"Can I have a glass of Lobster Red and a glass of water, please?"

"Coming right up."

While the bartender did his thing, Grace dropped to the only empty barstool, bumping her shoulder against the solid back of the man next to her.

Brady.

"Um. Sorry."

He did a slow one-eighty until his knees knocked into hers.

"Wow. You clean up well." Oh. Did she say that out loud? It was true. His cheeks, normally dusted with a fine layer of scruff after working in the fields, or trees, or wherever, was gone. His upper lip lifted in a slight smirk, and a dimple she'd never seen before appeared.

And, shit. Brady's eyes were gray. And green. And there could have been a swirl of blue mixed in as well. She'd never noticed before. She'd never been this close to him. The temptation to lean over and touch that cute little-indented spot on his cheek was overwhelming.

Oh. Was that her kidney? Stomach? Intestine? She didn't know what it was, but some organ in her core tingled and shifted.

"You look..." Brady paused and gulped a mouthful of air before continuing, "pretty."

His face strained, as if the compliment was difficult to formulate, so she tamped down that extra little flutter that occurred when he said *pretty*. Not nice or beautiful or stunning. Pretty. Like a ten-year-old.

Which was what he thought of her. A spoiled little kid. His dislike for her was sketched in his face. She should hit him up for a game of poker. She'd know every time he had a crap hand. His brows would furrow, he'd purse his lips, and he'd pause before tossing in his chips. Just like he did every time he spoke her.

"Yeah. Thanks," she did her best to sound flippant.

"I'm surprised you're still here." Alexis appeared next to her. "Hey, Brady. Good season for you guys this year, huh? I can't wait to sample the blueberry wine. We'll have to come up with a cool name for it. Something that blends our farms."

"That's kind of you. I'm sure whatever you and Ben come up with will be great. As will the wine. Speaking of, can I get you a drink?"

It was junior high all over again. Grace trying to get in with the older crowd, but all the guys wanted to hang out with her older sister. Alexis played football right up until her senior year. The guys who wanted to hang out with Grace only wanted to get into her pants.

And even then, she was always "Alexis' little sister," never known for being an individual. Not until Alexis buried herself with work on the winery was Grace able to make a name for herself.

A reputation Brady obviously hadn't forgotten about.

"I'm surprised you're not outside by the bonfire. Carter, Jimmy, Kev, and Max are all out there. I didn't think this was your kind of scene," Alexis said to her, sipping the wine Brady just purchased for her.

The insult stung. Jimmy, Kev, and Max were twenty-one-year-old farmhands, and even though Carter was her age, he acted ten years younger. It was obvious her sister didn't want her hanging around with her friends. The more sophisticated crowd.

"I was dancing and told Lily I'd get her a drink."

"Doesn't look like she wants it anymore."

Grace looked over her shoulder and saw Lily wrapped in Ty's arms in the middle of the dance floor. Alexis had embarrassed her twice in less than a minute. She knew when and where she wasn't wanted and was getting faster at reading the signs.

Alexis hadn't said too much when Grace had joined the book club and was quiet when Grace tagged along with a few of the girls' night out events. She hadn't meant to invade her sister's space, but no matter what she did, it seemed to be the wrong move.

Alexis made it quite clear she was disappointed and embarrassed that Grace took off for Europe, barely earning a degree in liberal arts. What good would that do? She'd never measure up, no matter how hard she tried, so why even try anymore.

Grace handed Alexis the wine glass. "Can you give this to Lily? I'm going to go join the crew outside." She took her water with her and with a forced smile. "Maybe Marshall Blue for your new label?" She said goodnight to Brady then Alexis and walked out of the function hall with as much dignity as she could scrape up off the floor.

• • • •

"MARSHALL BLUE. I LIKE it." His mom would get a kick out of having their name on a wine label. Especially one associated with Coastal Vines.

"What am I missing here?" Alexis took a sip of her wine and set it on the bar.

"Not sure what you're talking about."

"Bullshit. I've been watching you watch her. She's not right for you, Brady. And frankly, I'm surprised you're giving her a second glance."

Brady ran his hand through his hair and shook his head. "Not sure what you're talking about," he said again.

"Grace comes floating into town without a worry on her back and gallivants her way into everyone's life as if she's been here for the past six years working side by side with us all."

"I thought you wanted your sister to come home." Brady took a pull of his beer, confused as ever. He'd been good friends with Alexis since they were in kindergarten. They were more like siblings with farming and living off the land in common.

Alexis was as sweet and kind and hardworking as they came. And loyal to her family. She'd expressed her annoyance with Grace's absence many times, but Brady didn't think it was the extra pair of hands she wanted. Alexis was independent and knew Grace had no desire to get her hands dirty.

"I thought so too."

What she wanted, he knew, was her sister. There were years of some serious resentment built up inside his little friend. She may barely come to his chest, but Alexis was a spitfire. One to be reckoned with.

Grace had the height, the natural beauty, the sense of style. And with that, came a lack of respect, not only from her sister, but Brady took a long look at himself and realized from him too.

He'd been judging her based on past behavior. Since she'd returned to Maine, she'd helped her family with vineyard tours and pouring samples to guests. If rumors were true, she'd worked a few months at a retail shop in Camden. And now she was a store owner.

Hope, Lily, Jenna, and Mia had all taken her in as part of their group. If Grace was as snobby as the reputation that preceded her, Brady doubted the women would have accepted her into their social circle.

Unless they were doing it as a favor to Alexis. But Alexis didn't seem too happy with her sister's involvement in her life.

"And you've avoided my question."

"Not sure what the question was," he stalled. The band ended its dance number and announced it would be taking a five-minute break.

The dance floor emptied, and Brady glanced about the room hoping someone would come tear Alexis off him. Not that she'd pinned him with questions, but he could feel them coming his way.

"You're thinking below the waist. Typical guy. I know my sister is pretty, but seriously, Brady. She's so wrong for you."

There was no way Alexis could have read his thoughts earlier. No way she knew how his mind had wandered somewhere it shouldn't have gone, thinking about Grace in different circumstances.

"Your sister and I have barely spoken to each other. It's been business-related only. If anything, you should be having this talk with Carter."

The stupid wave of jealousy heated his cheeks. He shouldn't care if his brother and Grace were involved, now or before.

"I already have. They're friends. Like you and me. He said he'd have sex with her if she offered, but didn't want any type of relationship. He already asked if she'd go for the friends with benefits deal."

"He did?" His brother could be an asshole, but he didn't think he'd be that inconsiderate to a woman.

"You've met your brother, right?" Alexis smirked and picked up her wine again. Carter was a man whore. He loved women. Loved having sex with women, and they seemed to fawn all over him. Grace though? Carter usually kept his trysts out of Crystal Cove. "His proposition was a joke. Although he said he'd gladly take her up on it if she ever changed her mind."

He clenched his jaw and squeezed his bottle a little too hard. Loosening his grip, he set his beer on the bar top.

"Back to you. You're interested. I can tell."

"I'm not."

"And now you're defensive."

"Only because you don't know what you're talking about."

"My sister is trouble. She's a flake who can't commit to anything. When her fancy shop thing ends up being a bust and a money suck, she'll come crawling back home, taking back her childhood bedroom and mooching off our parents and whining to my husband."

"You don't have faith in your sister?"

Alexis gave him a stare down. Her lack of expression and the tilt of her head spoke louder than any words.

"She seems to be trying."

"Like I said. You have the hots for Grace."

"No, I don't."

"That's how she gets what she wants."

"Aren't you being a little harsh?" It was unlike Alexis to be so ... snide. This was another side of her he'd never witnessed. In the past, when she'd talked about Grace, it had always been bitter at first, complaining that her sister had left the family with all the hard work. But there was a longing for her sister to come back home. Deep down inside, Brady believed Alexis loved her sister.

They had issues, for sure.

"Look at her." He would have if she hadn't left the building. "She's not cut out for this town. She's forgotten what winter in Maine can be like. I give her until Christmas, and then she's out."

Something deep inside Brady felt bad for Grace. He'd judged her quickly, as had Alexis, and probably many others in town.

Whatever her reputation had been back in high school, Grace was now a business owner. She helped Ty find the perfect engagement ring for Lily and from the sounds of it, hadn't taken any of the credit.

Brady pushed to his feet. "Give Sophie a kiss for me." He placed his hand on Alexis' shoulder and squeezed. "I'm going to head home. Early mornings. You know how those go."

"Sure do. I promised Ben one dance," Alexis—always the tomboy—shuddered, "and then we're out as well."

"I'll see you around." Brady placed a few bills on the bar and picked up his fleece coat from the back of his stool.

Avoiding eye contact so he wouldn't get stuck staying any later, he ducked out of the hall and headed toward the back of the gravel parking lot to his truck.

The full moon illuminated a lone silhouette in the gazebo. The woman leaned against the archway, arms crossed, looking out over the grapevines. Even with her back to him, Brady knew the figure.

Debating whether to give her privacy or to say hello, or goodnight, or something, he ground his toe into the dirt and turned his head in a one-eighty. On the other side of the parking lot, a fire crackled, and deep voices laughed and echoed through the cool night air.

Brady kicked at a small rock and it flew out, ricocheting against an oak barrel and off the gazebo step.

Grace spun around.

"Hi." The whites of her eyes were big and round. "I didn't mean to scare you. Sorry."

"That's okay." She sniffed and rubbed her chin against her shoulder.

His legs moved of their own accord up the steps to the gazebo. Grace stepped away from him, and he stopped dead center.

"Are you alright?"

Her sister had been pretty rough on her.

"Sure."

He had no right talking to her about anything personal. Alexis had intentionally embarrassed her in front of him, and his heart hurt a little for her. He wasn't sure what the gentlemanly thing to do was.

"Nice night." *Smooth.* Brady tucked his hands deep in his fleece pockets and rocked back on his heels.

"Yeah." Grace nodded and looked away. The moon continued to play against her pale skin. She chewed on her top lip and sniffled again.

Shit. She'd been crying. That completely changed the game. What the hell did he do with a crying woman? If it had been his fault, he'd apologize. This wasn't his doing—thankfully—so now what?

"Can I get you anything?" Again, lame.

"Nope. Peachy hunky dory here." Grace let out a humorless laugh and shrugged. "I was just taking in some air before heading home. To think, a week ago all I'd have to do was walk up those stairs." She nodded toward the main house where she'd been living since back in Maine. "Now it's a whole ten minutes to town."

"Have you been drinking?" Brady couldn't help but be the responsible adult. It was ingrained in him now.

"Water. I hadn't planned on staying too long. I need to look fresh when I open the store tomorrow morning." Again, the smile that didn't reach her eyes.

"You always look fresh, Grace." The compliment slipped out.

Grace slapped a hand over her chest. "First I'm pretty and now I look fresh. And your face didn't make that look like it hurt to say it. I don't know what to do with all the compliments. And here I thought you hated me."

Brady stepped closer, those legs of his moving on their own again. "I never said I hated you."

"Please," she snorted. "You and Alexis couldn't look any-more down on me. I know what I do will never measure up to the work you two put into your jobs, but I'm not—"

First his legs, now his hand. Brady had no intentions of reaching out and touching her. He had no right, but his brain hadn't registered the thought fast enough to his hand. His fingers wrapped around her wrist, stopping it from swirling around as she spoke.

Those eyes, as green as the dress she wore, turned up toward his and hell, his knees nearly buckled.

Doe eyes. Scared, lost, passionate eyes. Frozen in the moment, he didn't know what to do or say next. Hell, if any of his body parts moved faster than his brain he would be in deep shit.

"Owning your own business, no matter what it is, is something to be proud of." Her skin was soft and delicate under his rough and calloused hands. He didn't want to squeeze too hard, afraid he'd break her. Proud of himself for resisting the temptation to stroke her wrist with the pad of his thumb, he let her go.

Grace rubbed her wrist with her other hand, those stormy sea eyes lowering to his mouth.

No. Don't do it.

She did.

The tip of her tongue traced her lips before she caught her bottom one between her teeth.

Shoving his hands back in his pockets, he stepped back and cleared his throat. "Can I give you a ride home?"

"I have my car," she said, her voice soft.

"Okay then. I'll, uh, walk you to it. It's late." He stated the obvious. Also obvious, they were in a no-crime town and her car couldn't be too far away.

"You don't have to."

"It's dark." *Way to go, Captain Obvious.*

Finally agreeing, Grace nodded and stepped past him, a trail of spice following in her wake. He walked elbow-to-elbow with her around to the front of the winery where he spotted her white sedan.

"Pretty soon we'll be running out to warm up our cars five minutes before we need to leave." This was why he didn't date. He said stupid things to women.

"I'm definitely not looking forward to that."

The casual bet Alexis made rang through his ears. *I give her until Christmas and then she'll be out.* He waited while she unlocked her car.

"Drive safely." Grace slid behind the wheel, and he held on to the door to close it for her. "Congratulations on your store. I'm sure it will be a great success."

"Thanks," she said, the doubt in her eyes as evident as the doubt in her sister's words.

"You have that drive. The passion. If anyone can make a store like that work in Crystal Cove, it's you, Grace."

She tilted her head up, her mouth open. He waited as she struggled to formulate words.

"That means a lot to me." She closed her eyes, scrunching them tight before opening them again. "There aren't many who have faith in me. I'd put you in that category as well."

"I'm sorry I've been..."

"An ass?"

"Something like that." He smirked. He'd been too quick to judge. No, she wasn't perfect, far from it, but she deserved a chance. A shot at achieving her dream, even if it seemed outlandish and nothing Brady could comprehend.

They were as different as different could be. Their interests were as far right and as far left as could be.

Yet something about Grace pulled at his heartstrings.

And damn, he was a sucker for those legs.

CHAPTER NINE

THE CLOSET'S OPENING week had been more than what Grace expected. Her friends had rallied, stopping by every day to visit and even buy a few pieces. Mia's social circle was the biggest, and she'd told her party girls to check out the shop.

And they did. The women weren't what Grace had expected. They were more like... her. Or rather, who she was in Europe. Shallow, superficial, and on the prowl for bigger and better. She was surprised Mia hung out with the women.

At six, she closed up and hurried up to her apartment to put the pizza dip she'd made this morning into the oven to warm up. It was her turn to bring snacks to the book club. While the dip heated, she changed into leggings and a pair of cute dark plum heels and pulled her hair up into a messy bun.

She'd finished the Sandra Brown novel two nights ago and even prepared a handful of questions for the girls to ponder over. They'd been on a roll the past two months actually talking about books and not just Lily and Ty's love life. Granted, now that they were engaged, the topic would be back to them and not as much on the books they were reading, which was fine with Grace.

The off-topic meets were her favorite. They made Grace feel a little more connected, one step closer to calling the girls her true friends.

Alexis' dismissal of her the other night still stung. She'd never come right out and said it, but Grace knew her sister wasn't thrilled with her return. Grace hadn't meant to prod her way into her sister's friends' lives. It just sort of happened.

It started with Hope's invite to a book night, then an invitation from Mia to join them in Rockland for a concert in the park, and then her connection with Lily. Grace didn't invite herself to anything and even declined the invitation to some of the backyard barbecues this past summer.

The once a month book clubs were her favorite though. She'd always been a reader. Books were what got her through those lonely days and nights when she didn't have a friend to call on or a sister to talk to. She could escape in a book and forget how truly alone she was in the world, despite living in a glamorous city like Paris and partying every weekend.

It had been her idea to prepare questions ahead of time. Alexis had scoffed at first, but Jenna and Lily were excited about it. Hope thought it was a decent idea as well. Mia didn't care either way.

The timer on the stove went off. Grace finished brushing her teeth and rushed into the kitchen. She picked up two potholders and opened the oven door. A wave of heat blasted her face, followed by the smell of sauce and pepperoni.

There were a few things she was good at. And while cooking may not be one of them, she was learning. Pinterest had been her new best friend. She'd always admired her mother's cooking, and when home these past months she started helping out in the kitchen.

Cooking was therapeutic. There were some major disasters, like when she drained lasagna noodles and placed the plastic strainer back on the hot burner. Or when she made a roasted chicken and forgot to take out the gizzards. Or when she added a fourth of a cup of baking soda instead of a teaspoon in her oatmeal raisin cookies.

For the most part, she could handle one recipe at a time. Multi-tasking was the challenge. That was when most of the blunders happened.

Placing the hot dish on the stovetop, Grace let out a sigh of relief as she inspected the perfectly bubbly cheese layer on top. She slipped off the mitts and took the baguette out of the plastic sleeve and sliced it into little rounds.

Not having anything fancy, she found a Ziploc bag and tossed the bread in it. Now how to transport the hot dip? She hadn't thought it all the way through. She scanned her kitchen, limited on supplies even with her mother's boxes of donated dishes and utensils.

The dip was in an eight-by-eight glass dish. Spotting the nine-by-thirteen glass pan, she set the dip inside. Not bad. Only it slipped around when she picked up the larger pan. Taking it out again, she wrapped a small towel around the dip and then placed it in the nine-by-thirteen pan.

"Perfect." Now to make it to Books by the Ocean without dropping it. The twenty-two steps to the bottom of her stairs didn't pose a problem now. In the winter they'd be brutal. She wouldn't dare juggle a hot dish if there was ice on the steps.

It only took a few minutes to load up and drive to the bookstore. If it was warmer out and she didn't have to bring the snacks, she would have walked. Hope, Jenna, and Lily were already there.

"That smells amazing." Jenna took the dish from Grace and set it on the square coffee table.

"Thanks. It's been so cold out lately I figured a warm snack was in order."

Lily opened the bag of bread and dipped it in the cheesy sauce. "Ohmygawd," she said around a mouthful of pizza dip. "My old oven made this?"

"Technically, Grace did." Hope followed suit, diving in as well.

Lily didn't like to cook. According to her, the only use the oven got in the apartment was to heat up frozen dinners.

"I want this recipe." Jenna dabbed her mouth with a napkin and sat down. "I hope Mia and Alexis can't make it tonight. More for us."

Jenna, always so sweet and kind, must really love the dip to wish the other two not come.

"I totally heard that," Mia said from behind the seating area. "And since I'm drink girl tonight, you're not getting any."

"As long as I don't have to share the dip, I don't care."

"It can't be that good. I brought hot toddies. My nips froze just walking across the parking lot." Mia set a bag down next to the food and unwound her purple scarf, tossing it on the back of the couch.

"Nice mouth," Hope scolded. "It amazes me why you don't have a boyfriend."

"They're overrated." Mia took out a thermos and poured the drinks.

Grace had to agree. She'd yet to have one who treated her well and made the effort worth it. Taking out her book, she settled on the couch next to Jenna.

"Weather forecast says it'll drop down to fifteen degrees tonight. Pretty cold for the first week of November," Hope said.

"Which will kill my grapes." Alexis blew into the store, cheeks flushed from the cold. "I can't stay long. Ben and I have a long night ahead of us keeping an eye on the crops."

"Don't you need cold weather to make ice wine?" Grace asked. Her sister had great success the past two winters with ice wine. The wine was delicious but so much work went into making it.

The right side of Alexis' face lifted in a snarly glare. "Not now. Not this cold. It's too soon. Don't you know anything about—"

"This is my first book club as an engaged woman," Lily interrupted, holding out her left hand across the middle of the table. She giggled and winked at Grace when they made eye contact.

While Grace hadn't bared her soul to Lily, her friend had picked up on the hostility between the sisters. She'd never been one who had to be the center of attention, and her tactic was clearly to break the tension in the room.

Grace blinked back grateful tears and sipped on the hot toddy Mia had made. After more *ooohs* and *aaahs*, everyone settled into the couches and chairs around the table.

"Grace, this pizza dip is totally kick ass." Mia wiped her chin with a napkin.

"Thank you."

"'K, ladies. Who came prepared with questions?" Hope, always the leader, attempted to bring the conversation to books.

"I have one." Jenna raised her hand. "When's the big day?"

Lily nestled into the cushions of the couch and laughed. "We're not sure yet. We wanted to check in with Ty's family and with you guys to see when would be the least obtrusive."

"You're too sweet. This day should be about you two though," Hope said. "Cam and I didn't want to wait, and we didn't care what others thought. No offense, ladies."

"I'm glad you didn't wait. I don't see the point," Mia said.

"Summer would be beautiful, but you're all so busy. Maybe early spring before it gets crowded around here? But fall is gorgeous too. I don't know."

For the next thirty minutes, Grace listened as Lily and her friends chatted about dresses, color schemes, and flowers.

"You're awful quiet," Jenna said, scooping up the last bit of pizza dip and bringing it to her mouth.

The side-eye Alexis cast her way all evening hadn't gone unnoticed. She wasn't welcome here.

"I guess my mind is preoccupied with everything I need to do at The Closet," she lied. There wasn't anything to do except more marketing. Foot traffic had already come to a halt in town with the festival being over, and Grace would have to rely on online sales to keep her afloat for the next few months. "I should probably go."

She stuffed her notes inside her book and stood.

"You're leaving?" Lily asked, her lips turned down in a pout as if disappointed. "I guess my blabbering about my wedding isn't as exciting to everyone else as it is to me."

"Oh! I can't wait to hear more. I'm really excited for you. Really." She tucked her book under one arm and reached out to grab Lily's hands.

"We haven't even talked about the book. You made notes." Lily pointed their joined hands toward the book.

"Of course she did. Grace is a planner," Hope said from her seat.

Alexis snorted from behind her. Again, Grace let her sister's passive aggressive disappointment roll off her. If they were still in high school, she would have had a snarky, bitchy comment. Time and life had taught her to take the high road.

"You're going to be a stunning bride. Ty's a lucky man." She didn't mean to meet her sister's eyes as she gathered her empty dish. The lines between Alexis' brows were deep, her eyes squinty, her lips pursed as if contemplating life's biggest mysteries. "Sorry to bail on you girls."

"Thanks for the pizza dip. I want the recipe," Jenna called out.

"Me too." This from Mia who never cooked anything.

"We should make a new rule that the snack keeper has to make something homemade. Maybe have themes for our food and drinks," Hope suggested.

"You're forgetting I can't cook anything other than scrambled eggs," Lily said.

"I'm limited on recipes and time," Alexis added. "Sophie skipped over the terrible twos and is making up for it now. Between her mood swings and her accidents, I don't know how I'll ever get anything done."

"I remember those days." Hope rubbed Alexis' shoulder. "Some days it feels like a hundred years ago, and other days just like yesterday. Delaney's almost fourteen. She's been begging for a baby sister or brother ever since Cam and I got married."

"Are you...?" Alexis covered Hope's hand with hers.

"Trying. We're trying."

Lily screeched. She was the girliest of the group. Grace would have too if she thought it appropriate. Glancing at Alexis, who smiled and patted Hope's hand, she hid her excitement.

"Dude. You two." Mia shook her head. "I'm surrounded by sex fiends and baby makers. You and Cam. And Alexis and Ben. I know you two will be making an announcement soon, and Ty and Lily. Like you're going to wait long to pop out gorgeous little Barbie and Ken dolls."

Alexis pregnant? Grace couldn't imagine. She adopted Ben's daughter when she was just a baby. How Sophie's birth mother could so easily pass her up, Grace didn't understand.

When she'd first heard the news that her sister was getting married, and then about the instant family, Grace was thrilled for her older sister. She pictured herself the favorite aunt, bringing her instant niece shopping, dressing her in poofy dresses and such.

Only Alexis shielded Sophie from her. When Ben and Alexis went out on the rare occasion, she asked their mother to watch Sophie. Grace would get down on the floor and play tea party and read books with her niece, but by the time Alexis returned, Sophie would be sleeping. She never witnessed Grace in the auntie role, keeping her daughter at a distance.

Their parents mediated from time to time, but for the most part, Alexis kept her distance from Grace. She had a life. A husband and daughter, a busy career running the vineyard. Grace just got in the way.

She helped with the tastings, but never the tours, not knowing enough about the grapes and the seasons. The giant wall Alexis built couldn't be knocked down in a day, and Grace didn't have the tools, the strength, or the knowledge to chip away at it. She respected her sister's space and kept to herself.

With loud chatter and playful arguing among the girls, Grace managed to slip away without drawing any more attention.

• • • •

BRADY HAD A KNOCKDOWN, dragged out battle with his mom—figuratively speaking—and finally won. He let out a sigh of relief when she finally buckled herself in the passenger side of his truck.

"You don't look well, Mom."

"Thanks. It's what every woman wants to hear."

"You know what I mean." He shoved his keys in the ignition and turned on his truck. "All these years you've demanded Carter and I see our doctor regularly, but you haven't been taking care of yourself."

"I saw Dr. Green eleven months ago. I'm not due for my annual check-up until December."

"You're also supposed to go when you don't feel well." Painful memories of his father's diagnosis replayed through his mind. His father had cursed doctors, saying they diagnosed people with random ailments so they could make money off suckers. Doctors and hospitals were for wussies. If you went to the hospital it was because you were dying.

Which was exactly when his father went. It had been too late. He'd had stage four pancreatic cancer and decided to let it run its course, opting out of chemotherapy.

Brady wouldn't let the same thing happen to his mother. No. She wasn't terminally ill. She had the flu, maybe. Or was anemic. Although if she was Dr. Green would have diagnosed that with her annual blood work.

"It's called old age. I hate to say it," his mother sighed and leaned back in her seat, "but Henry and Claudia may have the right idea. Giving the business to Alexis and Ben but still living on the land."

He'd been dropping subtle hints to his mother over the past year about doing the same. Taking a semi-retirement role from the farm. Do the baking and run the cash register while he, Carter, and the help kept up with the planting, cultivating, and overall management of the fields.

Like him, she liked to have her hands in the dirt. His mother couldn't sit still for ten minutes. Even when down with the flu, or whatever was ailing her.

"I think it's a great idea. You don't have to sell me the farm. Just let me run it."

His mother laughed. "*Let* you? You've been running Marshall Farm since your father passed away. I don't know what I would have done without you." She placed a hand on his knee and patted. "You and Carter. You boys are my world. You and the farm. Not to say I'm not itching to have a daughter-in-law and some grandbabies to keep me company. You should do like Alexis did. Find yourself a nice woman to help with the farm and I'll take care of my grandbabies."

The doctor's office came into view, putting a stop to that conversation. Brady wiped the bead of perspiration from his brow and helped his mother out of his truck.

Two hours later, he helped her back in. She clutched a folder with paperwork in one hand and her purse in the other.

"See? A total waste of time. I'm sorry you gave up your afternoon for this, Brady. Like I told you this morning, I could have driven myself."

"It wasn't a waste. It gave me a break." He closed the door and rounded the hood to the driver's side.

"A break." She *tskd*. "You forget who you're talking to. You and I, we're too alike. Your brother is just like his father. Full of life and fun. If your Daddy didn't have the farm to keep him grounded, he'd have—"

"Run off with the circus," Brady continued for her, familiar with the tale of his father's antics.

"Did I ever tell you about the time your father stacked ninety-eight bales of hay on the inside of the barn door, so when his daddy opened it in the morning he walked into a wall of hay?"

"And had to go cut down his own sapling so Grandpa could hide his ass with it."

His mother chuckled. "And then had to move all those bales of hay back with his rear end sorer than a cow after it's been prodded."

Brady listened as his mother rattled about other stories he'd heard dozens and dozens of times. She didn't want to talk about the blood test or the unspoken words from the doctor. *We'll have to wait for the results of the blood work and x-rays to come back, and then we'll talk.*

It wasn't good. The questions, scribbling of notes, quiet head nods and tapping of Dr. Green's foot spoke louder than any words, any diagnosis.

They'd continue the Friday as if it was any other day in November. He and Carter would ready the fields for winter. Next week they'd set up the greenhouses. And his mother, thankfully, could rest.

CHAPTER TEN

STUNNED. SHOCKED. SCARED.

Even though the doctor said it could be treated with chemotherapy and possibly surgery, Brady was scared shitless. The endoscopy she was called in for two days ago made it clear without a shadow of a doubt. His mother had cancer. Stomach cancer.

It explained the nausea, the loss of appetite, the stomach pains, and her lethargy. If he hadn't forced her to go to the doctor to get checked out last week, it could have been too late.

"We'll get through this." He reached across the wooden armrest of the chair and held on to his mother's hand. Carter, sitting to her right, grabbed the other.

"Is this hereditary? Are my boys at risk?"

"Smoking and unhealthy eating habits put you at risk," Dr. Green said from behind his desk.

"I don't smoke, and my cholesterol levels and weight are all within normal range."

"Ulcers can put you at risk. There is evidence you may have had one for quite some time."

And it was just like his mom to power through any pain she'd been experiencing.

"So what do we do now?" he asked.

The doctor had removed his white coat for the meeting. Despite the dreadful news he dropped in their laps, Brady liked him. He'd been the one to diagnosis his father and was the one Brady, Carter, and their mother visited once a year for their annual check-ups.

"I'm glad your boys convinced you to get some tests done, Dorothy. You have options." Unlike their father had. "You'll need to meet with an oncologist." He slid a file folder across the desk, and Brady picked it up. "Depending on how much it has spread, Dr. Moore may suggest surgery."

"Surgery? That sounds serious." Carter bounced his knee as he typically did when nervous.

"Surgery can get rid of the tumor and will stop the cancer from spreading to other parts of your body."

"What would the surgery entail?" Brady squeezed his mother's hand.

"That's for the oncologist to discuss with you, but if you do go that route, he would be removing a piece of your stomach."

"That's one way to diet," his mother teased, although the joke fell flat.

"There's also chemotherapy and radiation. The pamphlets I gave Brady give you a little background on each option. It will come down to what Dr. Moore finds. He's the best at his job. But if you want a second opinion, I can give you names of a couple doctors in Portland at Maine Medical Center."

"No. I'm not going to Portland. I want to be close to home."

Brady glanced across his mother at Carter. They gave each other the same unspoken message. If she needed to go to Portland, they would get her there.

"Is Dr. Moore here today? I'd like to get this over with as quickly as possible." His mother was never one for drama or emotion. Cut and dried, she was.

"I talked with him this morning and gave him your charts. I'll bring you to his office."

Dr. Green stood, as did Brady and Carter. Normally their mother would brush off their help, but she accepted their assistance in standing, a sign of how weak she'd gotten, and followed the doctor out the door.

• • • •

THREE HOURS LATER THEY sat around the kitchen table in their family farmhouse.

"You two need to move out. Immediately."

"We're not going anywhere, Mom. Especially now," Carter said, surprising Brady with his maturity.

"You heard what Dr. Moore said. My cancer is from asbestos."

"No." Brady corrected. "He listed that as one of the possible causes."

"We know it's not from any of these." She tossed a packet of information on the table, and Brady couldn't help but notice the tremble in her hands. "Working in a coal mine, smoking, being overweight. This house was built in 1892. It's filled with asbestos. You two are young and healthy. Get out now before you get sick."

Her face was ashen and the circles that had formed under her eyes last month had turned to a deep purple.

"Can I make you some tea?" Brady got up and filled the kettle with water.

"Don't change the subject. It's about time you two move out on your own anyway. A thirty-six and a thirty-one-year-old man living with their mother. Who's more pathetic? Me or you two?" She tapped Carter on the back of the head, which loosened a smile from his lips.

"I'm the baby, so I'd say Brady is the most pathetic. He'll be a forty-year-old virgin living in his mama's basement." Carter got up and helped himself to a beer from the fridge.

Brady wouldn't take the bait. There was no point in defending himself in age or in his sexual partners. He'd had plenty.

Well, maybe not plenty, but enough to keep him semi-satisfied over the years.

"I've been thinking about renovating the bathrooms and kitchen anyway. I can talk to Ty and see what he's got scheduled. Winter is usually slow for his construction company."

"We're not going into more debt because I'm sick. The hospital bills are going to be a challenge enough."

Marshall Farm wasn't exactly rolling in the dough, but they weren't losing money either. With their income dependent upon the weather, they never took a good season for granted. Still, it needed to be done.

"I'm hurting our finances as it is." The gray in her eyes was colorless, no longer full of life and spunk. "Carter, this winter you had big plans for your website design business. Don't stop because of me."

Brady's heart tugged. He wanted his brother to branch off and do something he loved. There was a layer of guilt inside him for keeping Carter on at the farm when his heart wasn't in it. Sure, Carter complained. Daily. But it was with a joke and a smile. Despite his carefree attitude, his brother was always there when Brady needed him. He wouldn't leave the family stranded, even though his heart wasn't in it anymore.

"No biggie, Ma. Great thing about a laptop, it's portable. I can work on my business anytime any place. Don't worry about me. We know Brady doesn't." Carter winked at his mom over his beer bottle and took a healthy sip.

He could read the worry in his brother's eyes. While he was better at masking his concern with jokes and banter, Brady could still read him like a book.

His mother placed a hand on Brady's. "I know how much you've had to pick up my slack around here this season. And I appreciate it. I hope to be well by spring planting. If not, you may need to hire more help. We can't afford to renovate the house now. Maybe after a few more good growing seasons."

"Work needs to be done to the house, Mom. We won't plan any major demolition unless Ty says we need to. I'll work out a budget with him. And I can do some projects as well."

"You're not exactly handy with a saw and hammer."

"I can Google. YouTube has a lot of instructional videos too." He poured the hot water in his mother's favorite pig mug and dipped a chamomile tea bag in it.

"You two aren't turning your lives upside down because I have a small medical issue." She took the mug from Brady and rolled her shoulders back. "Life goes on. You heard the doctor. I'm not dying. Some drugs. Maybe a piece of my stomach, and I'll be as good as new."

Which was true. Thankfully the tumor in her stomach was small, and Dr. Moore was hopeful it hadn't spread. More tests would confirm this.

"The house is in dire need of a reno, and this is the perfect time to do it."

"And risk exposing you to asbestos?"

"If that's what has caused your cancer we need to get it out of the house immediately, or you'll never heal. Think of it as part of your medical treatment."

His mother sipped her tea and slumped in her seat. Her eyelids were next.

"You should go lay down. Carter and I can handle dinner."

That stirred a reaction in her. "You each can cook about two meals and they both include the grill. I'll make a big batch of soup and a crockpot meal to last the week."

"You will not." Brady placed his hands under his mother's elbows and helped her up. "Go rest. Tomorrow is a long day. Next week will be even longer. Carter and I have this under control." He led her to her bedroom. When she took off her shoes and slid under the covers, he left, closing the door quietly behind him.

Carter lifted his head from the fridge. "We're screwed, man. You and I can't cook worth shit."

"It can't be that hard. Find a recipe online and follow the directions." Brady pushed past Carter and opened the cabinets to check out what ingredients they had to work with.

"Yeah. As easy as fixing a damn toilet."

• • • •

THE CHEMOTHERAPY HAD been harder on his mother than any of them expected. Dr. Moore said it was her body finally shutting down after decades of hard work. Dorothy Marshall wasn't one who liked to sit idle, and lying around helpless turned his normally optimistic mother into a bear.

Brady ladled soup from the crockpot into a bowl. His mother didn't have much of an appetite, or energy to even spoon-feed herself, but he'd continue to bring her meals and coax her into taking a few bites.

Claudia Le Blanc had been a godsend, bringing over dinners every few days. It gave Brady more time to prep the fields for winter and Carter more time to work on the budget. He'd passed on all the bookwork and accounting to his brother, freeing up another hour in the day to spend outside.

Carter was spending more time on his laptop, seeking new clients and branching out across other mediums. Brady didn't exactly know what that meant. Carter said it would bring in more money, so Brady didn't bug him when he holed himself in the downstairs office.

His brother shouldn't have to give up his income to help out with the farm bills. That was Brady's job; to run the farm, take care of the house and his mother. Carter deserved to have the life he wanted, not be forced into living on a farm for the rest of his life.

While his future may have been carved out for him as the oldest son, he didn't mind dedicating his life to Marshall Farm. It *was* his life, and Brady couldn't imagine doing anything else with it.

Working outside in the fields, watching seeds turn into tiny plants and saplings, and later produce fruits and vegetables he and the community would pick and bring home to eat, nourished something deep inside him. This was his calling.

And while computers didn't scare him, being stuck inside behind one all day held no desire to him.

Brady tucked a sleeve of crackers in his shirt pocket and dug around the silverware drawer for a spoon. He and his brother weren't slobs, but they didn't have much time lately to clean the house. Or do the dishes.

Claudia had come over a few times to help with laundry and tidy up the kitchen. He owed her big time.

Tapping his knuckles on his mother's door, he called out in a soft voice, "I have butternut squash soup." He pushed the door open with his hip and studied his mother's frail frame.

The bedside light was on, her reading glasses next to the lamp and an unopened book. Alexis brought a bag of books and magazines last week. As far as Brady knew, his mother hadn't rustled up energy enough to flip through them.

"Mom." He pushed her glasses out of the way and set the soup on top of the book. "It's time to eat." The sun had set an hour ago and the last time he'd offered her food, it had been high in the sky.

She ate a piece of toast at lunch and said it gave her a stomachache. Torn between forcing her to eat more for energy or letting her be, he'd caved and left her to sleep.

When his father was dying—not that his mother was, he had to remind himself—Dorothy did all the caring while

Brady and Carter filled in for him, running the farm. It had been August, and blueberry season was in full swing.

Brady had never worked as hard or such long days in his life. He didn't want to be a failure to his father or his mother and figured out problems on his own as they arose. He'd been working side-by-side with his father since he could walk, so it hadn't been anything new. But he didn't have his father to bounce ideas off of or to ask clarifying questions.

Douglas and Dorothy hadn't doubted his ability to run the farm. Not once. In all his grief of losing his father, he'd managed a sense of pride as well, not wanting to let his parents down. It was what got him through his father's death.

That fall, during his senior year, he'd decided not to go away to college and earn a degree in agriculture. Instead, he skimped on his studies, doing just enough to ensure he'd still graduate the following spring, and spent every waking minute working on the farm, making his father and mother proud.

Looking down at his mother, her hair thinning from the chemotherapy and radiation, he realized he had it easy back then. His mother had the brunt of the work, caring for their father, knowing he was dying and there was nothing she could do for him.

"Mom," he said again, gently, but loud enough to wake her. "I have soup." He sat at the edge of her bed and nudged her side.

"Hmm?" Her eyes fluttered before opening and squinted in the soft light from the lamp. "I already ate."

"You had half a piece of toast six hours ago. Mrs. Le Blanc made butternut squash soup."

"Ours?"

Brady smiled. "She was sure to tell me the squash came from our farm stand."

"I'll call her." His mother dug her elbows in the mattress and struggled to sit up. "Thank her."

"Eat first." He helped his mother into a seated position and fluffed the pillow behind her back.

Carter came up with the ingenious idea to use his laptop desk as an eating tray for the times when their mom couldn't get out of bed. Brady reached for it between the bed and the nightstand and placed it on his mother's lap.

He'd learned after a few trials and errors not to fill the bowl too full. Not only did his mother not eat much, it often spilled in the process of delivery.

"It shouldn't be too hot." He picked up the spoon and held it to her lips.

"I'm not an invalid." She took the spoon from him and fed herself. A good sign.

Her chemo treatment was three days ago, and she finally had a little life in her. Brady dreaded bringing her for her next treatment in the morning. If this round was like the last, his mother would be vomiting and in pain for a solid forty-eight hours after.

"I brought you crackers as well." He opened the sleeve and placed it next to her bowl.

"Thank you." She closed her eyes and leaned back into the pillow, a lonely tear escaping her eye.

"Mom?"

She sniffed. "I'm okay."

No. She wasn't. "Tell me what I can do."

Opening her eyes, she cast a sad smile at him. "You're doing it, honey."

"I wish I could do more."

She set the spoon in the bowl and blinked, her eyes closing for a few beats before opening again.

"You do *too* much. Always have." Reaching for his hand, she squeezed, not as hard as she used to do. "I worry about you."

"No need." He patted her hand. "I'm a big boy."

"Since your father..." she trailed off as if speaking wiped the little energy she had from her body, "died, you've sacrificed a lot. Your life."

"My life is here. On the farm. You know I love this land as much as you and Dad." Probably more.

"I want you to be happy."

"I am."

"You're alone."

Shit. He knew where his mother was going with this. The wife and kids thing. She wanted it for him, and he wasn't sure if he wanted to settle down to please his mother or because that was what he wanted.

A year ago he could have honestly told his mother he hadn't given it much thought. Now. Not so much. Not with his friends—even if he didn't socialize much—finding love and getting married.

Alexis. Ty. Hope.

"I'm never alone, Mom. Besides, you and Carter are always underfoot," he teased. "There are always people at the farm." Changing the subject, he pointed to her bowl. "You need to eat."

"Field workers and customers. Not the same." She picked up her spoon and sipped her soup.

The shrill of his cell phone in his pocket startled them both. "I want that soup gone by the time I come back."

He slipped his hand in his pocket and pulled out his cell, answering it on his way out of his mother's room.

"Hello?"

"Brady. I hope I'm not calling at a bad time."

He cradled the phone between his shoulder and ear as he ladled a bowl of soup for himself. "Not at all, Mrs. Le Blanc. I was just feeding Mom some of your soup. I'm about to indulge in a bowl myself."

"Glad to hear Dorothy is eating. How is she feeling today?"

"Better now that the chemo has worn off. She has another round tomorrow so..."

"It breaks my heart. I'm glad the doctors were able to detect the cancer before it spread."

"Me too."

The kitchen door swung open bringing in a rush of cold air, Carter following behind carrying a pizza box.

"I had planned on spending this weekend making casseroles for you and your family to freeze before Henry and I leave for vacation on Monday, but I've come down with the stomach flu, and I don't want to risk contaminating any of your food."

"You're too kind and have done more than necessary already, Mrs. Le Blanc. You need to take care of yourself. The flight to California is long."

Since retiring last year, Henry and Claudia had been flying out to Ben's family's vineyard in Napa twice a year. They came back tanned and refreshed, happier than ever. Brady wished his mother could do the same. At least go away somewhere warm during the winter with girlfriends.

She didn't have many close friends, spending all her time on the farm. The women in town were nice to her though, all calling up when they heard about the diagnosis.

"I asked Grace if she could fill in for a while."

"Grace?" He couldn't picture her in a kitchen. Fine linen tablecloths and waiters in bow ties seemed more her style.

Carter flipped open the pizza box and shoved a slice of pepperoni in his face. Brady shook his head and held up the bowl of soup. "How's Mom?" Carter whispered.

Brady shrugged and nodded. "The same," he mouthed.

"I taught her a few recipes while she lived here. She doesn't like my help anymore and has learned to be a fairly decent cook. She'll come by tomorrow with something for your family."

"She doesn't have to do that."

"If Dorothy is going in for another round of chemo tomorrow, you'll need our help. She'll come by with dinner for you and Carter after she closes up."

"Well, thank you. That was kind of you. Both of you."

"Give your mother our love."

"I will. Take care of yourself."

He disconnected and tossed his cell on the counter so he could pick up his bowl with two hands.

"You're saying no to pizza for a bowl of healthy soup? Shit. I hope I'm never as old as you."

"I'll have a slice when I'm done with this. I couldn't shove pizza in my mouth while talking on the phone."

"Sure you can." Carter took a bite of pizza, the cheese stretching from his hand to his mouth. "I do it all the time," he said with a mouthful.

He'd make a remark on his brother's lack of a girlfriend if he had a leg to stand on. Carter, despite his lack of manners, managed to always have a date or a girl at his side. Including Grace.

Speaking of. "Mrs. Le Blanc is down with the flu, so she won't be cooking for us anymore."

"That's too bad. Aren't they leaving soon anyway?"

"On Monday."

"We can order takeout until they get back."

"They'll be gone until Christmas. We're not eating take-out for six weeks. Mom needs healthy food."

"I can't cook worth shit, and you're not much better."

"Claudia asked Grace to make some meals."

"Grace?" Carter laughed and wiped his hands on a paper towel. "I didn't know she cooked."

"She's bringing dinner tomorrow. I'll tell her we're all set though."

"What's that saying about a gift horse and its mouth?" Carter opened the fridge and pulled out two beers. "Want one?"

"Sure." Brady took the bottle and set his bowl in the sink. "Thanks for the pizza," he said, helping himself to a slice.

They didn't order out often. No one delivered in this area and the time it took to drive to a restaurant and order, and then get back home again, they might as well had boiled a pot of water for spaghetti.

The nearest pizza joint was twenty minutes away. Maybe he could learn how to make homemade pizza. Their mother was a good cook but kept to the old-fashioned classics. Meatloaf, roasts, chicken, shepherds pie, lasagna. For dessert, pumpkin and apple pies, and oatmeal raisin cookies.

Good home cooked meals using as many of their home-grown fruits and vegetables as possible.

"I'm gonna contact a few clients. Let me know if you need anything."

"You just want out of kitchen duty."

"Damn straight."

Brady didn't mind. There wasn't much to clean up anyway. The soup needed to be stored in a container, the crockpot washed out, and the pizza box tossed in the recycling bin.

"Mom's got chemo at eight. We need to leave by seven."

"I'll be ready." Carter stole one more slice from the box and padded down the hall.

So would Brady, physically. Emotionally, he'd fake it.

CHAPTER ELEVEN

GRACE REALLY WISHED her mother hadn't volunteered her to cook for the Marshalls. She couldn't say no though. She'd go straight to hell for refusing to cook for a woman battling cancer, even if she'd been a cranky old bat toward Grace in the past.

She didn't have much time to plan, prepare, and cook after her mom had called last night. Scrolling through her Pinterest page until midnight, she'd searched for an easy and wholesome meal she could prepare for the Marshalls that would also transport well.

Lasagna popped up a dozen times. She'd made it before. Boil noodles. Mix ricotta, eggs, cheese, and herbs, dump some jarred sauce over it. Done.

There was absolutely nothing wrong with jarred sauce, but she knew Mrs. Marshall made her own from the bazillion tomato plants they had. Grace had to at least attempt it, so she searched sauce recipes and found one with nearly a thousand five-star reviews, using canned tomatoes.

Before she opened the shop this morning, she'd sped to the store, bought all the necessary ingredients and put the sauce on to simmer. The good thing about working practically downstairs from her apartment, she could run up every hour or so to give the sauce a stir. The blend of tomatoes, garlic, and herbs smacked her in the face every time she opened the apartment door.

Since no one had come into The Closet in the past hour, heck, since lunch, at five o'clock she flipped the sign on the front door to *Sorry, We're Closed* and wrangled into her winter coat. There wasn't much time to layer all the ingredients and get it over to the Marshalls before dinner.

Running up the stairs to her apartment, she remembered her mother had said Mrs. Marshall had chemotherapy this morning and wouldn't be eating, but Carter and Brady would be hungry. They'd expect her to burn dinner, or to be a no-show, or to be an epic failure in some way. Alexis thought that way about her, and since she was so close to the Marshalls, Grace figured they'd feel the same.

She unlocked her apartment door and stepped inside. Once again the aroma of garlic and herbs filled the air. The reviews had to be right. If the sauce tasted anything close to how it smelled, she'd totally impress the Marshalls.

Not that she cared. Carter would eat anything. Toss him a bologna sandwich and he'd be in heaven. Mrs. Marshall probably wouldn't be hungry today, but Brady would, and for some reason, his opinion mattered to her.

Shrugging out of her coat, she tossed it on one of the kitchen chairs and opened the fridge for the beef and sausage. She filled a pot of water to cook the noodles and preheated a pan for the meat. While that cooked, she clicked on her phone to find the recipe and mixed the ricotta, eggs, cheese, and seasonings.

Bustling around in the kitchen had been fun in her parents' home, but making something for someone else was even more exciting. Like making the dip for the reader group last week, mixing together ingredients and watching her friends' faces light up when they tasted it. Like finding the perfect outfit for a customer, doing things for others that brought a smile to their face made her happy. Maybe she wasn't the selfish bitch her reputation had caused her to believe.

Still nervous about straying from the recipe, she measured the oregano, basil, and salt, and added another clove of garlic to the cheese mixture. The sauce had required four cloves. She thought it looked like a lot, but the smell... To die for.

Giving the mixture one last stir, she checked on the meat, stirring that as well, and dropped the noodles in the boiling water. She'd gotten the multi-tasking thing down. Sort of.

While the noodles cooked, she ran back to her bedroom to change out of her skirt and blouse, noticing splotches of red on her sleeve. Maybe she should have changed *before* cooking. She tossed her lavender blouse in her dry cleaning pile and dug out a pair of black leggings from her drawer.

Only a few weeks into the retail business and she already regretted having so many dry clean only clothes. Fine for Paris, not so great for Maine. In the morning she'd contact Arianna about designing fashionable blouses and dresses that could be tossed in the washer. Or at least hand washed. Maria and Lacey's designs were washer friendly, but not as dressy.

Going for super casual tonight, Grace pulled on her favorite sweatshirt and finger-combed her hair back into a ponytail. Something else she should have done before finishing dinner. She prayed there were no loose hairs in the food.

"Crap." Remembering the noodles, she ran to the kitchen, still holding her hair with one hand. The sauce had bubbled over and the noodles looked more than cooked. Quickly tying her hair back, she scoured her tiny kitchen with her eyes searching for the strainer.

"Where are you?" Once her hands were free she squatted in front of the cabinet where she kept her pots and pans and spotted it.

A few minutes later, the noodles were drained and cooling, the meat had joined the sauce, and she was ready to put it all together. There was no time to taste anything. Assembling it just as the recipe listed, she stepped back to admire her masterpiece.

"Not bad, Le Blanc." She covered it with foil and scribbled the heating directions on a post-it note.

Careful not to fall on her ass on the way to her car and drop the lasagna, Grace took her time down the steps. Was it only twenty-two steps? It felt like at least eighty-nine.

It was just past six o'clock when she'd pulled up to the Marshall farmhouse, and the sun had already set some time ago. Her headlights must have triggered her arrival. By the time she closed the car door behind her, Brady was at her side.

"Thank you for making this. You didn't have to." Brady took the pan from her.

"Yeah. I kind of did."

He paused in his steps and cocked his head toward her. "I'm sorry. I didn't—"

"I'm kidding. It was no trouble at all. Mom told me about your mom. I'm sorry she's suffering. How did today go?"

Grace hadn't meant to start a conversation. Drop off dinner and go was her plan.

"Today was... rough." Brady closed his mouth and sucked in his lips as if trying to keep too much information from spilling out.

"I'll leave you guys alone then." Grace turned to her car, but Brady stopped her with his words.

"Why don't you stay for dinner?"

"Oh. I can't."

"I'm sorry. Of course, you have other plans."

Those sad eyes turned down, and hell if he didn't look like she'd run over his puppy.

"No plans. I don't want to intrude though."

"You went out of your way to make us dinner. I don't think that's an intrusion."

"Your mom..."

"She's sleeping. She won't be eating anything tonight. Maybe by dinner tomorrow. Something bland."

Kicking herself for not researching what foods Mrs. Marshall should be eating, Grace covered her face with her hands. "I'm an idiot. I'm so sorry. I made lasagna. I should have asked—"

"Carter and I are excited to eat a real meal that doesn't include soup, toast, or take out. This smells amazing. Why don't you come inside and join us?"

Why was he being nice to her? He'd been sweet to her a few weeks ago at the festival as well. It excited and confused her. He did say *us* though. If Carter was there it wouldn't be as awkward. And she didn't want to be responsible for the kicking the puppy look.

"Sure. Thanks." They walked side by side until they reached the back steps. "Don't all farms have a dog? I expected one to greet me last month when I came to work on my website with Carter. Figured he was out in the fields with you."

"Bandit died last year. He was fifteen."

Aaaand there goes the kicking the puppy look again. "I'm sorry, Brady." She remembered the dog from her high school years. A chocolate lab, if she remembered correctly.

"We talked about getting a couple rescues from the shelter once the busy season was over. But with Mom..." he trailed off and opened the door for Grace.

Shit. She did it again. Puppy. Mom. What was next? Remind him of the father he lost?

"We rescued Bandit a few months before my Dad died."

Yeah. True talent in bringing up sad memories.

"I remember him. He used to run away. We'd find him wandering through our vines."

"The shelter said he'd been abused by men before, which was probably why he gravitated to your farm. Better female-male ratio."

Brady set the lasagna on the table and went back to the mat by the door to remove his shoes. Following suit, Grace kicked off her sneakers as well. The floor creaked, and she had the sense of being off balance. It wasn't Brady's clean, fresh scent that gave her a stumble. The orange and yellow linoleum floor was warped in places, curling up at the seams.

The cabinets had to be original to the house. Solid, heavy wood, and doors that hung slightly off-kilter. The red and white checked curtains above the window at the sink were the only feminine touch in the room. The rest, from the low, cracked ceiling to the floral wallpaper, was like walking into a time warp.

Brady's tall frame filled out the space making him incongruous to the room.

"You can leave your shoes on. Our floor has seen its share of... mess. In fact, I've been talking with Ty about renovating a few rooms. Checking to see if we have asbestos while we're at it."

"Do you think you do?"

"Mom does." Brady read the post-it on the foil-covered pan. "Three-fifty for an hour? I don't know if I can wait that long. It smells amazing."

Warmed by his compliment, she didn't even try to hide her smile. "Let's try four hundred and see what happens. It's all cooked. Except the cheese mixture. There are eggs in it."

"Eggs?" Brady quirked his lip. "My eggs?"

The lopsided grin transformed Brady Marshall from serious, stubborn, pain in the ass farmer to charming and sexy boyfriend material. Wait. Boyfriend material? No. Just because he had sex appeal to him didn't mean he was right for Grace. Or her for him.

Friends. Maybe. They could possibly be friends. Until Alexis reminded him how flakey and irresponsible she could be. The party animal not fit for a family guy like Brady.

"I don't know about that." She eyed him up and down. The flirting came naturally. She couldn't help it. "You don't have the right plumbing for making eggs."

Carter stepped into the kitchen barking out a laugh. "Dude. What the hell did I walk in on?"

Brady lifted the lasagna and turned toward the oven. "Grace made us lasagna."

"And your brother is taking credit for making the eggs."

"I didn't mean it that way, and you know it."

"You might want to take off the post-it on the lasagna. Wouldn't want it catching on fire," Grace pointed out.

Carter laughed again and Brady opened the oven door, peeling off the note.

"That would be one way to rush renovations on the kitchen." Brady crumpled the note and tossed it in the trash. "Can I get you a drink while the lasagna cooks?"

"Sure. Whatever you have is fine."

Carter opened the fridge. "Water, milk, and beer. Sorry. Slim pickings around here."

"She's not going to want a beer, Carter. Her family runs a vineyard."

Like that mattered. Sure, Grace loved wine. Vodka was good too. And beer she didn't mind in the right setting. Drinking it on her own, not so much. At a party or with two handsome men, yeah, she could keep up with the rest of them.

"Grace's been drinking beer since high school. I bet you can still do a keg stand," Carter said.

Who needed her sister to lower Grace's ego and keep her reputation at the bottom of the pig pile? Carter and her old high school friends could do it just fine. He didn't mean any harm in his teasing and had no way of knowing her party past was a sore wound still not healed.

"I'll have water, please."

Brady got her a glass and set it on the table. "Have a seat."

The air grew uncomfortable and thick, and it wasn't just from her lasagna.

"I really don't want to be in your way…"

"I've been sitting across from his ugly mug for too long. Bout time we have a pretty face in the kitchen. No offense, Mom," Carter called over his shoulder, not loud enough to wake her if she was sleeping.

"Are we going to disturb her out here?" Grace hadn't had a full tour of the house, but had spent some time with Carter in the office space down the hall from the kitchen and had used the small bathroom across from it. The door past the office had been open, and she'd caught a glimpse of a four-poster bed and an off-white and green patterned quilt. Too feminine to be the boys.

"She's exhausted. Nothing's going to wake her except pain." Carter turned a chair around at the head of the table and straddled it. "I've got first shift. Brady's on at midnight."

"That sounds…" Terrible. Exhausting. And wonderful of her sons to care so well for her. "Challenging."

"Yeah. If you wanna go up and get some shut-eye now I'll keep an eye on the food. And our guest." Carter winked at Grace and sipped his beer.

Brady pulled out a chair across from her, his jaw tight, shoulders stiff. "I'm good."

Carter craned his neck behind him and picked up a deck of cards off a shelf. "We can pass time shooting the shit or playing cards. Lady picks."

"Cards?" she shrugged.

"Good choice," both Marshall men said at the same time.

Shuffling the deck, Carter called the first game. "Poker. Jacks and twos wild."

"I didn't bring any money." Not that she had any to spare.

"We can play strip poker," Carter joked, wiggling his eyebrows.

"We have poker chips, or we can play with something else," Brady offered.

"If we're just playing with chips, I'm in." Grace rubbed her hands together. She'd never played a live game with real people, only online while sitting in her bleak apartment outside Paris on a Friday night. And Saturday. And Sunday. And pretty much any day she wasn't working or with Robert.

His wife had been first priority, so Grace settled for online poker while sitting in her apartment all alone.

"Jacks and twos it is." Carter dealt the cards, and Brady divvied up the poker chips.

Thirty minutes later the oven alarm went off, as did Carter's phone. "Shit. I've gotta take this. Potential client. If Mom needs anything, can you cover for me?"

"Of course." Brady waved him away and slipped on the hot mitts. "I haven't smelled homemade garlic sauce in ages." He set the pan on top of the oven.

"The directions say to let it rest for fifteen minutes."

"I don't know if I can wait that long."

Grace bit her lip at the compliment. Brady had been quiet during their card game. Carter had teased it was because the pile of chips was all in front of Grace. Now that Carter wasn't in the room, the Brady from earlier was back.

The one with the hook in his lip and warmth in his gray-blue eyes that warmed the tips of her toes all the way up to the tips of her ears. She couldn't help the smile that erupted on her face.

"That's the nicest compliment anyone has ever given me."

Brady's head flinched back slightly, and he frowned. "That wasn't exactly a compliment."

"Oh." Didn't she feel like a fool? "It felt like one." Grace tried to brush it off, embarrassed at misinterpreting his comment. "Where are the plates? I'll set the table." She got up and stood in front of one of the cabinets, not daring to open it without his permission.

"You're not who I thought you were," Brady said quietly. He brushed his hand on the back of his neck and scratched.

"I. I'm sorry. I'll just... I'll let you and Carter..." She backed away into the corner where her shoes were and bent to pick up her sneakers.

"Grace." Brady squatted beside her. "Don't go."

"I..." She made the mistake of tilting her head and locking her gaze with his. Damn. The crooked grin was gone, but the sincerity in his eyes was real. No one had looked at her like that in ... ever. Like he really wanted her to stay, and not in a sexual way.

Sex was easy. That look she recognized. Heated stares that focused more on her chest and lacked anything real. Anything substantial.

Brady's eyes weren't full of lust. It was the warmth and sincerity that did her in.

"I want you to stay. Keep me company, will you?" He took the shoe from her hand and dropped it to the floor, rising to his height, taking her hand in his so she had no choice but to stand as well.

"Are you sure?"

"Absolutely." He licked his lips and she couldn't help it if her gaze dropped to his mouth, wondering what his tongue and lips would taste like.

Embarrassed at her staring, she lifted her chin to apologize again—for what, she wasn't sure—and caught him doing the same, staring at her mouth. She unconsciously licked her bottom lip then trapped it between her teeth.

Brady closed his eyes and dropped his hand from her elbow. "I think the lasagna is ready." Grace nodded in agreement. "You went to the trouble to make this for us, so you sit. I'll get the plates."

"But you—"

"No." He put a finger to her mouth, and she all but moaned at his touch. Brady must have noticed her reaction, but he kept it there, rubbing lightly along her bottom lip. "Sit."

She wasn't one to take orders from anyone, especially a man, but she didn't think her legs could hold her up much longer. She nodded and slipped into the chair she'd vacated a few minutes ago, her back, thankfully, to the counter. And to Brady.

CHAPTER TWELVE

SHIT. HE CROSSED THE line. Grace didn't come over to be hit on. If anyone should be putting the moves on her it was Carter. A man closer to her age and her lifestyle. Free-spirited, social, and wanting to discover the world.

Not a man who had no desire to leave his hometown, much less his land. Taking a minute to gather his composure, he stood in front of the cabinet and opened the door, staring blankly at the white and blue chipped plates.

They were old when he was a kid; even older now. Not something Grace Le Blanc would dine on. Heck. The beat up farmhouse table wasn't fit for someone like her to eat at. She'd spent the better half of a decade traipsing around Italy, then France. Dining at chic restaurants and shopping in designer stores.

Not that he knew firsthand. It was what Alexis had told him over the years. She resented her sister gallivanting in Europe while she stayed home to work the vineyard. Brady had asked Alexis why she never left Maine, never traveled.

Her response was exactly what he would have said if ever asked.

"This land is my lifeline. To run your hands through dirt and seed, and watch something you plant grow and mature into a vine, later producing grapes you turn into wine. The process, the science, the natural beauty of it. No other job could complete me like this one does."

Brady hadn't thought anyone other than his mother understood his love. Alexis had. And yet there was never a spark between them.

Her sister, however, was another story. With nothing in common other than neighboring family farms, one she wanted nothing to do with, Grace triggered a visceral reaction in him.

One he tried desperately to ignore. He wanted to dislike her. Especially after all the stories he'd heard Alexis tell, and that one incident on her prom night.

Brady wanted to scoff at her silly idea to run a fashion boutique in the anything but fashionable Crystal Cove.

He wanted to push her away because, at first glance, she appeared selfish, not caring for family values.

With her sitting so close, smelling like angels and garlic, he wanted to wish her away. Or, at the very least, wish away the desire building within. Wish away the ache in his fingers as they tingled with the need to touch. Wish away the awareness of his rapid heartbeat every time she was near.

Brady reached for the plates, chipped and stained with memories as old as the farm, and blinked away his wanting, his wishing.

"I didn't think of making a salad," he said, setting the plates on the table. "I can make a vegetable. We have zucchini."

"Don't bother on my account. I need to get going as soon as dinner's done anyway," Grace said without looking up at him.

"Sure." He turned to the stove and picked up the glass dish, forgetting to slip on the hot mitts. "Damn!" At least the burn on his hands distracted him from the burning in his gut.

"Are you okay?" Grace jumped to his side and gathered his hands in hers.

"Fine. Stupid is all. I thought maybe the dish was cool enough to handle," he lied. No point in telling Grace it was her soft words and softer lips that made him forget.

"Here. Run them under cold water." Keeping his hands in hers, she led him to the sink and turned on the faucet.

The cool water didn't simmer the heat emanating from her hands. Her touch burned more than the dish and hurt almost as much. Hurt because he couldn't act on the chemistry.

Grace wasn't here long term. And he was. Getting involved with his neighbor's daughter, his good friend's sister, was not a good idea.

Not one bit.

But her hands. Soft like her lips. One more touch. That's all he wanted. To touch her lips.

"How do you feel?"

"Confused."

"Your hands?" Grace tipped her chin toward him.

"Oh. Those." It was the beer. Although he'd only had one. The lack of sleep. The stress. Being alone with a woman. The perfect storm to mess with his brain and put words in his mouth he didn't intend to say, make body parts he had no intention of moving move.

"Are you okay?"

A stirring in his pants brought things to a whole new level. "Fine. Go sit." He didn't mean to bark at her. If she stood next to him a second longer she'd feel how not okay he was.

If eyes could flip him off, hers just did.

"I'm sorry. It's been a long day. Longer week. I didn't mean to snap." He stuck the handle end of a spatula in his pocket.

"You don't owe me an apology, Brady," she said from the table.

And hell if her sweet voice didn't irritate him even more. Where the hell was Carter?

Carter. That's right. Wasn't it only a few weeks ago she was laughing with his brother? And thirteen or so years ago he found her naked in his fields after a night with Carter?

Brady had no right to look or think of Grace with anything other than neighborly friendship.

Using the hot mitts this time, he set the dish in the middle of the table and pulled out the spatula.

"Do you want the honors?" He held the spatula to her and waited for her to accept it.

"Sure. I'm not sure if it will look pretty when I serve it."

"Honey, if it tastes anything like it smells, you don't need to worry."

Damn. She did that biting of her bottom lip thing again. He didn't mean to toss the endearment her way.

Grace took the spatula from him and, using the thin metal end as a knife, cut two neat rows. "I'm assuming you want a big piece."

"The bigger the better." Shit. He did it again. Why was everything coming out like an innuendo?

Grace gasped and continued slicing. Brady held up his plate for her, and she placed a healthy serving on his dish.

Her slice wasn't even half as big as his. "Is that all you're eating?"

"I don't know how it tastes yet. If it's good, I'll take some more."

"So I get to be the guinea pig?" Brady smiled. He didn't mind. His stomach was in knots from hunger, or from her, he wasn't sure. Scooping up a heaping forkful, he blew on it, then bit down on the steamy layers of red sauce, cheese, and noodles.

The first sensation was hot. It hadn't cooled all the way yet. The second was of the rich marinara, and then, the garlic. Holy mother of garlic. Brady swallowed and picked up his beer to wash it down. He must have bit on a chunk of it in the sauce. It was good, a bit potent, but good.

"Something's wrong, isn't it?"

"No. It's awesome." He took another forkful hoping he avoided another chunk of garlic. Not so much. Was garlic supposed to be spicy? To burn? To make his eyes water? He chewed and swallowed quickly, again chasing it with another healthy gulp of beer.

He watched Grace take a delicate bite of her pasta and waited for her reaction. Her green eyes grew round and she frantically chewed and swallowed.

"Water. I need more water." She pushed back on the chair and jumped to her feet, filling her glass at the faucet and gulping it down while standing at the sink.

"You okay?"

"Holy crap. What is that? I didn't use any spicy ingredients."

"Tastes like garlic."

"Garlic isn't spicy." Grace filled her glass once more and brought it back to the table.

"I guess it depends how much you use."

"It called for three cloves. It looked like a lot but I followed the recipe to a T."

"Three cloves isn't a lot. Are you sure that's all you put in?"

Grace picked at her lasagna with her fork. "Yeah. It took forever to peel. After the first one, I Googled faster ways to peel. I learned how to smash each little piece with the side of the knife. The skins come off much easier that way. Some of those cloves have like twenty pieces to them."

"Wait." Brady covered his mouth with his hand and laughed. "You put in three cloves or bulbs?"

"There had to be about twenty bulbs in each clove. It looked like a lot, but it smelled great."

"Oh, honey." Brady sat back in his chair unable to contain his laughter anymore. He laughed until his eyes watered, or that could have been from the garlic. At this point, he was sweating it out of his pores.

When he finally calmed his laughter down, he looked up at Grace who was anything but amused. Arms crossed and lips turned down in a scowl, he needed to let her know.

"My mom grows garlic in her garden."

"Of course she does," Grace pouted. "I don't see what's so funny. Does grocery store garlic taste different than Marshall garlic?"

He got up and went over to the pantry, retrieving a braid of garlic bulbs. "This," he said, holding out an odd shaped ball, "is a bulb." He cracked open a bulb and held five cloves in his hand. "Each of these is a clove."

Grace's mouth hung open in shock. Her eyes grew round as saucers, hell, round as a garlic bulb. "Oh. My. God."

"No worries about vampires anywhere in the vicinity tonight."

"That's not funny."

"It is." He snickered.

"No, it's not." Grace leaped from her chair, the force and motion knocking it to the floor, and rushed to the door.

"Grace."

"Shut up." She shoved her feet into her sneakers, her heels sticking out over the backs, and yanked her coat off the hook.

"Come on. Let's finish dinner."

"I am finished."

He swore he heard a sniff followed by a curse. In a matter of seconds, she yanked the door open and was flying down the porch steps. Brady rolled his shoulders back and followed her outside.

"Grace. Wait."

"Leave me alone."

Shit. She was crying. Fumbling with her keys and crying.

"Grace." He wormed his way between her and her car and put his fingers under her chin, lifting it until her eyes met his. "I'm sorry. I was only teasing."

"I don't need you or anyone else to tell me what a screw up I am."

"I didn't—"

"You did. And you enjoyed it. Just back off." She pushed at his chest, but he didn't relent.

"I didn't mean to hurt your feelings. I apologize."

"Really? Making fun of me for not knowing the difference between a garlic clove and bulb? Warning off vampires? Yeah, have your fun, Brady Marshall. Tell the world Grace Le Blanc couldn't even follow a stupid lasagna recipe. Tell them she's a major screw up, just like everyone pred—"

He cut her off with a searing kiss. It wasn't gentle like he usually gave on a first date or the first time kissing a woman. He'd never kissed a woman before with the intent of shutting her up.

Not that this was his intent. He wanted to stop her tears. Stop her self-deprecating rant. Stop her doubt.

He softened his kiss when he felt her relax under him. Sliding his fingers from her chin to the side of her face, he massaged her scalp, pulling her gently into him. He sipped at her lips, full and plump now from their kiss.

She loosened her grip on his shirt and skirted her hands up his chest and to his neck. She didn't choke him, and he took that for a good sign.

Coaxing her mouth open, he slid his tongue along the seam of her lips until she invited him in. It may have been frigid around them, but in their tight circle, arms around each other and chest to chest, he felt nothing but warmth and satisfaction.

Her tongue slipped past his lips into his mouth, teasing him. They played until she moaned. Sliding his hands forward, he cupped her cheeks, turning their kiss deeper until she touched something unfathomable.

"Brady."

He opened his eyes and studied her features. Her long lashes feathered out under her eyes, her cheeks red from their passion. She must have felt his gaze on her and opened her eyes.

The spell broken, Grace released her lips from his and dropped her hands from his neck.

"I like them there." He picked them up and put them back up on his shoulders.

"We shouldn't be doing this."

"Why not?" He'd gone through a dozen reasons why not before dinner. But he couldn't think of a single one of them now.

"We're not... you and me. You don't even like me."

"Oh." He grinned. "I like you plenty."

"I'm not right for you."

He didn't like the seriousness in her eyes, the doubt someone put there.

"Says who?"

"I'm not."

He didn't budge, forcing her with his stare to open up.

"Besides"—a beginning of a smile formed on her lips—"you have terrible garlic breath."

He opened his mouth to protest and clamped it down again. Grace giggled and slipped from under his arms and into her car.

"You had garlic too so you couldn't smell mine," he said over the roar of her engine.

"That's a myth." She closed the door on his face with a smile and sped off into the dark.

Brady stood alone in the driveway and watched until her taillights could no longer be seen. Holding up his hand to his mouth he breathed out and sniffed.

Shit. His breath stunk.

CHAPTER THIRTEEN

GRACE LIFTED HER FACE and closed her eyes, sighing into the warm spray from the shower. Her body melted into the water, the steam and warmth wrapping around her body after a mentally exhausting day.

She'd screwed up big time with last night's dinner and had been on the defensive, waiting for Brady to make fun of her. To put her down. Insult her ability to do... anything.

Twenty-four hours later and she could still taste the lingering drudges of garlic.

And Brady's kiss. She expected to be shunned, the door slammed in her face, not kissed senseless in his driveway. That kiss got her through nine hours of work. Not that it was *work* work. Standing on her feet all day, she filled online orders, placed strategic ads on websites, made some targeted Facebook ads, and searched for new recipes.

In the spring and summer, she'd stay open seven days a week. For now, she decided to make winter hours: closed on Monday and minimal hours on Tuesday and Wednesday. Hopefully, her online sales would keep her financially afloat for a few months.

She turned so the water could massage her back. She pictured Brady's strong hands behind her, touching, rubbing away her insecurities. He grew up just down the road from her, she'd known him since birth, and never, ever had she fantasized about him before.

Granted, he'd never kissed her before. Normally she liked her men tall, dark, and lean. Brady had the tall part down, and even a bit of the dark. Her hands had the luxury of touching his chest, hard from working outside all day. She knew the rest of him had to be just as solid. Maybe rugged was more her style.

Those gray and green eyes weren't bland and didn't look at her with disdain. Instead, they'd darkened, even crinkled around the corners when he smiled. And not to make fun, she now realized.

Fun. Not a word she'd use in the same sentence with Brady Marshall. His brother, sure. Carter oozed fun. Took all the fun genes in the family leaving his older brother with nothing but seriousness.

And responsibility. He was the male version of Alexis, which was why they didn't get along. Or rather, hadn't gotten along until last night.

He wasn't angry with her for screwing up the dinner. Instead, he reacted the way she expected Carter to. Even after dealing with his mother's cancer, taking care of her physically and emotionally, he didn't snap at Grace.

He kissed her. She liked to believe she'd been kissed like that before. With passion and humor, but she couldn't remember a time. Back in high school, she kissed a lot of boys. There was definite humor involved. She never got too serious with a boy.

In her twenties, she kissed men who had connections. Men who wanted her for her body. There was no humor there, just passion. Lust.

With Brady, there'd been a combination of everything. Anger, confusion, lust, humor, even friendship.

Well, maybe friendship was going too far. They seemed to have stepped off the ledge from strong dislike to... not disliking each other.

Turning off the water, she shook her hair like a wet dog and stepped out of the shower. She reached for the giant, fluffy lavender towel Lily got her as a housewarming gift and wrapped it around her body. Twice.

Padding across the hall to her bedroom, she debated on leggings or sweatpants. Glancing at the clock, she opted for sweats. No one was coming by at eight o'clock. Her friends were home with their husbands or out with other friends.

Mia had called earlier asking if she wanted to join her and Jenna at karaoke in Camden, but she was tired. And she wanted time to herself to process what had happened last night with Brady.

Finishing off her outfit with her black T with a picture of the Eiffel tower on the front, she finger-combed her hair on her way back to the bathroom. Finding her wide-tooth comb, she ran it through her hair, then twisted it up in a bun and secured it with a clip.

She glanced in the mirror and froze. Two dots donned her nose.

"Great," she mumbled. She found a blackhead remover strip and stuck it across her nose. Good thing she didn't have any plans for the evening.

Since dinner consisted of a salad, she decided to make brownies for dessert. From scratch. If they came out well she'd bring them along with tomorrow's dinner, chicken tetrazzini, to the Marshalls.

Gathering the ingredients she'd written down, Grace hummed to herself, wishing she had enough money to buy a stereo system. Her phone would do.

Searching her playlists, she selected the two-thousand dance party mix. Nothing like Cypress Hill and Eminem to get her moving around the kitchen.

With the wet ingredients mixed and waiting, she started on the dry. One and a half cups flour, leveled with the back of a butter knife—she'd learned that trick from her mother. A knock on her door scared the crap out of her, and she jerked her hand, flour flying everywhere, including all over her front.

"Seriously?" Some of it landed in the bowl, the rest on the counter, floor, and her shirt and navy sweats. Whoever it was, wasn't getting any brownies.

Pushing a loose strand of hair off her face, she marched to the door with a growl and a sigh.

"Who is it?" she asked as she opened the door.

"Shouldn't you wait to see who it is first?"

Six feet of Brady stood on her doorstep. "What are you doing here?"

"I came to apologize. And to offer a peace offering." He held up a plastic shopping bag and a Cheshire grin.

"What is it?"

"Apple pie. I took it out of the freezer about an hour ago. It might still be cold. We can warm it up in your microwave." He held up another bag. "And I have vanilla bean ice cream as well."

The pie and ice cream were tempting but not nearly as tempting as Brady. Now to figure out what he came to apologize for. If it was for the kiss, she'd crawl in a hole and die. It meant too much to her to be apologized away.

If it was for insulting her cooking, well, the lasagna was a bit... ripe.

"Can I come in?"

"I guess." Grace stepped back and waved him in.

"I was worried I'd be interrupting your night." He stood in the middle of her living room, taking up too much space with his bags and his kind eyes.

"So why didn't you call?" Grace crossed her arms.

"I was afraid you wouldn't answer."

She cocked her head to the side and inadvertently jutted out a hip as well. "So you came by my apartment instead?"

Damn, that grin. "Harder to turn me away in person. Especially if I have pie."

"What if I don't like apple pie?"

Brady flinched as if she'd said something ridiculous like buying eggs from a store.

"Everyone likes apple pie."

"I'm sure there are people who don't."

"You're not one of those people... are you?"

Grace unfolded her arms and walked past him to the kitchen. She had forgotten about the mess. Brady's fault.

Wetting a paper towel, she wiped the countertop then crouched to clean the floor.

"What've you got going on in here?" She heard the freezer open and shut and the rustling of the plastic bag as he removed the pie from it.

"Brownies."

"I love brownies."

"I'd have them in the oven by now if I wasn't interrupted." She swiped one last time across the floor and stood, tossing the paper towel in the trash. Picking up her cell phone, she turned off the music.

"I take it you're still mad at me about last night." Brady shrugged out of his winter coat and draped it across the back of a chair. "I can leave if you want me to."

"Yet you took off your coat." *Ah! Fish hook. Leave his mouth alone.*

"I figure it will be harder for you to kick me out if I already have my coat off."

"Pushy much?"

"Not usually."

"All that garlic must have gone to your head."

Brady tipped back his head and laughed. "It was strong. Good, but strong. I gave Carter a heaping plate full. He was so hungry he was about ten bites in before he stopped to breathe and actually taste it."

"Oh no." Grace scrunched her nose and bit her bottom lip. "Is he okay?"

"No worse for the wear."

"Good thing he didn't have a date last night." Instantly Grace regretted her words. She didn't want to bring up their kiss. It was a knee-jerk reaction, she was sure. Brady had no interest in her other than as a friend of the family. They had mutual friends and would be running into each other more frequently now that he wasn't needed on the field twenty-four-seven.

His mother, however, needed him.

"How's your mom doing?"

The laugh lines around his eyes dissipated, his face growing somber. "Last night was tough for her."

"You've been up all night?"

He lifted a shoulder. "At least I'm not in pain. My mother..." he trailed off, sagging into a chair. Brady leaned over, his hands on his knees, his head hanging loosely.

"Brady?" Grace squatted in front of him and covered his hands with hers. "What can I do to help?"

She watched as he closed his eyes and swayed from side to side. His breathing was labored, loud and slow. He looked up into her eyes and stopped moving.

Grace hadn't noticed the dark circles under his eyes when he first came in. The charming smile gone, replaced by a vacant stare. His full lips flatlined, his jaw somewhere between tense and relaxed, Brady finally swallowed.

Movement. That was good. She'd give him time to compose himself. He didn't seem the type of man who openly talked about his feelings, especially with a near-stranger-not-quite-a-friend like Grace.

Absently, she squeezed his hands and he came to life, turning his palms up and threading his fingers through hers.

"You're doing it."

"Doing what?" Her thighs began to shake from squatting.

"Distracting me."

"I'm sorry."

"No." This time he squeezed. "That's good. I needed to get out of the house for a bit."

"Oh, so the apple pie really isn't an apology but an excuse?" she teased. It worked. That grin that didn't happen often enough appeared again.

"Both. I call it multi-tasking." Brady drew himself upright, taking Grace's hands with him. "I'm really good at it."

The sparkle in his eyes did funny things to her knees. Or it was the squatting. Either way, she stood and slipped her hands from his.

"I, on the other hand, am not. You interrupted my brownies. I need to get the dry ingredients measured and mixed."

"Can I help?"

She didn't trust him—okay, she didn't trust herself—to work side-by-side with him. "You sit there and look pretty. I've got this under control."

The cute and loud laugh barked from his solid chest again. "Pretty? I think we have the roles reversed, honey."

The compliment, forced or not, it didn't matter, caused a stirring in her belly. "Can you cook?" She tried not to be distracted by his cuteness as she measured out the flour again, and the sugar, cocoa powder, baking powder, and salt.

"I can follow a recipe. Sort of. You cook a lot?" He leaned back, draping an arm across the back of the chair.

"I'm still learning. Like you, I can follow a recipe. It's just a matter of understanding what it says. Clove. Bulb. Tomato tom-ah-to."

"Who says that? Tom-ah-to?"

"The British."

"Did you like it? Living in Italy and France?"

Talking about her time in Europe would only remind Brady of how far apart their lives, their worlds were. Which could be a good thing. They weren't right for each other, and acting on the chemistry sizzling between them would be stupid.

Things wouldn't work out, and Alexis would blame her for ruining Brady.

"I did." For the most part. Up until the last year. "The wine was amazing in Italy."

"Your parents had said you were touring vineyards and learning from the best. Did you enjoy it?"

"Some of it." She measured the baking powder and dumped it in the bowl. "The sampling, yes. I didn't like working in the vineyard at home and didn't care for it in Italy either. Dressing up and playing hostess and barmaid was more my thing."

There. Take that, lust. Tuck those gorgeous eyes away, and stop looking at me like I'm a brownie bowl and you want to lick me.

"So when did you decide fashion was your thing?"

Was that genuine interest in his voice or small talk while he waited for pie?

"I attended school in Italy. I guess you could compare it to an online vocational school. Majored in liberal arts. I'm not one to commit to anything, you know?" She looked up from the brownie bowl, anticipating a condescending brow. Nothing. Poker face. She continued scraping the batter into the pan. "A few classes here, a few classes there. I gave Italy my all, but it wasn't anything I wanted to do long term. Enter Paris."

"I can picture you in Paris."

"Yeah?" She licked the rubber spatula and tossed it in the sink. Eyeing the oven, she realized she forgot to preheat it. Eh. She'd just tack on a few extra minutes to the cooking time. She set the temperature and placed the brownie pan in it.

"Sure. It looks good on you."

Wiping her hands on her sweats... oh God. Her sweats. Grace looked down at her shirt where Paris was written out in all caps under the Eiffel tower. Two pebbles beaded out on either side of the tower.

Shit. No bra. Brady looking so sexy and smug across the kitchen. She crossed her arms, tucking her hands under her armpits and dashed off to her bedroom.

The full-length mirror laughed at her reflection. Hair a mess, headlights shining their high beams at anyone who passed—who happened to be Brady—and the most unflattering sweats she owned. She had no butt in them, lost under the baggy folds of soft material.

To change now would only make it looked like she cared, which could go one of two ways. Brady would remember how shallow and superficial and totally wrong she was for him, or he would think she was dressing up for him.

Neither appealed to her. Grabbing the nearest bra, she strapped it on and tugged her shirt over her head. The temptation to fix her bun was at the tip of her fingers. Tucking her loose strands behind her ears instead, took a closer look in the mirror.

She gasped in horror and ripped the zit strip off her nose. Completely mortified, she contemplated not leaving her bedroom. Instead, she took a few calming breaths and strolled to the kitchen with the pretense of being cool, calm, and collected.

Brady had two plates and two forks on the table. "I helped myself to your cabinets. Don't tell my mom. She'd be ashamed of my manners."

Not wanting to bring up the painful topic of his mother, she continued with distracting him. "I don't have a real pie server or ice cream scoop. A knife and a spoon will have to do." She handed him each and turned to the freezer for the ice cream.

"Works for me. Do you want your pie warmed up?" he asked as he sliced through the perfect looking crust.

"Duh." She took the plates from him and put them in the microwave. "I'm assuming you want yours warm as well."

"Warm is good. Hot is better."

Oh, it was definitely getting hot in here. His comment didn't seem to affect him in the least. Sweat broke out across her back and under her arms. Attractive and dignified she was not.

The microwave dinged, and she took out their plates. Brady topped them with healthy scoops of ice cream and slid one across the table in front of the empty seat.

"Thanks." She cut her fork into the pie and slid it through the melting ice cream. "Ohmygawd," she said around a mouthful of amazingness. "Thisissogood."

"They sell like crazy. Carter and I have to hide some in the freezer or she'll put them all out for customers." He took a healthy bite and nodded. "Good."

"Can't she just make more?" Grace dropped her fork and covered her face with her hands. "I'm an idiot. I'm sorry."

"It's okay."

"It's just... I don't know your mom very well, but any encounter I've had with her over the years she's always been so... strong." Strong-willed and sharp-tongued as well.

"I know." She heard the *clink* as Brady dropped his fork. He rubbed her forearms and spoke softly. "I think that's why this is so hard. My mom has been our rock. She's not one to let a cold slow her down. Being helpless is killing her."

Grace dropped her hands and gasped. "She's not—"

"Bad choice of words. On a positive note, her doctors see no reason why she won't make a full recovery. They believe they caught the cancer before it spread, but she'll need to have a lot of follow up appointments."

"How many more chemotherapy treatments does she need?"

"She's scheduled for five more."

"Wow."

"Yeah. She thinks she'll be back to her full strength by spring planting."

"Will she?"

He picked up his fork and played with his pie. "Knowing my mom, yeah. I guess it depends how bad this kicks her spirits. Last week she fought through the pain. Yesterday and today?" Brady shook his head.

"She's lucky to have you and Carter by her side."

"I feel bad." He took a bite of dessert and swallowed. "I've always been a homebody. The walls never felt like this. Like they're closing in around me. Even in winter when I can't be out on the fields, I enjoy coming home after a day or night of plowing and sitting back in our old-fashioned living room with a book."

"You read?"

"I am literate."

"I didn't mean it like that."

"I know. I'm kidding."

At least she got the glimmer back in his eyes. Wait. That wasn't her intent. She didn't want to see him sad over his mother either.

Remembering the brownies—and that she'd forgotten to set a timer—she got up and checked on them. They seemed cooked enough, so she set them on the stove and returned to her seat across from Brady, enraptured by his stories.

"Besides plowing for the town, what else do you do when the ground is frozen and covered with snow?"

They talked over pie—seconds for her and thirds for him—and laughed at silly tales he told her from growing up on the farm. When her laugh turned into a yawn, Brady stood, picking up their plates.

"I didn't mean to keep you up so late."

Grace squinted to read the clock on the oven. Almost midnight and they hadn't left the kitchen. She couldn't remember a time she sat across from a sexy man and talked the night away.

"I'm not the one who has to be on call all night." Noticing the brownies on the stove, she took out some foil and covered the pan. "Here. Take these with you."

"I couldn't..."

"I was planning on bringing them over with dinner tomorrow night anyway."

"You're coming over for dinner?" Brady paused, one arm in his coat sleeve, the other holding on to the zipper.

"*Bringing* you dinner."

"You'll need to stay. Eat with us."

Grace worked her bottom lip between her teeth. "That wasn't my intent."

"Don't make me eat another meal alone with my brother. You'd be doing me a favor."

She remembered the walls closing in remark from earlier in the night. All night they bounced from one topic to another, never digging too deep in one direction.

Grace read between the lines. He was lonely. And sad. And emotionally drained. She recognized the vacant and sad stares, the exhausted shoulders. The way he easily perked up with the mention of company. She'd done the same when Lily, Hope, and the girls befriended her.

"I suppose I can stay. I'll make sure to sample dinner before bringing it over."

"I'm sure whatever you make will taste amazing. We're grateful you're helping us out."

Grace handed him the brownies and followed him to the door. "Thank you for the pie. I'm not going to even attempt to make one. Hopefully, my brownies didn't turn out like crap. You'll have to let me know."

Brady leaned in, brushing his lips across hers. "We'll sample them together tomorrow night."

"You don't have to wait."

"It'll be worth it." He kissed her softly again. "Apple and vanilla. Much better." With a wink and a chuckle, he let himself out of her apartment.

Grace touched her lips with her fingers. Apple and vanilla. Yes. Much, much better.

CHAPTER FOURTEEN

THE LAST PERSON GRACE expected to see knocking on the glass door to The Closet was her sister. Not only did Alexis have no time for her, but she was a tomboy at heart. Jeans, flannel, and sweatshirts were her go-to outfits.

"I went to your apartment first." Ah. That explained it. Not the visit, but why her sister stood in the middle of a boutique.

"I'm not technically open today. Needed to get out of the apartment though. I feel more inspired when I'm here."

"Sure," Alexis said with a shrug, sounding like she didn't understand or care what Grace meant.

"Hey. How's my favorite niece?" Grace stepped around the counter and knelt in front of Sophie. Despite Alexis' effort to sway her from all things girly, Sophie was a princess at heart.

"I'm Cinda-lella today." She twirled around, her poofy tutu style skirt billowing around her tiny frame.

"And Cinderella never looked so beautiful. Come give your auntie some love." Grace opened her arms, and Sophie leaped into them.

Ah. The smell of baby shampoo and Goldfish. "What are you and Mommy doing today?" She'd have better luck talking to an almost three-year-old than to her sister.

"Mommy and me are going to wunch."

"Are you having lunch at Hope's restaurant?"

Dark curls bobbed up and down. "I'm having mac and cheese."

"Which is why we don't go out to eat all that often. It costs me sixty-five cents if I make it at home."

"I'm sure Hope gives you a friend discount."

"I don't mooch off my friends." Alexis hiked the diaper bag higher on her shoulder. "Sophie's naptime will be here before we know it. I only have a sec. I need to talk to you about something."

Of course, she didn't come by for a social visit. "We wouldn't want to mess with Miss Sophie's nap." Grace rubbed her nose against her niece's and set her down when she started to wiggle.

If Alexis mentioned anything about Brady, she'd... kick her out. Not that there was anything to discuss.

"Ben's surprised me with a quick family getaway."

"That's good. You never leave the vineyard."

"Yeah, well, it's only for two days, and Mom and Dad won't be back until Christmas."

She couldn't be asking Grace to help out at the vineyard. She didn't know anything about it.

"We're leaving next Wednesday and will be back Friday night. Ben promises the vineyard will be fine for a few days without us there."

Phew. Narrow escape. "Have fun. Where are you going?"

"Not far. Canada, near Niagara."

"Is that where those vineyards you like so much are? The ones that showed you how to make ice wine?" See? She paid attention. She could be a decent sister.

Alexis looked at her with surprise. "Yeah."

"Need me to watch Sophie?" That could be fun. Auntie and princess sleepover for a few nights.

"No. She's coming with us."

"Well... have fun." What else could she say?

Alexis blinked and jerked her head. "You'll be... okay?"

"Sure." It wasn't like she'd even notice if her sister had gone on vacation. The only time they saw each other was at book club meetings and when their mutual friends had get-togethers.

"We're not meeting next week anyway because—oh. It's Thanksgiving." So now her parents *and* sister would be away. They hadn't talked about the holiday yet. Had Alexis been around, Grace wasn't sure she'd be invited to her Thanksgiving table anyway.

"I didn't know if you had any plans." Alexis shifted the bag again. Could it be she actually cared about Grace?

"I hadn't thought about it yet. Don't worry about me though. You three have a good time."

Alexis darted her gaze around the store, her fingers intertwining and playing together as if nervous to be with Grace. They had their issues, more than the usual sister issue crap.

Besides being totally opposite and having none of the same interests, Alexis seemed to despise Grace. Similarly to how Brady used to look at her. He'd gotten past whatever his beef was with her, but Alexis still snubbed her nose down—or up, since Grace was five inches taller—at her.

"You're not mad?"

"Mad?" No. Disappointed, yes. "Were you expecting me to have a hissy fit or something? I'm not a toddler upset about missing out on mac and cheese. No offense, Sophie," she said to her niece, who was playing obliviously with a pair of four-inch stilettos.

"Turkey and stuffing is a far cry from mac and cheese."

"Mom's mac and cheese or the boxed stuff?" This elicited a smile from her sister. "There's always work to do. I can conference call with my girls since they don't celebrate Thanksgiving."

"Lily? She'll be with Ty's family. Hope has—"

Grace's voice hitched. "Not them." Wow. Alexis interpreted *my girls* as their mutual friends. Maybe she didn't hold her in content. "Arianna, Kendall, Lacey, and Maria. They're my top designers and live overseas. No Thanksgiving for them."

"Oh. I didn't realize."

Because she never listened. Grace had explained the situation a few times over dinner at their parents' house. Alexis was there. So was Ben. He listened, asked questions, offered tips.

"It doesn't matter. Anyway, I'll keep busy. You guys have fun." She turned her back on her sister to scout out her curly topped niece. "Bye, princess. Eat lots and lots of mac and cheese, okay? Next to Gramma's, Hope's is the best."

"I want mac and cheese now."

"You don't want to keep a toddler in waiting." Grace took Sophie's hand and led her to the door.

"Toddlers need to learn to wait," Alexis said from behind. The edge wasn't as sharp in her voice, but it was still there.

"Waiting is good. Teaches you patience."

"Since when have you had patience?" And here came the claws.

Keeping her tone even, Grace held the door for her sister and her niece. "I've changed a lot over the years, Alexis. I'm not the same girl I was when I left Crystal Cove. Maybe someday you'll see me for who I am today."

She turned away and went back into her store, hoping her sister would see the light and take the time to get to know the new Grace.

With her creative mojo now in the crapper, she powered down her laptop and zipped up her winter coat. She needed to start the prep work for dinner anyway.

An hour later, she sampled the most amazing chicken tetrazzini. It wasn't a dish her mother had ever made, so she didn't have to worry about measuring up there, not that her parents or sister were around to sample.

Hopefully, Mrs. Marshall didn't have this on her repertoire. If she cooked like she baked, there'd be no impressing Brady. Or Carter.

Her meals weren't supposed to be about impressing; they were to help out a family in need. In emotional need. Not something easy to assist with. If food helped, and by the look on Brady's face it seemed to, she had no problem providing the support.

His kiss last night was anticipated yet unexpected. All night she oscillated between wanting to push him away and wanting to bury him under the covers with her and cuddle forever.

It was loneliness that drove him to her, and she didn't want to take advantage of that. What else could he find attractive in her?

Needing to put some distance between them, she sent Carter a text asking if he had time to take a look at her website tonight. He texted back immediately with a thumbs up emoji.

Carter could play interference and babysitter all in one. Satisfied she wouldn't manipulate or take advantage of Brady's weakness anymore, she covered the tetrazzini and added it to the tote bag with the rolls and bagged salad.

Ten minutes later she stood on the Marshall's back porch and knocked on the door. No one came. She rapped her knuckles again.

Nothing.

It was too cold to leave the dinner on the porch, but she didn't want to not leave it. Trying the doorknob, she paused when it twisted. Should she let herself in? The lights were on upstairs and down the hall where Mrs. Marshall slept.

If she was in pain Grace would slip out, hopefully undetected. Taking a chance, she pushed at the sticking door and stepped into the dark kitchen, closing the door behind her.

The chicken dish was still warm so she set it on top of the oven along with a box of noodles still needing to be cooked. She found a tiny notepad stuck to the side of the fridge and a pen in an old coffee cup at the end of the counter.

Scribbling down heating directions for the food, she caught movement behind her.

"Now there's a site for sore eyes." Carter flipped on the kitchen light, momentarily blinding her.

Blinking away the shock to her pupils, she glanced up at Carter. Shirtless, hair still wet from a shower, and looking sexy as sin. Only his naked torso didn't cause any stirring inside. He was nice to look at though. Very nice.

Even though she'd seen more of Carter's naked skin than Brady's, it was the older brother who warmed her from the inside out.

Who would have thought?

"What's for dinner tonight?" He towered over her, lifting the foil from the pan. "Smells good. Not too garlicky."

"Sorry about that."

"Who am I to complain? Beats frozen waffles and cereal for dinner every night."

"I sampled the tetrazzini before I came. It's safe. Promise."

"Again. No complaints here." He scratched his naked chest, and Grace caught the lingering effects of his soap. Nice. Clean.

Still not Brady.

"I'll see you later." Grace moved past him toward the back door.

"You're not going to eat with us?"

"No. You guys enjoy."

"Let's at least go through your website. You mentioned wanting to change one of the windows?" Carter opened his laptop on the kitchen table and patted the seat next to him. "Show me what you want." A wicked grin escaped his lips. "Interpret as you may."

Grace laughed and shook her head. "You're pathetic."

"You love me anyway."

She parked herself next to Carter and took the laptop from him, logging into her account.

It didn't take him long to add a new window and the graphics she found on a free photo site.

"It's perfect. Thank you."

Carter bumped his still naked shoulder against her. "For you, doll, anything."

"What's going on?" Brady's deep, yet soft voice asked from the archway. His hooded gaze was dark, his lips tight as if holding back an angry tirade of words.

"Just hanging with our girl here. She made us dinner."

Brady's glare didn't budge from his brother. "You could put a shirt on."

Carter must have sensed a trace of jealousy or annoyance in his brother. He broke out into a shit-eating grin and stretched his arms back, one resting casually on Grace's shoulder.

Brady clenched his jaw and sniffed. Still, his eyes remained fixated on his brother. A low moan from down the hall had him spinning around and rushing off.

"Your mom's having a rough day?"

"Yeah. That's what Brady said." Carter dropped his arm, his shoulders following suit. "I took on three new clients this week. Left for Portland at the ass crack of dawn, and I just got back."

Which meant Brady was with his mom all day long. "I should go. All three of you must be exhausted." Grace pushed back her chair and stood.

"You sure I can't convince you to stay for dinner?"

"I appreciate it, but you three need to rest. I'm sure your mom doesn't want company in the house when she's suffering."

"Stay," Brady's voice said from behind her.

Carter smirked over the top of her head at his brother. "Guess I should get dressed if we're going to have company for dinner." He clicked his tongue at her and strolled out of the kitchen.

Grace avoided Brady and helped herself to the cabinets, finding a pot and filling it with water. Once it was on the stove, she put the chicken dish in the oven to warm. Needing a bowl for the salad, she turned and bumped into Brady's chest.

"Oh. Sorry."

"You apologize a lot for a woman who's done nothing but help us out." Brady's eyes darkened, trapping her with his gaze. "Me out."

"You've had a long day." Having a will of their own, her hands reached up and stroked his chest.

Brady dropped his gaze from hers and looked down at her hands. Nodding, he sighed. "This is the highlight of my day."

They were entering the danger zone. Two innocent kisses—well, one not so innocent, the second one sweet—later and a night of talking over pie, and they were already headed in the wrong direction.

Or was it? Brady was the type of man who, when he kissed a woman, he wanted something more. Not in a sexual way, although she wouldn't complain. He was relationship material. She was not.

Why did he have to say such sweet things to her? Look at her as if she was a kitten and he wanted to pet her all day, and then look at her like a bowl of brownie batter he wanted to lick? It wasn't fair.

"How's your mom?" she asked, knowing it would change the direction of his thoughts. Her tactic worked. Scratching his fingers across his face with a loud sigh, he lowered his head, resting his chin on his chest.

"She's mad at me for making her rest. Four times I caught her in the kitchen scrubbing the counter or organizing the fridge. She's not one to sit idle."

"Did the doctor say it's okay for her to be up and about."

"Yeah. If she can handle it."

"You don't think she can?"

Brady moved in closer, trapping her hands between them, and rested his chin on her head. "If it was anyone else, I'd push them to get up and move around. Not Dorothy Marshall though. She'll overdo it and relapse. She's too stubborn to see the danger in over-extending herself."

"How long has she been in bed?" Grace rested her head against his shoulder, melting into his embrace.

"Pretty much since her first chemo. I've brought her for short walks outside, but the past few days it hasn't hit above freezing. I'm not letting her out in the cold."

"She must be going stir crazy."

"She is. But every time she gets up and moves around, she gets sick."

"Is that normal?"

"Unfortunately. Sleep is the best medicine for her. Well, that and chemo."

She didn't know what else to say. What to do.

"You need to take care of yourself as well, Brady. It won't do her any good if you or your brother gets sick."

"That's what I've been doing." He lowered his head and nuzzled her neck with kisses.

She was a distraction. That, she could handle. As long as he didn't have any expectations of a future together. Her future plans were to leave this place. Set up shop somewhere more glamorous, where the action was.

"I could say this is a surprise, but I'd be lying." At the sound of Carter's voice, they pulled apart. "You don't hide your feelings very well, big bro."

Humiliated at being busted, Grace hid behind Brady's body and dumped the pasta in the boiling water and stirred. And stirred. She couldn't turn around and face Carter.

"Make yourself useful and set the table," Brady snapped.

"What are you going to do while Grace is cooking and I set the table? Continue groping the hel—"

"Enough."

Carter chuckled but dropped the jokes.

"Sorry about that," Brady said so only she could hear.

Grace flashed him a quick smile and returned her focus to the boiling noodles. "Do you have a bowl for the salad? And a strainer? And can you put some dressings on the table?"

He did as asked, and when the noodles were done she dumped the water into the strainer.

"Can you get me some butter?"

Brady complied while Carter opened the bagged salad and dumped it into the bowl. She took the chicken out of the oven and stirred the noodles into the mixture. Once combined, she carried it to the kitchen table.

"Think Mom will want real food tonight?" Carter asked as he served himself salad.

"I'll make her a small plate after dinner. It sounds like she's finally sleeping."

"She was up all day, huh? So I may have it easy if she sleeps all night?"

"I hope she does." Brady scooped out a healthy portion and placed it on Grace's plate before he served himself. "What kind of dressing would you like?" He handed her the ranch, Italian, and balsamic vinaigrette.

She hadn't thought Carter rude for serving himself first. Brady, however, was the impeccable gentleman, treating her like a real lady.

They ate in silence with the occasional, "So good," from Carter as he shoveled his food down his throat.

"You'd think he hasn't eaten in years."

"I'm a growing boy." Carter patted his flat stomach. "I didn't have time to stop for lunch today. Thanks again, Grace. This is amazing."

Compliments were still relatively new to her. She blushed at the praise and took her last bite. It was good. Hearty and filling. Hopefully, Mrs. Marshall would like it as well.

Carter got up from the table and rinsed his plate. "I'll do the dishes later. Just toss them in the sink for now." He sliced into the brownies and wrapped one in a napkin. "For later. I'm gonna be in the office getting some work done. I'll keep an ear out for Mom. You two," he winked, "behave your-selves."

When he was gone, Brady turned her chair so she faced him and then spun his body around as well, trapping her legs between his.

"I'm sorry if I embarrassed you earlier."

"You didn't." Yeah. Total mortification there.

"I did." He rubbed his big, calloused hands on her knees, and his fingers made circles on her thighs. "I like you, Grace Le Blanc."

"I like you too." Too much.

"I wasn't expecting anything like this to happen between us."

Because her sister had made him believe she was a spoiled, self-centered bitch. She was. Maybe still was in some ways.

"I know I don't have a lot to offer, especially now with my time caught up on caring for my mother, but I'd like to..." he ran his tongue across his teeth, clearly uncomfortable with what to say next.

If he were any other man, he'd say he'd like to have an affair. Keep it on the down low. That had been perfect for her in the past. Not being tied to a man but having a guy around to sleep with was a win-win.

Relationships weren't her thing. They didn't suit her goals in life. Fancy dinners. Expensive gifts or exotic getaways in exchange for no-strings sex suited her just fine.

Brady couldn't offer any of those. Not even the no-strings sex. He didn't have to say it; she knew. She could tell. He was the marrying type.

Not wanting him to finish his statement with ridiculous words like date, see each other, commitment, or relationship, she continued for him.

"I'd like to as well." There. Whatever happened she could blame it on miscommunication.

That cute, little boy smile like someone offered him a triple scoop ice cream cone lit up his face.

"You understand I can't—"

"Shh." She placed a finger on his lips. "Your number one priority right now is taking care of your mom. The rest will fall into place."

"Grace." His fingers dug into her thighs, and she found herself being pulled into his body. When her knees hit his chair, he picked up her legs and draped them over his. Those magic fingers of his skirted up her sides and into her hair. "Grace," he said again, drawing her into his body until they touched torso to torso.

His lips were heaven on hers. Soft, pillowy clouds of sweetness, Brady kissed her with meaning. With gratitude. With passion. His hands never stopped moving, massaging first her sides, then her back, and up to her shoulders.

Her mind floated in and out of consciousness as his mouth made love to hers, not leaving one centimeter of her mouth untouched.

The passion flowed through her body from head to toe. With just a kiss, he managed to make her feel thoroughly loved, as if his lips had kissed every inch of her body. His hands moved to her face, cupping her cheeks in his palms, making her feel small with his powerful touch.

Not small as in weak. Brady didn't dominate, he gave. Her nurtured. He made her feel safe.

Ironically, the only danger that existed was falling for him.

CHAPTER FIFTEEN

THE KISS HAD TAKEN things to a new level with Grace. Brady warmed up a bowl of soup for his mother and put the rest of the food away.

"Your girlfriend gone?" Carter tossed something in the trash and helped himself to another beer.

"Grace left a few minutes ago," he said, ignoring the girlfriend comment.

"Did you try the brownies?"

"Not yet."

"Don't. They're crap."

"I watched her make them. I'm sure you're overreacting." Brady cut off a healthy size chunk and tossed it in his mouth. Coughing—or choking, he wasn't sure—he banged on his chest and swallowed. Hard.

"Here. You need this more than me right now." Carter handed him his beer.

The cold ale helped wash the bitter, salty mess down his throat. "What was that?"

"You're the one who was there when she made them. You tell me."

Brady hadn't focused on the ingredients as much as he had the movement of her hands, noticing her long, feminine fingers. When he wasn't zeroed in on her hands, he studied her lips. She spoke with them, not only literally, but figuratively as well. When nervous, she worried her bottom lip between her teeth. When flirting, she pursed them. When angry, she tucked them in.

And when passionate, she opened them to him, letting him explore their softness, their taste. Which unfortunately had been erased by the bitter, salty brownie.

"She must have replaced the sugar with salt. Or measured wrong. I don't know." He eyed the pan. They looked amazing, just like the lasagna had. Deceiving. "I'll throw them out. Don't tell her though. It'll only make her feel bad."

"Damn. You're whipped already." Carter laughed, taking out another beer from the fridge.

"It's called being polite."

"Uh huh. That for Mom?" He jerked his head toward the bowl on the counter.

"Yeah. She had a half piece of toast this afternoon and felt nauseous. Try to get some liquids in her. I'm worried she's going to be dehydrated."

"Why not make her a smoothie or something?"

"Tried." Brady set his still full beer bottle on the counter and scrubbed his hands across his face. "Dairy doesn't agree with her. Found that out the hard way when I made her one for breakfast."

"Man." Carter slouched in a chair. "Think we should bring her back to the doctors?"

"I called Dr. Moore's office earlier. Spoke with a nurse. Said if she doesn't get any fluids in her she'll need to come in. Have an IV."

"Mom's not gonna want to do that."

"I know. And she needs company other than you and me. Someone to lift her spirits. Mrs. Le Blanc is away for another month. Mom doesn't have many friends."

"What about Alexis? She can bring Sophie over. Mom loves little kids."

"Now that, my idiot brother, is the best idea you've ever had."

The next morning Brady managed to help his mother into the shower while keeping her dignity and his sanity. Once she was dressed, he called Alexis, who came over right away, daughter in tow.

They hung out in the living room while Brady went out to the barn to work on the equipment. Not long before his father died, he'd taught Brady how to inspect the tractors. How to clean out the carburetor, fuel lines, and run multi-point inspections. He was diligent about keeping his equipment running smoothly and spent nearly the entire winter in the barn inspecting every piece.

Brady followed in his father's footsteps, only he also made time for his plowing business. Along with the tractors, he also inspected his truck and made sure the hydraulics on the plow were functioning properly.

Sometime later, his stomach alerted him it was time to eat. And time to check on his mother.

He found the three of them, Alexis, Sophie, and his mom having a tea party on the floor in the living room. The space wasn't large. Just enough room for the woodstove, a camelback couch that he and his brother had always hated, and his father's favorite recliner.

It had seen better days eighteen years ago and hadn't fared well since then, yet was still comfortable. His mother had covered it with a quilt his paternal grandmother had made for their wedding, which covered up the worn and frayed green and blue checked print. They would have gotten rid of it years ago if it didn't hold so many memories.

The pictures on the wall above the couch hadn't been updated since Carter's senior year of high school. Brady's and Carter's graduation pictures were the only ones added since their father's death.

His parents' wedding photo, pictures of each of the boys sitting on their dad's lap on the tractor in the middle of the fields, their mother sitting on a blanket, surrounded by blueberry bushes, and Brady leaning over her shoulder and Carter swaddled in her lap. Memories that made their place a home.

"Bwady." Sophie pointed at him and held up a miniature teacup.

"Hey, Sophie. Are you having a nice tea party?" He was surprised the little girl even knew who he was. They saw each other from time to time, but it was usually in passing.

Sophie danced around his mom and Alexis and picked up a baby doll, feeding her pretend tea.

"I'm going to warm up some food. Would you like to stay and have lunch with us, Alexis?"

"Oh, you don't need to go to any trouble." She got to her feet and joined him in the doorway.

"No trouble at all. We have a ton of leftovers. Your sister's been keeping us well fed."

"*My* sister?"

"Yeah. She's a good cook." He wouldn't mention the garlic or brownie mishap.

"I guess if it's not too much trouble. Sophie's incredibly picky so I doubt she'll eat anything. She can pick off my plate if she's hungry."

"I can make her a peanut butter and jelly sandwich."

"Nah. I'll wait until she asks to eat."

He watched his mother struggle to get up from the floor, knowing she hated how weak her body had become. She needed food. In one quick stride, he was by her side, lifting her to her feet. "I'm making you a plate as well. Do you want to sit at the table or out here?"

"I forgot how exhausting a toddler can be."

"Oh, Mrs. Marshall. I'm so sorry. I'll take Sophie home and let you rest."

"Don't you dare. Sophie's an angel. She's exhausting me in the most wonderful way. I love listening to her constant chatter and watching her play with her dolls."

Brady kept a hand on her lower back, following her to his father's chair, where she lowered herself into the quilt.

"If only my sons would give me a grandchild of my own."

Alexis snorted. "You can borrow Sophie anytime, Mrs. M."

"I plan on taking you up on it. You two go eat lunch. I'll keep an eye on her. Promise."

Brady followed Alexis into the kitchen where he took out the chicken tetrazzini and three plates.

"Did my sister make that?"

"Yup." He scooped some onto a plate and slid it into the microwave. "It's amazing. Your mom was making meals for us and asked Grace to fill in while she was gone."

"I'm surprised she didn't ask me."

"You've got your hands full. Sophie. The vineyard. Your own husband."

"True. Grace doesn't really have anything going on."

He wanted to come to her defense, to tell Alexis how proud he was of Grace for following her dreams. He never would have thought of Alexis as the snarky sister, but her comments last month at the festival were a little snotty toward her sister, yet Grace didn't argue back.

Interesting how people weren't necessarily as they seemed.

"How's your mom doing?" Alexis asked.

Brady was grateful for the change in subject. He didn't want to talk about Grace with Alexis right now. He filled her in on the chemo, the slow recovery, the depression that was ultimately settling in.

"I haven't seen her this happy in a long time. You and Sophie are good for her." The microwave *dinged,* and he took their lunches out. "Maybe she'll eat a little with you here." He scraped a small portion on a salad plate and brought it to the living room.

Curled up in her lap was Sophie, book in hand.

"Oh, that's too cute," Alexis said softly from behind. "*Pinkalicious* is her favorite book. I hate it. I think that's why Grace bought it for Sophie. That and a zillion princess books."

"Let me guess. You got her the farm and sports books." Of course, Grace would buy her niece girly books. Instead of rolling his eyes as Alexis had done, he smiled inside.

"You know it. I've been avoiding this book forever. It's so annoying. Of course, Sophie's obsessed. I already read it to her four times today. I'll gladly pass on the chore to your mother."

"This is the cutest book," his mother said from across the living room. "Having two boys, I never got to indulge in stories like these. Make a note of it, son. Marriage. Grandchildren. Lots. Especially girls."

"I'll get right on that," Brady laughed. Grace's bright smile came to mind. Her big green eyes. Her soft lips. Her kind soul. She may not be a farmer at heart like him or her sister, but she had other wonderful traits. "Do you want lunch?"

"After my snuggles. I think someone is getting sleepy."

"Looks to me like two someones," Alexis said.

They retreated to the kitchen and ate their lunch listening to giggles from the other room.

"Your mom is good with her."

"She's in heaven. Thanks for coming by. You've really made her day."

"Any time."

They talked about the weather, their hopes for next year's crops, and Ty's plans for a remodel.

"He offered to come by next week. Said business is pretty slow before and after Thanksgiving. No one wants their house torn apart during the holidays."

"Good for you. Oh, speaking of Thanksgiving." Alexis scraped her plate, pushing the last of the chicken on to her fork. "Ben and I will be going away for a few days. I'm sure everything will be fine, but if you hear of any shenanigans at the vineyard, will you let me know?"

"Sure. Do you need me to watch Hemmy as well?" Her gigantic Bernese Mountain Dog was a gentle giant. Could be therapeutic for his mother as well.

"Really? We planned on bringing him with us. Are you sure he won't be an inconvenience?"

"Not at all. We thought about getting a rescue dog this winter anyway. Might as well get used to having one under foot by babysitting Hemsworth."

"You're awesome."

He picked up their plates and rinsed them off in the sink. Knowing his mother wouldn't want her food too hot he didn't bother reheating her plate. She'd only use the temperature as an excuse to put it aside.

When he and Alexis entered the living room they both chuckled at the scene. Both were out cold, Sophie draped across his mother's lap, the old quilt wrapped around them.

"Isn't that sweet? I almost hate to disturb them."

"You can leave Sophie here if you want. I can text you when she wakes up."

"I appreciate it, but she's a bear if she doesn't get her one and half hour nap. She won't sleep long like this. I can get her back to sleep when we get home if I leave now."

Brady helped with her bag and both doors, watching as Alexis buckled Sophie in her car seat.

"Thanks again for lunch. If I don't see you before we leave, I hope you're able to have a nice Thanksgiving."

"We may skip it this year. Carter and I aren't the best in the kitchen. I'll give my hand at it, but may end up eating frozen dinners."

"I feel bad. If we were home we would have invited you up. Maybe for Christmas we can get the families together. My mom would love to hang out with your mom."

"Sounds like a great idea."

He hugged her and stepped back as she drove off in her SUV.

The Le Blancs were away. Alexis and Ben would be away. So where would Grace be spending Thanksgiving?

She needed company, and he needed help in the kitchen. Not that he'd use that as an excuse when inviting her to Thanksgiving dinner.

He'd keep the real reason he wanted her at his dinner table a secret.

He was falling for her. Deeper than he should, faster than was safe. Maybe a chic store owner and a poor farmer had more in common than he thought?

CHAPTER SIXTEEN

"FOR REAL?" GRACE NEARLY tripped in her heeled boots and dropped the crockpot of minestrone soup in the middle of Brady's kitchen. "You want me to help you make a turkey? And stuffing and ... all the other stuff?"

"I know I'm asking a lot. You probably have other plans."

Brady took the crockpot from her, and she tried to ignore the tingles that shot through her legs when their fingers touched.

"Actually..." Actually, her family completely ditched her without a second thought. Sort of. It surprised her when Alexis came by to tell her of their family plans. She probably scheduled the mini-getaway to avoid having to invite Grace over for Thanksgiving. "My parents are still away, and my sister and Ben are going to Canada to visit some wineries."

"I heard about that."

"You did?" She propped a hip against the counter and watched Brady lift the lid to the soup and dip his face into the steam. If he knew, this was a pity invitation.

"Mom is going to love this."

"I had a bowl for lunch. It's safe."

"You don't have to convince me every time you bring us food. The beef stew the other night was perfect."

"I forgot to take out the bay leaves. You're not supposed to eat them."

"I didn't know that, but my mom did. She ate an entire bowl and had another the next day for breakfast."

"That sounds disgusting."

"When you haven't eaten in weeks and you finally have your appetite back, I guess anything goes."

"Desperate—"

"No." He hushed her with his finger on her lips. "I didn't mean it that way. She didn't scarf down your food because she was desperate and would eat anything in sight. She ate it because it was delicious."

"I'm glad she liked it," she said around his finger.

"You don't take compliments well, do you?" Brady dropped his finger and put his hands on her hips, drawing her into his body.

They didn't often come her way, but she wouldn't say that to him. She didn't need a pity invite to Thanksgiving, and she didn't need pity compliments. Brady and Carter were raised on manners and knew how to treat and talk to a lady. Even when her food did taste like crap, they sang her praises.

She'd like to believe some of the compliments were genuine though and not stemmed from proper good old-fashioned etiquette.

Ignoring his question, she went with a distraction. "I didn't have time to make dessert, but I brought ice cream. It's in the car." Still in her winter coat and high-heeled boots, she hustled backward and tugged open the kitchen door.

Brady was waiting for her when she came up the steps and took the bag from her hand. "You're spoiling us."

"I have to eat anyway. Might as well share." Not that she normally cooked every day. Once a week, maybe, until lately.

"Speaking of." Brady put the ice cream in the freezer and then reached for an envelope propped between the salt and pepper shakers. "This is for you."

"What is it?" She slid the white envelope between her fingers.

"Grocery money."

"I'm not taking your money." She held the envelope out toward him.

"You've been feeding us for two weeks now. Carter and I eat a hell... excuse me, a heck of a lot more than you do. Your grocery bill had to have quadrupled."

Actually, it had. And she hadn't given one thought about it being because of Carter and Brady. Eating healthy was more expensive than eating crap foods. It didn't seem right. She could buy a bag of chips, a carton of ice cream, and a high calorie, high sodium, high-fat meal for less than ten bucks. But to make a healthy salad with all the fixings would cost just as much, if not more, and wouldn't be as filling.

She enjoyed cooking for them. Loved how they made her feel like a princess. No. A queen. Doing nice things for people—especially two very handsome men—made her feel good. So cooking for them was partly selfish.

And as a side bonus, most meals ended with savory kisses from Brady. The reward far outweighed the time, effort, and money she invested.

"I have to cook for myself anyway. It's not a problem."

"I doubt you'd be cooking so much. Or so often. You work all day, slave in the kitchen, then drive over here. The least I can do is cover your expenses."

"I'm not taking your money." She shoved the envelope against his chest and let go. It fell to the floor between their feet.

"You're stubborn," he grumbled, bending down to pick it up.

"Likewise."

Brady straightened with a smile. "So how about this." He unbuttoned her coat and slid it off her shoulders, hanging it up on the hooks behind the door. Returning to her, he threaded his fingers in the loops of her jeans and yanked her tight into his body.

Her heels had her stumbling ungracefully into his chest. Which he seemed to like. "You're looking rather smug right now, Mr. Marshall. What is it you're planning?" Grace slid her hands up his chest and snaked them around his neck.

"A date."

"A date?"

"A date. Someplace nice where you don't have to worry about lifting a finger."

"Pizza works fine for me." She didn't want him to spend his well-earned money on overpriced food.

"We can do better than pizza." He dipped his chin and drew her bottom lip between his. His hands worked their way down her back, stopping at the top of her butt.

Lower she wanted to tell him. Anytime they kissed he kept his hands in respectable places. Her hips. Her shoulders. Her cheeks. Oh, how she loved when he cupped her face in his palms. Swoon-worthy.

Never the ass. Never a brush against her breasts, unless it was his chest crushing into hers. Always the gentleman.

His tongue found hers and coaxed and caressed as he rubbed her lower back. Maybe if she stood on her tiptoes his hands would drop to her cheeks.

Nope. Even in her three-inch heels, he didn't let his hands dangle.

The other night when he kissed her goodbye, she'd leaned into him against the car and felt his arousal. The primal instinct to rub against him had been strong, and she did. Immediately Brady had pulled back and toned down their kiss.

While she didn't want to jump into bed with him—well, maybe she did, just a little—she wouldn't mind going from first to second base.

Finding herself dangerously close to his arousal once more, she resisted the temptation to rub herself like a cat—a cat in heat—against him.

She tugged at his hair, lightening the moment. "You need a haircut." The first time she kissed him she could sift her hand through it and it barely threaded through her fingers. She liked being able to tug, to grab ahold of it, but shorter was definitely sexier on him.

"No time," he said between kisses, trailing his lips along her jawline.

A noise from behind had her dropping her hands. "I think your mom is awake."

With a sigh and one last brush of his lips against hers, he stepped away. "She'll be happy to see you. With all the times you've been over, she has yet to come out of her room and thank you."

Yeah. If the snubbing she got last month was any indication, Grace didn't think Mrs. Marshall would be overly ecstatic to see her.

"Mom." Brady left Grace to wrap an arm around his mother.

Grace retreated to the door and unzipped her boots. When she looked up she did her best to control the shock in her eyes. She'd never seen Mrs. Marshall so frail. So thin. So dependent on another human being. In all her encounters with her, granted they were mostly from her childhood years when her family walked down the road to pick blueberries and apples, the woman had always been a pillar of strength.

She remembered hearing Alexis boast about Mrs. Marshall, and how she could drive a tractor and toss a bail of hay over her shoulder. Grace had worried their own mother would be envious of their neighbor. That was never the case.

Dorothy Marshall may have been the epitome of physical strength, but Claudia Le Blanc had a quality more dangerous. She could peer at Grace or Alexis and force the truth to come out with one look from her deep brown eyes. No one stood a chance with their mother.

Which was why Grace had avoided her family as much as possible. With Alexis as the goody-two-shoes and a mother with a sixth sense, all Grace had was her ability to sweet talk her father into siding with her.

On many occasions, he had. But when push came to shove, no one disagreed with Claudia.

"Brady says you've been bringing dinners over while your parents are away. Thank you." The last two words came out strained.

"You're welcome. How are you feeling, Mrs. Marshall?"

"Like a woman who has been pricked, prodded, electrocuted, stomped over, and hung up to dry. I can only imagine if I hadn't been in better condition. If I'd had a desk job my whole life instead of being outdoors."

A passive-aggressive jab. She and Alexis must have taken lessons in it.

"Have a seat, Mom." Brady kicked out a chair and gently eased his mother into it.

"I made minestrone soup. Will that be okay tonight, or would you like something more bland?"

"You been telling stories?" she asked Brady.

"The whole town knows what you're going through. Everyone cares. You've read the cards from others, those who've been through chemo before."

Mrs. Marshall cleared her throat and folded her hands on the table. "I'd like a cup of chamomile tea. And I'll try the soup. If it's too spicy I won't be able to eat it."

"Fresh herbs only. Well, as fresh as we can get in Maine in November."

"Did you use the herbs from my garden?"

Was that an accusatory tone or a hopeful one? Grace wasn't sure what the right answer was. She went with honesty. "I got them at the whole food store in Rockland."

"Those places are stealing money from people. You can grow and harvest your own food and save yourself thousands of dollars every year."

"I don't have much of a green thumb. Or the space at my apartment."

"Your mother told me you were planning on moving out. Young people these days." She shook her head in disappointment. "Thank you," she said to Brady when he handed her the cup of tea.

"It's Lily's old place, right next door to my shop."

"Mmhm." She sipped her tea, not yet making eye contact with Grace. "Nothing wrong with your parents' place as far as I can tell."

Grace didn't want to stand there defending herself or her decisions. Knowing dinner would only be more stressed with her there, she forced a smile and her manners.

"It was nice seeing you again, Mrs. Marshall. I'll let you and your family eat in private." She reached for her coat on the hook by the door and shoved her feet in her boots. Damned things wouldn't go in smoothly. She should have worn sneakers. Or flip flops for a faster getaway. Bending down as gracefully as she could, she zipped up her boots over her skinny jeans and tipped her head to Brady.

"Have a good night."

"I'll walk you to your car."

"No." She held out her hand to stop him. "Eat dinner with your mother. I'll be by in a few days... if you still need me."

"Grace," he pleaded.

She avoided eye contact and lowered her head, letting herself out of the kitchen.

The night had turned brisk, which was perfect for cooling her cheeks and her temper. She knew she shouldn't let people get to her so easily. It was the passive-aggressive, condescending attitude people gave her that cut her to the pulp.

Sniffing back angry tears, Grace started her car and sped off, not waiting for it to warm up. It had only been parked for a few minutes anyway.

Just long enough to have a thrilling make out session with Brady, and then get cut down by his mother.

Why she thought the two of them had a chance, she didn't know.

Besides. A year from now she wouldn't be in Crystal Cove anymore. Her store would be run by someone else while she opened up a bigger place closer to one of the fashion capitals. By this summer she'd hire a couple potential assistant managers.

Life was good. She didn't need a master kisser and his evil mother ruining her plans.

She could ruin them just fine all on her own.

CHAPTER SEVENTEEN

WITH ENOUGH SOUP IN the crockpot to last two nights, Grace hadn't planned on going to Brady's tonight. It wasn't expected, and she'd sort of set up that routine anyway. When the meal was big, she skipped a night. When it was gobbled up in one sitting by Brady and Carter, she came back the next night with another dish.

Secretly she'd wished she'd made a smaller pot of soup last night so she would have to come by again. Well, not *have* to. Brady had made it clear she wasn't expected to do anything and had even tossed money in her face.

The money would have helped her financial status. A lot. But it couldn't buy the happiness cooking brought her.

Grace snorted, hoping the woman in the dressing room didn't overhear her. Imagine her saying that out loud.

Money *can* buy happiness. It was why she needed to grow and expand her business. Sales had dipped, which was expected. With Black Friday specials planned in a few days, hopefully, she'd see some momentum before everything went static again.

Winter months were planning months. In the spring she hoped to regain some of her investments. At times she'd felt like a cheap whore taking the money from Robert, but she didn't let pride get in her way. She'd needed the cash, and he was an asshole. A win-win.

The woman came out of the dressing room holding two dresses in one hand and a sweater and scarf in the other. Her Dooney and Bourke bag and her Burberry scarf were in-

206

congruous to this little section of Crystal Cove. It was what Grace had hoped she could lure into her shop, but at the same time offer something nice to those who preferred to wear jeans and work boots.

"How did you do?"

"You're a terrible person," the lady huffed, her generous diamond momentarily blinding Grace.

Her chest caved in, and she rounded her shoulders at the reprimand. Backing away, she braced herself for another tirade of insults. Unlike Mrs. Marshall, this woman didn't sound like she was going to go the passive-aggressive route.

"I'm... I'm sorry."

"Oh. You should be. I'm going to give my husband your phone number when he gets the credit card bill."

Confused, Grace straightened. "I... I..."

"Here." The woman tossed the clothes in Grace's arms. "Go ring them up. I have no need for those dresses. I don't have anywhere to wear them. I'll have to ask my husband to take me out, which he hates to do, just so I can show them off."

"Oh." Realization set in, and Grace bit back a smile.

"And then he'll get annoyed with me because I'll ask him if he thinks I should wear the navy or the plum."

Grace brought the clothes behind the counter with her and hung them on the rack so she could drape a garment bag over them.

"I'm sorry I didn't get to see you in them. Arianna's designs are fabulous, don't you think? The cut of her dresses is flattering on almost every body type."

"Which is why I had to buy two of almost the exact same dress."

The plum had capped sleeves while the navy had lacey long sleeves; other than that, the style and hemline were identical. The sixty-something-year-old woman could pull off just about anything in the store, her figure curvy and in shape.

"Our anniversary is in two weeks. It often gets overlooked with the holidays. I'll tell Preston this is his gift to me. The dresses and dinner."

Grace scanned the tags and picked up the blouse and scarf. "Did you want these as well or should I put them back on the rack for you?"

"Don't you dare. I've been searching for a scarf with those colors. My girlfriends are going to be so jealous. The emerald green is simply stunning, don't you think? And the traces of red woven through are just enough to make it festive without looking like a Christmas wreath. Brilliant design. Who is it, did you say?"

"Arianna. She's a Scottish designer."

"Those Scots know their green."

Grace totaled the order and read the amount.

"It's actually not that bad. I'd planned on going to Boston for a dress. You saved me money on gas and a hotel." She handed Grace her platinum credit card.

"I'm here to serve."

The woman, Delores Powell, signed her name on the receipt and tucked her credit card in her bag. "Do you have a business card? I don't want my friends shopping here and stealing my clothes, but my daughter's allowed."

Grace laughed and handed her a few cards. "You can tell your friends to shop online. I don't have all the clothes in the store. Most are actually online."

"Well then. I'll tell them to come here and keep your online store my secret."

"I appreciate whatever word of mouth you can give me. Let me help you carry these to your car."

"Nonsense. I'm not that old." The bell chimed above the door, and both she and Delores looked up. "Well now. Looks like you have company. He's obviously not here to shop unless it's for a girlfriend. But, by the way he's looking at you..." Delores purred as she walked off with her purchases.

Brady held the door for her and laughed at whatever she said to him.

"Sounds like one happy customer."

"I have a feeling I'll be seeing her again."

"I'm proud of you."

Grace squinted in confusion. *Proud?* Why? He wasn't her father, wasn't any relation, they weren't in a relationship; he didn't know any of the trials and hell she went through to get here. How could he be proud?

Or was that one of those things he said to anyone? Like when you praise a toddler for their beautiful picture when you haven't a clue what it's supposed to be. She wasn't a toddler. She didn't need meaningless praise to make her or him feel better.

That was what this was all about. Ass kissing to make up for his mother's rudeness. And now that she thought back, he did the same after Alexis insulted her in front of him.

"Yeah, well. I'm really busy right now." He looked around the empty store. "With online stuff. Like you don't have plants and stuff to worry about in the winter but you do other stuff. I may not have customers, but I have stuff to do." She hoped she made sense and didn't sound like the blundering idiot she was.

No, that *he* was.

"Grace."

Oh, how she hated how he said her name, all sweet and gentle, and with a layer of sexiness to it. She didn't need to hear her name purr off his tongue.

"Busy." She opened her laptop and blinked her eyes into focus, bringing up her website.

"Hey." He closed the laptop, pinching her fingers inside.

"Hey yourself." She snatched her fingers away before he could do damage to her manicure.

"You're mad."

"I'm busy."

Brady leaned his elbows on the counter, bringing his hands together and resting his chin on top of them. "Talk to me."

"Like I said. Busy."

"I'm sorry about my mom. She's not... she's not herself lately."

"This has nothing to do with your mom."

"Then what?"

"Busy."

"Grace."

The man was relentless with those smoldering eyes he so innocently used to stir up emotions in her head. Needing some space, she leaned against the wall behind her, bracing one foot on the baseboard.

"We're not a good match, you and me."

"Says who?"

Everyone. Your mom. My sister. The world. "Me."

Brady stood to his full height and whipped his head back as if she'd slapped him. "I'm not good enough."

"What? No."

"At first I thought my job, my simple lifestyle was beneath you, and then you proved yourself to be more than *that* kind of girl." He zipped up his coat and shook his head in defeat, in disgust, in shame. She wasn't sure which. Maybe all. "I guess I was wrong about you."

"No. It's not you. It's me."

Brady snorted and headed for the door. "Original."

She couldn't let him walk away thinking he was the problem. "Brady. Wait." He didn't turn around. Grace pushed off the wall and ran after him, gripping on to his coat sleeve. "Please. Don't go like this. It's not what you're thinking."

"Then what is it?" he asked, facing the door, staring blankly through the glass instead of looking at her.

"I don't have a problem with *you*. The problem is *me*."

"So you said."

"I'm not one to gush about my feelings to a guy. Especially a guy who..."

"Who you're not interested in."

"No." She tugged him harder, forcing him to turn a smidge toward her. "A man I'm too interested in."

His eyes, filled with questions, met hers.

Grace wasn't ready for this. To open up. To reveal her thoughts, her secrets, her passions. If he knew too much he'd see her ugly skeletons. But if she didn't tell Brady enough he'd think he was the problem.

"I'm afraid once you get to know me better you won't like me anymore."

"Why would you think that?"

"Your mom has a beef with me already. I won't ever be able to measure up to her high standards. I have a past I'm not proud of."

"Are you still living in the past or trying to make a future?"

Sensing he wasn't going to leave, Grace let go of his sleeve. "I'm trying to make a future. A good one. I believe I've changed, but there are people who won't ever believe in me." People close to him. Those in the fashion industry with connections to Robert and Brielle Powers.

"One thing I've learned over the years is you can't live your life for everyone else. You have to live it for yourself."

"You're one of the lucky ones. You knew what you wanted to do with your life before you even graduated from high school. You're kind and caring. Manners ingrained from birth. I'm... an embarrassment to you. To your family."

"If this is because of what my mother—"

"Yes and no." She held up her hands in question. "I don't understand why you even want to be with me. We're cut from two different swaths." Grace stepped back needing her space. As long as he didn't walk away thinking he was the problem, she could live with the decision to let the nicest man who ever entered her life slip through her fingers.

"See. Now I think you're fishing for compliments." That Marshall grin was back, stirring up all kinds of trouble in places that hadn't been touched in ages. A-ges.

"That's not what I meant."

"I think," he said, taking a step closer to her, "that you're scared."

Hell yeah, she was scared. Scared he'd find out about her past. Scared he'd break her heart into a million pieces. "You have a lot on your plate right now."

"As do you."

"Not like you do." She stepped back and bumped into the counter. "How's your mother doing?" Bringing her up always seemed to darken the mood.

Brady licked his lips, the predator in his eyes still zeroing in on her. "She feels bad for being so snippy and would like to invite you to Thanksgiving on Thursday."

"I highly doubt she wants me there at her table. I can bring a few dishes over for you though. Help with the turkey in the morning." She made a mental note to buy a practice turkey tonight after work and scour the Internet for recipes and tips.

"You're not going to slave all day catering to us and not enjoy the food yourself."

"Brady." She sighed. Needing space—and an object between them—she moved behind the counter. "My intentions were never to eat any of the meals I prepared. They were a gift to you and your family. A way for our family to help yours. That's all."

"That's all? Really?" He resumed his earlier position, elbows propped on the counter, chin resting on his hands.

Looking away, she nodded. "I've been doing my mom a favor. It was her idea. Her suggestion."

"Did she suggest we kiss after each meal as well?"

Grace gasped and jerked her glare at him. "You..."

"What? Curious minds want to know. Was this your mother's way of setting us up?"

"Of course not! She had no idea anything would come of me bringing you guys food."

"So it's fate."

"I wouldn't call it that." Fate was too strong a word. Fate had never been in her favor.

"What would you call it then?"

"Boredom?"

"I'm not bored. You?" He shifted so his palm cupped his chin.

"You're a difficult man to talk to, Brady Marshall."

"I'm actually as straightforward as they come. I don't say things I don't mean. I don't do things I don't agree with. And I don't waste my time on lost causes."

Like a panther scoping out his prey, Brady slowly prowled around the counter, trapping Grace between him and the wall.

"What are you doing?" she squeaked.

"Do I bore you, Grace?" She shook her head. "Do you want me to back off? To leave you alone?"

She licked her lips, and her heartbeat quickened when his gaze dropped to her mouth.

"I don't..."

"I'll walk away. Just say the word. If you don't want to pursue us, to see where things can lead, tell me now," he said, his voice soft and raspy and not at all forceful.

Yet the force from his eyes, the heat from his body, all but made her forgotten parts explode.

"Grace. You're a saint!" Lily said excitedly as the door chimed and a cold rush of air blew into the shop. "Oh. Brady. Grace. Hi. I, uh, I'll come back."

"I was just leaving," Brady said, moving away from her. "Thanksgiving. Yes or no?"

Grace's breath quickened. "I..." she glanced over at Lily, who had an enormous grin on her face. "I..." and back to Brady with an impatient and worried tick in his brow. "Okay."

The worry turned to victory. He leaned in and gave her a peck on the lips.

"Oh."

"I'll be at the hospital all day tomorrow with Mom. They're running more tests. I'll call you tomorrow night to figure out dinner details." He gave her a chaste kiss again and spun on his heels. "Nice to see you again, Lily."

"You too, Brady."

Grace and Lily watched as he walked out the door and took a right toward the parking lot.

"What. Just. Happened?" Lily squealed and rushed behind the counter. "You and Brady? I had no idea. You two are adorable!" She jumped up and down while hugging Grace.

"Easy." She placed her hands on Lily's shoulders, stopping her from bouncing anymore. "It's not a big deal."

"Not a big deal?" Lily clutched at her chest. "That man's got it bad. Holy hotness. I've never seen his eyes go so dark. You sly thing you." She swatted the air between them. "And here I was feeling bad you'd be all alone on Thanksgiving. Ty told me Alexis and Ben are going away tomorrow. I came over to invite you to Ty's parents."

"I don't know what I'm doing for Thanksgiving." Grace ran a hand down her hair, smoothing it from Lily's excitement. And Brady's kisses.

"Brady just said—"

"He invited me over. To make dinner for them."

"I'm sure he wants you over for more than just dinner." Lily giggled. "Dessert too."

"Oh, shut up." Grace couldn't help but laugh as well. "This thing with Brady... it's new, and I don't know where it's going."

"From what Ty's said, Brady's never had a long-term girl-friend."

"Which is why I don't think we're good for each other."

"You think he isn't relationship material? I think he hasn't found the right one yet."

"No. The exact opposite. I think he *is* relationship mate-rial. I, however, am not."

"So take things slow. See what happens. Brady wouldn't be kissing you in public if he didn't like you. A lot. From what I've seen, he's a lot like Ty. Private. Keeps to himself. Loyal. Good boyfriend material."

"I'm not doubting that."

"You're doubting yourself."

"I'm doubting the concept of us. I'm in it for a quick fling."

"Does he know that?"

"I'm not really good at that kind of stuff. Communicating."

"I think you want more than a fling."

"What makes you think that?"

"The way you turned all mushy when he kissed you," Lily teased, wiggling her hips with jest.

"You're all caught up in lovey-dovey la-la land and are seeing life through rose-colored glasses. It was a kiss. Sure, I wouldn't mind sleeping with the man. If he wants more than that, I'm out."

Now why couldn't she lay it all on the line like that with Brady? Instead, she let his sweet lips and intense eyes talk her into something more. When he called tonight to discuss dinner, she'd tell him how she really felt.

Sex only. No relationship. Take it or leave it.

CHAPTER EIGHTEEN

GRACE DISCONNECTED her phone and tossed it on the kitchen counter. So much for telling Brady she only wanted him for sex. When he called Tuesday night, he filled her with accolades and told her stories about fighting off the mother hens in his chicken coop; she couldn't tell him she only wanted him for sex.

Hell. She loved talking to him on the phone. Loved sitting across from him at dinner. Loved being on the receiving end of his kisses.

They planned Thursday's dinner with a list of recipes and another list of ingredients. Still new to the cooking game, she didn't feel comfortable preparing all the food at his house, under his mother's watchful eye.

He wasn't thrilled with the idea, but she only agreed to come if she could make the mashed potatoes at home. He and his mother would start the turkey and stuffing in the morning, and she'd come over with the potatoes.

They'd make the green beans and carrots at his house and would defrost one of his mother's pumpkin pies for dessert.

That didn't sound too bad. At least she got out of hanging around his house all day while the turkey cooked. The less time she had with Mrs. Marshall, the better. Carter would be a nice distraction, taking some of the attention off her.

And after they ate, she'd tell Brady she wasn't interested in a relationship. Not now. Not when she planned on moving away in less than a year.

Only he'd screwed up her plans once again by calling this morning to say he was picking her up. It seemed kind of silly since she only lived ten minutes away. He insisted and hung up on her, leaving her without any options.

Well, she could refuse to answer the door. Glancing at the clock, she noted she had just over an hour until he'd be at her doorstep. The potatoes were boiling and the sweet potatoes were roasting in the oven. They hadn't talked about sweet potato pie, but it was one of her favorite dishes her mother made.

She'd called her last night and asked for step-by-step instructions, which sounded pretty simple.

Tossing a kitchen towel on the counter, she scurried to her bathroom for a quick shower. Shampoo, conditioner, and a few swipes with her razor up and down her legs—just in case, not that she would be dropping her pants for Brady—and she was out of the shower in no time.

Today wasn't a day to put on all the war paint, even though she'd be facing the brutal Mrs. Marshall. Going with a light foundation, simple brown tone eye shadow, and her shorter false eyelashes, Grace looked done up but not overdone.

Since she'd be cooking at the stove and bending over the oven to baste the turkey, unless Mrs. Marshall had the energy to do so, Grace dried her hair and stuck it up in a twist. At least her hair was fairly simple to do. Thin and straight, it was boring, but never too much of a problem.

Knowing the Marshalls were informal people, she didn't want to overdress for the meal, yet wanted to look nice.

Rummaging through her closet, she settled on a pair of chocolate brown pants and a simple beige sweater.

One of Arianna's scarves would go perfectly. Finding the burnt orange and red swirl infinity scarf, Grace looped it around her neck and finished off the look with brown dangly earrings.

"Not bad," she said to herself in the mirror. Remembering the stove, she hustled to the kitchen and stuck a fork in the potatoes.

You couldn't overcook mashed potatoes, could you? Plopping the strainer in the sink, she dumped the potatoes and even went the extra step of measuring the butter, milk, and salt. Her mother never measured unless baking. Grace wasn't there yet and didn't want to take a chance at ruining Thanksgiving.

The oven timer beeped as she finished whipping the potatoes, and with her new multi-tasking skills, she shut it off, opened the door so she wouldn't forget, and scooped the pile of white clouds into a pretty bowl she borrowed from her mother's hutch.

She covered it with foil and then worked on the sweet potatoes. Again, she measured, even though her mother gave her guesstimates on how much brown sugar, orange juice, and marshmallows to use.

Sampling the mixture, Grace licked her spoon with a grin. "That's awesome." Mom was right. It was easy. She scraped the orange mixture into a pie pan, dotted it with more mini marshmallows and chopped pecans, and covered it with foil.

The thud of boots coming up her stairs told her there was no time to wash the dishes. They weren't going anywhere anyway. She opened the door the same time Brady held up his hand to knock.

"Anxious to see me?" He leaned in for a kiss, not waiting for a reply.

Anxious, yes, but not only at seeing him. "Good timing. The potatoes are ready. I may need a hand carrying them."

"That's what I'm here for." He followed her into the kitchen and picked up one dish in each hand and quickly set them back down again. "The bottoms are still hot."

"I literally just finished making them. Let me look for a box or something to carry them in."

"I've got it. Just need to carry it differently." He picked the mashed potatoes bowl up by the sides and eyed the covered pie pan.

"I can carry this one."

"You sure?"

"I had planned on it anyway. Before you said you were going to pick me up, which I still think is silly."

"I'm bringing my girl to Thanksgiving, and she's helping my mother prepare the feast. The least I could do is pick her up." With both their hands full, he could only lean over for a quick kiss.

Grace ignored the girlfriend comment. She'd be crushing him tonight when she said she preferred a different title. Girl on the side, maybe. Friends with benefits. Booty call.

Something less personal. Something more associated with her rep.

He followed her down the steps to his truck, where she waited for him to open the door for her. Even Robert with his Mercedes and his eight-figure salary didn't open doors for her. He did for his wife when the paparazzi were around. Never for his mistress though.

"Mom had a pretty good night and was up at eight to put the turkey in."

"She's got to be exhausted already."

"Maybe. She won't admit it though. Her internal clock has always gotten her up at five, so eight is sleeping in. She's been on and off her feet for the past three hours. I'm hoping she's sitting down now with me gone. I think she's trying to put on a strong front for Carter and me. Thanksgiving has always been a big deal, even with just the three of us."

Grace wanted to ask about his grandparents, but his cell phone rang.

"It's Carter," he apologized and answered the call. "Everything okay?"

She heard Carter's voice on the other line, but couldn't make out any of the words he said. Brady chuckled, agreed to whatever his brother said, and then hung up.

"Everything okay?"

"Yeah. Mom's taking a nap in Dad's recliner. Carter says to drive around for a bit to give her time to rest. Knowing Mom, she'll jump out of that chair the second she hears my truck pull in. Well, jumping may be a challenge these days, but she'll be up."

"Brady, is it because I'm going to be there? I don't want to make your mom uncomfortable."

"You're not. You won't." He rubbed his hand up and down her thigh, giving her a gentle squeeze. "My mom wants me to be happy, she's said it a dozen times. More like hundreds, really. And you make me happy."

Weren't guys supposed to be all clammed up about their feelings? Brady defied the stereotype of the tall, dark, handsome rugged male, apparently secure with himself enough to pour his heart and soul out on Grace, who didn't deserve as much as a friendly hug from him.

He circled around town taking the scenic route along the ocean. She changed the subject, and they talked about the water, seafood, fishing, and nearby lighthouses. Thirty minutes later he pulled into his driveway.

It had never been this comfortable before, talking with a man without it being sexual, especially a man who'd kissed her before. Never before had she kissed a man—on multiple occasions—and not been in his bed already.

This was nice. For the first time in her life, Grace felt special, worth something. She actually felt like *someone* and not just a some*thing*.

"You ready?"

"Do I have a choice?"

"You're adorable when you're nervous." Brady leaned across the potatoes and kissed her soundly. It wasn't a passionate kiss, but one of familiarity and kindness. It was meant to comfort and soothe. And hell, it did.

When they got inside, Dorothy was hunched over the oven basting the turkey.

"Smells amazing, Mom."

"It's the herbs. This year's sage and rosemary crop were more than I could keep up with. I even sold bundles in the stand last month."

"I'm learning to cook with fresh herbs. They make quite a difference compared to the dried ones you buy at the grocery store." Grace rolled her shoulders back for Brady, letting him take her coat for her.

Mrs. Marshall acted like Grace wasn't even in there, closing the oven and setting the baster on the counter. "The turkey will be ready to take out in thirty minutes. It will need to rest before carving. I'm going to shower."

"She looks better," Grace said, putting the sweet potatoes on top of the stove.

"She's doing better."

Wanting to change the subject, she looked around for Hemmy. "I thought you were dog sitting."

"Sophie threw a fit when they tried to drop off Hemmy yesterday, so they ended up bringing him with them." Something dropped in the bathroom, and they both looked down the hall. He kissed the top of her head. "I'm going to see if she needs help with anything else."

"Okay. I'll start on the vegetables."

An hour later the four of them sat around the kitchen table. Mrs. Marshall at the head, Carter on one side, and Brady and Grace on the other.

"The turkey is delicious, Mrs. Marshall." When she didn't get a response, Grace sliced into the tender white meat and dragged it through the gravy. Thankfully Brady's mom felt well enough to make the gravy; Grace didn't think she could manage it under so much pressure.

Carter monopolized the conversation at dinner, keeping the focus on him, his new business, and asked the occasional question of Brady about spring planting.

"Your sweet potato pie tastes amazing, Grace. Are these marshmallows?" Carter asked.

"Yes. My mom makes it every year. It was always one of Alexis and my favorite holiday dishes."

"Your mother is a good cook," Mrs. Marshall said, taking a bite of sweet potatoes. It was the closest she came to giving Grace a compliment.

Brady slid his hand under the table and squeezed Grace's thigh. "Grace is following in her mother's footsteps."

When no reply came from his mother, Carter pointed his fork at her. "Much better than those brownies."

"My brownies? What was wrong with them?" She'd laid out all the ingredients ahead of time, including the measuring cups. She turned to Brady for clarification.

His jaw clenched, his eyes big and round, darting daggers across the table at his brother.

"Sorry. Thought she knew about that."

"Tell me," she ordered Carter, knowing Brady would stay mum.

"You might have added too much salt."

She looked up at Brady, who still avoided her gaze. "Were they terrible?"

"It's my fault," he conceded, squeezing her thigh again and making eye contact. "I watched you make them and should have asked if you meant to fill a measuring cup with salt instead of a spoon."

"Oh, no." She covered her face with her hands. "Why didn't stop me?"

"Aw, you two. So cute, distracting each other into doing silly things," Carter teased.

"I'm going to go lie down." Mrs. Marshall twisted her body to the side and used the table to help prop her up.

Both men jumped to their feet to help their mother, who swatted them away. "I'm not an invalid. Finish your dinner."

They waited until she disappeared down the hall before sitting down again. For some reason, Mrs. Marshall didn't like her. Whether Brady was in denial or too attached to his mother to pick up on her insults, Grace wasn't sure.

It was another sign they weren't meant to be together. She'd end things with him when he brought her home, no matter how much he sweet talked her into continuing on with whatever was happening between them.

When the three of them finished eating, Brady stood and picked up her plate. "Thanksgiving leftovers for the next few days. My favorite."

Which also meant she wouldn't feel obligated to bring over meals. With his mom having a little more energy and being able to be up longer, Grace wasn't needed anymore. Which was good.

She did the dishes while Carter picked at the turkey and Brady put the food in containers.

When everything was clean, she draped a kitchen towel over the lower cabinet door under the sink and touched Brady's arm.

"Having company exhausted your mom. I should go home now."

"You won't stay for dessert?"

"I'm too stuffed right now."

Brady wrapped her in his arms, his hands resting on her lower back. "Which is why you should stay a little longer. We'll have dessert, and then I'll bring you home."

"Seriously, you two," Carter said, coming into the kitchen from bringing the trash out. "Get a room."

Grace moved out from Brady's arms. "Thank you for having me over, Carter. And for picking the turkey. That used to be my job. I hated it."

"I think I ate more than I saved." He patted his belly. "Thanks for brightening up our table." He yanked her in for a rough hug.

Brighten the table, she did not. Her presence was a cloud of disapproving gloom over the meal.

"I'll keep an ear out for Mom. Don't rush home, big brother." Carter slapped him on the back. "I'll see you in the morning." He wiggled his eyebrows and clicked his tongue before spinning on his heels and chuckling his way down the hall.

"I'll get your coat." It was less than ten feet away from them, but Grace let Brady do the gentlemanly thing by helping her into it.

He took her hand in his as soon as he fastened his seatbelt. They didn't say much on the way back to her place. She mentally prepared herself for the sort of break up. It wasn't that they were in a committed relationship. A few kisses. Not even groping.

What they had was a junior high thing. Only the kisses were more passionate and the feelings deeper. Not that she'd expressed any.

She wouldn't let him distract her with kisses this time.

He parked the truck, and she waited for him to open her door. He helped her down and kept his hands on her waist longer than necessary. Avoiding his gaze and his mouth, she slipped away and started up the steps.

"I, um... thank you for inviting me to dinner." She kept her back to him as she unlocked the door.

"You're welcome. Thank you for all you did for us." He pushed her hair to the side and nuzzled her neck. With her big scarf in the way, he didn't have much access but made enough contact with her skin to cause shivers all the way down to her toes.

Once again she slipped away from him and pushed her way into the apartment.

"Do you mind if I stay for a bit?" Brady set her dishes on the kitchen table and unzipped his coat.

"Actually." She kept her coat buttoned up and shoved her hands deep in her pockets. "We need to talk."

"Is this going to be the same conversation we had in your shop two days ago?"

"You distracted me."

"Fair play. You distract me." Brady licked his lips and mimicked her stance, tucking his hands into his pockets.

"I'm serious."

"Me too." He rocked back on his heels like this was a game to him.

"Like I said before, we're not right for each other. I'm not..."

"You *are*."

"Your mother hates me."

"She doesn't hate you." He stopped rocking, and his playful eyes turned soft. "She's going through a lot."

"She knows how wrong I am for you, Brady."

"My mother doesn't determine who I date."

"There are things about me you don't know."

Brady paused and then removed his coat, draping it on the back of a chair. He moved in closer, and Grace stood her ground.

"Are you married?"

"What? Of course not." What a ridiculous thing for him to ask.

"Are you seeing someone else?"

Grace snorted. "Not even close."

"Because those would be definite no's for me. I'm glad to hear you're single and available."

"I'm single, but emotionally, I'm not available." And she knew he wanted her more than physically. Not being able to connect on a deeper level would turn him off. It had to turn him off.

"Slap me if this question is rude and out of line, but have you slept with anyone in the past... month?"

Since they first kissed. "Try over a year."

That elicited a giant grin from Brady. Too much information.

"You've already told me the problem isn't me, it's you." He worked to free the buttons of her jacket one by one. "And personally, I don't see any problems with you." He freed the last button and slid her coat off her shoulders. "Not a single one."

"Brady," she whispered. She wanted him in the worst way and feared he could read the desire in her eyes.

"I've never wanted to be with a woman more than I want to be with you, Grace," his words whispered across her cheek.

"Your mother..."

"Does not choose who I'm with."

They were both single. Both two consenting adults. She'd been honest with him about not being right for him. About not wanting a relationship. She'd said that, hadn't she?

And yet here he was, kissing her skin with words, perfect words. No man had ever been so kind, so caring, so thoughtful.

She couldn't say no. Couldn't turn him away. She wanted to be loved and cherished by Brady Marshall.

All. Night. Long.

CHAPTER NINETEEN

GRACE'S SCARF COVERED most of her neck, so Brady nuzzled it away with his nose, finding the soft spot under her ear.

"You smell amazing. I'd like to stay. With you. Tonight," he said between kisses.

"It's the turkey you smell. The stuffing too. Your mom makes good stuffing."

He didn't want to bring his mother into this conversation. Grace had used her as an excuse for them not to be together. Sensing her reluctance even now with his lips on her neck, he gently bit on her earlobe and pulled away.

"If you want me to leave, I will." He eyed his coat, hoping Grace wouldn't call his bluff. No, it wasn't a bluff. He wouldn't force himself on her.

She had it stuck in her head she wasn't good enough for him. Funny, since he'd thought the same thing about her when he crossed her path a few months ago. He wasn't ashamed of being a farmer. Marshall Farms was an icon around these parts. Being the great-grandson of Peter Marshall who started a farm in the middle of nowhere and helped cultivate not only the land but the town as well, was something to be proud of.

Brady picked up his coat and draped it over his arm. Grace worried her bottom lip between her teeth. Oh, how he envied her teeth right now.

"I don't..."

He paused, his eyes meeting hers. "You don't... want me to stay?" Brady had made his intentions known. It was up to Grace to decide how far they'd go.

"No." Grace twisted her hands together in front of her.

"Still unclear here." If she was that nervous, he'd cut her some slack. Maybe she was afraid to say no to him. Not one to ever force himself on a woman, he gave her another out. "Let's call it a night, okay? We can talk about... this some other time."

He kissed her softly on the lips and stepped back to put on his coat. Grace didn't budge, so he walked across her small apartment to the back door. He'd placed a hand on the knob when Grace called out behind him.

"Don't go."

He stilled and took a deep breath before he turned and leaned against it.

"Don't go," she said again.

"If I stay, we don't have to... do anything." The last thing he wanted was for Grace to think he only cared about sex. Hanging out with her for a few hours would be fine by him.

"I want to do something."

"Yeah?" He crooked his head.

"I want..." Grace crossed the room with new confidence. "I want you to stay the night. With me."

"There's no other woman I'd rather stay the night with." Still, he waited for her to come closer, to make sure she was ready. "Are you sure?"

"There's no doubt in my mind how much I want you."

"Could have fooled me." He toyed with the scarf around her neck.

"Oh, I've wanted you naked for a long time."

Brady choked and banged his chest to allow air to pass through. Tears filled his eyes, and he swiped them away. "Honey," he said when he could speak again. "All you had to do was ask."

"Are you sure you want *me*?"

His heart did that little flippity thing it did the first time he'd kissed her. Despite her persona of being in control and independent and confident in her ways, Grace Le Blanc was the most insecure woman he'd ever met.

"What I mean is, I freak a little when I'm around you."

"That's not good."

"You're this... perfect guy."

"I'm far from perfect."

Grace ran her hand along the zipper of his coat.

"You're kind and understanding. You have this incredible sense of family loyalty. You're a true gentleman."

"Sweetheart, everything I'm thinking about right now is as far from gentlemanly as can be."

"I doubt that."

Her innocent flirting, incongruous to her sexy style, stirred his insides into a tumultuous sea of lust.

"So much so"—reaching for her scarf, he tugged until her body crashed into his—"I'm almost afraid of how much I want you right now."

"Oh." She gasped, her sweet, beautiful mouth turning up to him. "Show me."

He came undone. Lifting her in his arms, he carried her to her bedroom, kicking the door open with the toe of his boot. The caveman show wasn't his gig, but Grace brought out the reckless side of him. A side he didn't know was buried within.

Setting her down on her feet next to the bed, he took a moment to study her. Her cheeks, red with embarrassment or excitement, her lips, begging to be kissed. He would. In time. First, he needed to look.

Still covered head to toe, even in her fancy boots, Brady pictured what she looked like underneath the layers. The clothes were fine but covered up her beauty. A beauty she tried to keep hidden.

There were secrets buried deep he wanted to unlock. Hurt buried even deeper he wanted to soothe. Tonight, though, was about getting under the first layer. Her clothing.

In time he'd work on the other layers. The layers that kept them from connecting at a level he wanted to be with her.

Slowly, he slipped her scarf from around her neck and laid it on her dresser. She stood there, an innocent angel, waiting for him. He removed his jacket, tossing it on the floor.

He slipped his hands under her sweater and moaned at the meeting of her skin against his hands. So smooth. So soft. He moved his hands across her ribs and around to her back, finding the clasp of her bra.

"Can I take this off?" he asked, whispering in her ear. She nodded, and with one flick, the clasp was undone.

Grace's hands settled on his hips, rubbing up and down his sides until she had his shirt bunched up and her hands on his chest.

The urge to strip them both down in seconds and toss her on the bed came in full force. Later. Maybe next time. Their first time would be slow and passionate. He'd show her how much she meant to him and leave no inch of her body unloved.

Sliding his fingers under her bra strap, he had them down her arms until they were trapped in her sweater.

"This needs to come off too." He sipped at her earlobe and left a trail of kisses along her jawline, avoiding her lips, even when they shifted toward him, begging for his touch.

He skimmed his fingers along her stomach and moved them along her sides, grazing against the edge of her breasts. Her hands left his chest as he lifted her arms above her head to remove her sweater and bra.

The garments joined her scarf on the dresser, and he took a moment to take in the view.

"Beautiful," he said, his eyes trained on hers. "Grace. You're perfect."

She blinked and let a smile escape her gorgeous mouth. "You're still dressed."

"You've got a way to go as well."

In her heels, they were closer in height, and Grace moved in until their thighs brushed each other. She lifted her hands between them and worked the buttons on his shirt. When it was free, she pushed it to his sides and lifted his undershirt by the hem.

It was a struggle, literally, to keep their bodies in contact and to finish removing the shirt. Normally he would have taken off the button-down and then slipped the undershirt

over his head. Grace, obviously not thinking it through, tried
to yank both over his head.

He managed to free his arms from the dress shirt and
tossed the wadded-up ball on to the floor.

"That didn't go as smoothly as your move." She laughed.

"I like your determination. We'll keep practicing."

"Not now, I hope. I rather like your torso naked like
this." Grace scratched her nails on his chest and weaved them
through his chest hair. "You're very Supermanesque."

"Supermanesque?"

"Mm," Grace moaned, kissing his left nipple.

He wanted to continue touching her and not carry on
with the conversation, but he liked the sparkle in her eyes.
"What exactly does that mean?"

"Very Henry Cavill."

"You're comparing me to another guy?" This was not
good. Sure, he'd sort of asked about sexual partners earlier,
but not while they were naked.

"You do know who he is, don't you?"

"No. Should I? I don't watch a lot of TV." Or get out
much, he could add.

Grace grinned and looped her hands behind his neck,
rubbing her naked chest against his.

"Henry Cavill plays Superman. Farmboy. Sweet. Almost
nerdy. Until he takes off his shirt. A truly heavenly swoon
moment for every female in America. Heck, the world. You
resemble him."

"The nerdy part?"

"No, the chest." She kissed the spot right over his heart,
and he nearly went weak in the knees.

"Does this mean you're going to be thinking about some movie star while I make love to you?"

"Who?" she asked coyly. "And are we going to make love or are we going to stand around all day talking about it."

This was more like it. The confident, funny, sassy Grace. Picking her up in one swoop, he cradled her for a moment while he kissed her roughly, then tossed her on the bed, enjoying the brief show as she bounced.

"Take those pants off before you climb into bed, cowboy."

"It's farmboy." He shucked his boots, jeans, and underwear and climbed on top of her. "And your pants need to go as well."

Brady hovered over her, his hands on either side of her head, and lowered his mouth to hers, tasting her sweetness. Her hands touched him all over. His chest. His shoulders. His stomach. When they headed further south, he pulled back, resting on his knees, straddling her.

"You're still overdressed for this party."

"I could use some help."

"At your service." He trailed a line of kisses from her lips and down her chest, not making contact with either breast, even when she tilted herself up into him. Continuing his trail, he stopped at the waistband of her pants.

With his eyes still focused on her face, reading for signs of nerves or playfulness, he undid the button, then the zipper, and slid her pants down her legs.

They snagged at the top of her fancy boots. Inching his naked body down her legs, he rested at the foot of the bed and unzipped each boot, chucking them behind him.

"That's very sexy, you know."

"Taking off your shoes?"

"Yes. You naked, at my feet."

"Grace," he growled, making quick work of her socks and pants. He pounced up toward the head of the bed, capturing her lips in his again.

They kissed with passion, with heat, their naked bodies rubbing into each other until he could hold back no further. He needed to be closer.

"Condom. I have one in my wallet."

"Such a boy scout."

"It was wishful thinking."

He stumbled out of bed and found his wallet in the back pocket of his jeans. Tossing it on the bed next to Grace, he climbed back on and pleasured her until she lay spread eagle like a limp noodle under him.

"I'm done in," Grace panted.

Brady sat back on his knees and looked from the naked woman under him to the condom wrapper in between his teeth. He hadn't opened it yet. If she was too tired to finish...

She swiped the condom from his teeth and opened it for him. "I'm not that done in. Saddle up, farm boy, we've got a long night ahead of us." With a force he hadn't seen in her before, she pushed him on his back and showed him just how much energy she had.

• • • •

"I WON'T NEED TO GO to the gym if we keep this up." Grace snuggled into Brady's side, laying blissfully in the aftermath of an evening and morning of the most amazing, tender, meaningful sex in her life.

"Always happy to oblige." Brady kissed the top of her head and tucked her in closer.

She draped her arm across his chest and played with his chest hair. He really did resemble Henry Cavill. She didn't know why she hadn't picked up on it before.

Maybe because she'd never seen Brady naked before. Now that she had, she could barely remember what Henry looked like. Sort of.

"I hate to say this—"

"You have to go. I know."

"I have a meeting with Ty at the house in an hour."

"I almost forgot about that." Grace propped herself up on one elbow and stared down at Brady. His hair was disheveled, and he had a sexy amount of stubble on his chin. Stubble that had scratched her in all sorts of sensitive places.

Grace clenched her legs and wiggled.

"You keep doing that and I'll have to reschedule."

Grinning with satisfaction, Grace kissed him on his cheek and pinched his sides. "I'll make you breakfast." She rolled to her right and grabbed a long shirt from her dresser drawer.

"You don't have to do that. I can scrounge up something at home."

"You have fifty minutes before you have to leave. How I look at it, we can do one of two things."

"Oh yeah?" Brady hopped out of bed and cornered her with his naked body. "What are those two... things?"

"One"—she placed a finger over his lips—"is breakfast. I've come pretty close to mastering French Toast."

"And the second?" he asked around her finger, sticking his tongue out to lick it.

"We can go out to breakfast. The Sunrise Diner has pretty quick service." She squeezed his lips together when she knew he'd protest and tried to rush away, giggling as he trapped her with his arm around her waist.

Playful banter after sex. Not what her mornings after usually consisted of. She liked this too much. She liked Brady. Too much.

"That's not what I was thinking as a second choice."

"Oh yeah?" she giggled some more, hunched over, her butt poking into his groin. "What were you thinking?"

"I was thinking we could do this."

Brady whipped her around, trapping her lips with his, and showed her exactly what he meant.

CHAPTER TWENTY

GRACE FLOATED ON RAINBOWS and clouds every morning after being with Brady. It was when the unicorns and fairy dust wore off that she started with the self-doubt.

They couldn't have a forever relationship, not with her leaving by the end of next summer. Not that their relationship would last that long anyway. In the meantime, she did her best to appreciate what they had going and pushed back her reservations.

After one week, the magic dust was starting to really settle in, shrouding her doubts and reservations as to why this wasn't a good idea.

Brady had been extra busy with the renovations and caring for his mom. She'd been more independent lately, he'd said. Grace used the excuse of their own privacy to avoid going to his house.

Mrs. Marshall never seemed happy to see her, and instead of bringing up the sore subject again and again, Grace invited Brady to her apartment for dinner then sent him home with leftovers the next morning.

Carter didn't mind having night time duty now that their mother was sleeping better through the night, while Brady stayed home during the day, working on demolition with Ty.

It was best on so many levels for Grace to stay away.

Lost in her daydreams about last night's playful sex and the leftover whipped cream, she didn't register her cell phone ringing until it clicked over to voicemail. Looking down at the number, she saw it was Alexis.

They hadn't spoken to each other since before Thanksgiving. Two weeks wasn't an uncommon time to go without connecting. Usually, they only interacted on book club night.

She dialed back and waited for Alexis to pick up.

"I was in the middle of leaving you a message."

"Sorry. I didn't hear my phone ring." Which was totally true.

"Listen. I need a favor."

Shock would be too mild a word to use. Alexis never needed anything from Grace.

"Sure. What can I do to help?" If she needed manpower in the vineyard, she'd have to say no. Especially with the frigid temperatures and snow on its way.

"Mom usually takes care of Sophie when Ben and I are working."

Babysitting, she could do. She'd been wanting that responsibility for months, but like Mrs. Marshall, Alexis always gave her the cold shoulder snub.

"I'd love to watch her."

"She's not easy. She uses her cuteness to get away with whatever she wants and loves to wander off. This would require you to pay attention to her every second."

"I've watched her with Mom before."

"With Mom is the key. This time you'd be alone and won't be able to rely on her to—"

"I got it. I swear on my life I'll keep Sophie safe."

"Today is story hour day at the library."

"Today?" She'd only been open for an hour. Granted, foot traffic would probably be nonexistent today. She did have online orders to fill though.

"I didn't think it would be an issue. You can close your store whenever you want, can't you?"

Grace didn't like the condescending attitude coming from her sister. Yes, she could. She didn't need the snarky attitude though. Maybe it was motherhood, or being in a relationship, but Alexis wasn't the sweet, humble girl she'd been back in the day.

Granted, Grace wasn't the obnoxious self-centered bitch anymore either.

With a loud sigh, she closed up her laptop. "What time do you want me over?"

"Sophie, honey. No!" Alexis yelled through the other end of the phone. "I have to go. She's eating Hemmy's dog food again. I thought she outgrew that a year ago. Come now."

The phone went silent. Her sister hung up on her expecting Grace to be at her beck and call. If it wasn't about Sophie, she'd tell her sister to shove it.

No. She wouldn't. Too much shit to make up for.

She shoved her arms through her winter coat and tugged on a hat. Her heels clicked on the wood floor as she hustled to the front door. A quick change of clothes would be necessary if she'd be chasing around a toddler.

However, Alexis' tone sounded urgent at the end. Maybe Grace should pick up Sophie first and then come back to change on their way to the library.

Opting for the latter, she unlocked her car and headed toward her sister's house.

"Really?" Alexis shook her head and sneered at Grace a few minutes later. "You're going to watch an active toddler in heels and a tight skirt?"

Not even through the front door and already getting picked on.

"In case you didn't notice by the clock on the wall, we hung up eleven minutes ago. I thought you needed me AS-AP."

"You live fifteen feet from your store."

"Twenty-two steps up and twenty-two steps down. Plus time to change. I could have squeezed it in, but figured you needed me more than my feet needed flats."

"Auntie Gwace," Sophie squealed, running across the kitchen.

"Now that's the greeting I've been looking for." She swooped her niece up in her arms and twirled around. "You ready to have an Auntie and Sophie day today?"

Sophie nodded, her ponytail bouncing, and wiggled to be put down.

"You need to get dressed, sweetie. Aunt Grace will bring you to the library."

"I am dwessed." Little sassy pants stuck her fists on her hips with a huff.

Oh, she had some of her auntie in her for sure, even if they weren't blood-related. Grace didn't know how Sophie's birth mom could have given her up so easily, just hours after she was born.

"You're not going to the library in your princess dress."

Sophie, in all her princess glory, spun around, her Cinderella blue dress swinging out in a big poof. "Auntie Gwace has a dwess on."

"Hey, princess." Grace squatted in her heels, keeping her knees close so her pencil skirt wouldn't rip, or slide up her thighs revealing her pink thong. A thong she'd hoped Brady would get a glimpse of later. "We're going to stop at my apartment so I can change. I'm thinking leggings with a pretty top. Do you want to be twins with me? I bet you have a million leggings in your dresser drawers."

Sophie, deep in thought with the suggestion, stuck her tongue out to lick her lips. Staring straight in front of her at Hemmy's back, she let out a loud gasp as if the light bulb went off over her head. Spinning on her pink polished toes, she ran off down the hall and banged on the gate at the bottom of the stairs.

"I need up," she called.

"I've got this. You go... do what you need to do. Let me know when you want her home."

Her sister, seeming a bit stunned, nodded slowly. "Ooookaaay." She scratched her head. "Getting her out of that dress is a surefire way to bring on a toddler meltdown. I'm impressed."

"We're not out of the woods yet."

"She's asking to go upstairs and change. That's more progress than I've made in months."

Grace warmed at the first compliment her sister had given her. At least, the first one in a long, long time.

"Should I bring her back here for a nap or see if she'll sleep at my place?"

"Naps are her specialty. You can ask where she wants to crash. But make sure she gets there before she's out. If you wake her in the middle of a nap, she won't go back down. And then those terrible three's come out. They're wicked."

"Noted." Grace tipped her head when Sophie hollered again. "The princess calls." She spun, not as gracefully as her niece, on her three-inch heels and went to turn a princess into a comfy toddler.

An hour at the library, followed by a visit to the bookstore to see Ty's mom, Celeste, and buy a new book, followed by a mac and cheese lunch at the Happy Clam, and a pedicure for two at the Sea Salt Spa, left Grace and Sophie exhausted.

"Want to sleep at Auntie's apartment?"

"Mhm." Sophie's head nodded, but Grace wasn't sure her niece was coherent enough to understand the question.

Picking her up and placing her on her hip, Grace carried the now sleeping princess up the stairs to her apartment. Who needed cardio class when you had a toddler and two flights of stairs?

Carefully, she unzipped Sophie's coat, took off her hat, mittens, and boots, and rolled her over under the blankets. She slept in a toddler bed at home, but it wasn't as high up as Grace's bed. Not wanting to leave her alone, she shucked her shoes and slid under the covers to snuggle.

Her leg vibrated, then chimed. *Shit.* She forgot to take her phone out of her pocket and turn it on silent. Reading the screen, her heart did a little *pitter-patter*. She clicked on the *I can't talk right now* button and then scrolled over to her texts.

Grace: *I'm taking a nap with Sophie.*
Brady: *Sounds like you're still awake.*
Grace: *I forgot to turn my phone off. Princess is out cold.*
Brady: *Sorry to wake you. We can talk later. Dinner?*
Grace: *It might be the three of us.*
Brady: *As long as I can see you.*
And boom. There went her heart.
Grace: *It's a date. Come over when you can.*
Brady: *As you wish.*
She replied with a bunch of silly emojis.

Sleep was out of the question now. She figured she'd see Brady tonight, but having it in writing, that he still wanted to be with her, was reassuring. Her book sat on her nightstand, unread. Normally the other women fell behind in their reading. With no life, no job, and no boyfriend, she'd had plenty of time to read in the past.

Being the slacker of the group this month meant her life was turning around. Being too busy had never been a problem before for Grace. It made her feel... like an adult.

Thumbing to her bookmark—only on chapter four—she focused on the words in front of her and read while the princess slept.

CHAPTER TWENTY-ONE

WITH EACH DAY, HIS mother regained her strength, and then she'd have a chemo treatment and be set back again. Brady wanted to believe his mother's cantankerous mood was from her illness and not because she didn't like Grace.

There was no reason not to. Grace bent over backward to help his family out and asked for nothing in return. As far as he knew, his mother had no reason not to like her.

So the mood had to be from her illness.

"I'll be back in the morning."

"You've been spending most of your nights over *there*." His mother gathered her blanket together at her neck and settled into the couch in front of the woodstove. "Your brother's been getting up in the middle of the night to put wood on the fire. I'm sure he would like a good night's sleep."

Carter was not the issue here. Could it be his mother was jealous? Maybe it had nothing to do with Grace and everything to do with another woman in his life. Brady mentally smacked himself for being so inconsiderate.

He and Carter were all his mom had after their father passed away. Here she was, suffering through a terrible disease, and he was ditching her every night to get laid. No wonder she felt betrayed by him and Grace.

"Mom," he said gently, sitting on the coffee table across from her. "Are you okay?" He laid a hand on her knee and she avoided eye contact, staring at the blank television.

"Of course I'm not okay. I have cancer."

"You have one more chemo treatment. You did really well with the last one. I can see the color coming back in your face, and you've had more energy lately."

"I've had to pick up the slack with you being gone all the time."

"Mom." She'd never laid the guilty treatment on him. Ever.

"Brady." She covered her face with the quilt and wept.

"It's okay." He soothed her the best he could, coming around the chair and hugging her tight. "It's going to be okay, Ma."

She was scared, and one thing Dorothy Marshall did not like to show was tears and fear. She'd been the pillar of strength for their family even before their father died.

"I'm sorry. That was," she sniffed, "cruel."

"You're going through a lot right now. It's okay."

"It's not okay." She wiped her eyes with the quilt and looked up at him. Her nose and around her eyes were red and blotchy. She was frail and tired. Two words he'd never associated with her before. "You've given up your life for me for the past nineteen years. I don't know what I'm going to do without you."

"Mom." He hugged her tighter. "Who says I'm going anywhere?" Other than to Grace's at night, but that wasn't what she was referring to.

"It's my own fault. It's what I wanted for you. To find a wife. Settle down. I didn't think it would be someone like…"

Brady craned his neck and clenched his jaw. His mother wouldn't openly insult his girlfriend.

"I don't want you rushing into a relationship with her—anyone."

"I'm a thirty-six-year-old man living at home with his mother and brother. I wouldn't say I'm rushing into anything."

"You spend your nights... away."

"I could bring Grace back here, but wasn't sure how you'd feel about that." Even Carter, with his girlfriend of the month, had never brought a woman home for a sleepover.

It wasn't that Brady was embarrassed to be living with his mom—he looked at it as taking care of her—it was because he respected his mother too much.

His mom shrunk into the quilt, letting it swallow her still-frail body. It had been two months since her diagnosis, and Christmas was only three days away. She'd want to make prime rib on Christmas Eve and an array of brunch dishes to eat all day long on Christmas.

This year he hoped to have Grace join them at the table as well. Maybe even spend the night on Christmas Eve.

But her parents were home, and she'd have her own family traditions. He hadn't asked her what her plans were, and she hadn't asked him. Between her days at her store and his working on the house with Ty, and the snow that seemed to only come during the evening hours, their time together consisted of late night sleepovers. He'd tried to reassure her she wasn't a *booty call*, as she liked to call herself.

It was always said with a flirtatious laugh and with her hands on his body. Their lovemaking was fun. They laughed, talked—sort of—played. It was a new sexual experience every night even though they never did anything kinky.

There was no need.

"That's not a good idea."

Afraid he'd spoken his thoughts out loud, he released his arms from around his mom and sat down on the coffee table. "No?"

"I'm not ready for you or Carter to have overnight guests. I know you're both old enough, and God knows you two have been sexually active since—"

Brady held up a hand. "We don't need to have this conversation. I respect your home, Mom. Don't worry about it."

"It would be nice if you were home in the mornings." The guilt treatment again.

It was hard as hell tugging himself away from Grace's warm body and climbing out of her bed every morning at four o'clock. His internal clock wouldn't let him sleep much later than that. But he wouldn't mind challenging it or just cuddling with Grace in the morning.

She slept like the dead, not stirring an inch when he left. Mornings weren't her thing, she'd said a dozen times. And that was fine with him. Brady never needed a lot of sleep.

Often he'd be up until almost midnight pricing out parts for the tractors, or seeds, or making budgets and working on the farm's finances. And on stormy nights, sometimes he didn't make it in at all trying to keep up with the snow. He could fully function on five hours sleep. Four if he had to.

Sleeping Beauty, however, needed at least nine.

"Are you getting up earlier? Usually, you're still in your room at five." If she was ready to start her day at the crack of dawn he'd come home earlier.

"You come home at five?"

"I'm not ignoring my responsibilities."

"I don't want to be your *responsibility*." She sniffed.

"I didn't mean you. You're my mom. My only mom. I'm here for you twenty-four seven if you need me. You know that." And he was. Mentally. Physically too, if that's what she needed.

Having a break from the responsibilities of the farm and his mom was a welcome change though. Grace and her apartment were a sort of refuge for him.

No wonder his brother spent so many nights in women's beds. There were many reasons, Brady was sure; escape and change of scenery were two.

"The tractors are in good condition. I inspected them, changed the oil, cleaned out the—"

"I'd never doubt your commitment to the farm."

There was more power in what was left unsaid. She questioned his commitment to her. His gut instinct had been right. His mother thought she was being replaced.

"I love you, Mom. You know that, right?"

She brought a wadded ball of tissues out from under the quilt and dabbed her eyes. "I know you do. You're the best son a mother could ask for. I worry about you though. You wear your heart on your sleeve."

Some would say he'd been wearing layered long sleeves for too long. Never had a woman seen that heart. Only Grace.

"You're like your father. A good man. It doesn't take much for a woman to fall in love with someone like you both. For her to forget what she wants in life and give up her dreams for him."

Him? As in her and his father? He'd never known anything but marital bliss between the two of them. His mother's dreams had been to live on the farm as well, hadn't they? For as long as Brady could remember, Dorothy Marshall was as much a representative of Marshall Farms as was Douglas Marshall.

"Did you have other dreams? Dreams before you met Dad?"

His mother's eyes grew warm and sad at the same time. "Your father was everything a girl could dream of. And more. You are too, Brady. Be careful about stealing hearts. Make sure she's not blinded by... you."

He wanted to argue that he wasn't much to brag about. Low to middle class, uneducated beyond a high school diploma, still living at home, and running a farm that depended on fickle Maine weather to make a profit each year.

If he insulted himself to her, he'd be insulting her as well.

"You worry too much. Want me to help you to bed?"

"No." She wrapped the blanket tighter around her. "I can get there on my own. Feed the fire though, please?"

Brady placed two more logs inside the stove and brushed off his jeans when he stood.

"I love you, Ma." He kissed the top of her head on his way out.

He'd always thought his mother's dream had been to live on the farm with his father and raise a family. Never once had he heard her speak of regret or throw the farm in his father's face if they were arguing, which they rarely did.

His parents' marriage was a love story for the books. His mother's parents weren't part of their lives, and Brady and Carter grew to accept that when they were young.

"My parents are too old to come up to Maine. They like their life in sunny Florida. Maybe someday we'll visit them," was the common reply their mother would give them when they asked about their grandparents.

Their paternal grandmother died two weeks after Carter was born, and their grandfather passed away the summer before Brady started high school. There were distant aunts and uncles who would visit every few years, but no one close.

Was that why his mother was so lonely now? Were there secrets she kept buried to keep her family happy?

What were her dreams she gave up to have a family with his father?

• • • •

"I TOLD YOU NOT TO GET me anything." Grace pushed Brady's hand away. They'd filled themselves on prime rib at his house and drove to her parents' house for Christmas Eve drinks and dessert.

Mrs. Marshall had prepared the entire meal herself, with little help from Brady and Carter. Brady hadn't picked up Grace until dinner was ready so she didn't have to lift a finger.

Now back at her apartment, stuffed from all the food, and a little bit tipsy from her family's wine, Grace moved to the other end of her couch.

"That was one request I wasn't going to listen to."

"One? You've ignored many other requests." She crossed her arms and pretended to pout.

"I'm not going to let you pay for dinner when we go out to eat."

They'd only been out three times in the two months they'd been dating, and both times he refused a dime from her.

"I wasn't talking about that."

"Oh." Brady wiggled his eyebrows and slid across the couch until their thighs smooshed together. "And I'm not going to *stop* when you really want me to continue."

He was referring to the other night when he'd pleasured her until she could no longer move, her legs collapsing from under her in the shower. He'd carried her to the bed, and she'd told him she didn't have the energy to make love.

He proved her wrong, not asking for her to do anything but lie there and let him love her.

Which he did.

So freaking well.

"You're blushing."

"Am not." She clasped her palms over her cheeks.

"You're thinking about it." Of course, she was. How could she not? "It's Christmas, and I want to give you a present."

"I said no gifts."

"I never agreed to that."

"Brady."

"It's not much, so don't get your hopes up thinking otherwise."

He didn't have a lot of money, only one of the reasons why she'd said no gifts a few weeks ago when he'd asked her what she wanted for Christmas.

The other being she didn't want to get too attached.

Yeah. Too late for that. Still. The no gift thing was supposed to create the illusion that they were just doing the friends with benefits thing.

"So it's not diamond earrings?" she teased.

Brady's lip quirked, but didn't remain up for long. Money had been a sensitive topic for him. It was like he thought she came from it when he lived across the road from her family's farm.

She'd spent nearly everything she made when working in Paris. And The Closet wasn't exactly bringing in buckets of money.

"Whatever it is, you shouldn't have." Grace took the box from him. Wrapped in candy cane paper with a shiny silver bow, it fit in the palm of her hand. "And I love it."

Grace wrapped her arms around Brady's neck and kissed him. He received her with open arms, and she wiggled her way onto his lap until she was straddling him.

Opening her mouth wider, she invited him in and kissed him deeper, deeper until their bodies melded into one. Her free hand—one was preoccupied holding the unopened gift—moved across his shoulders, clutching him as she rocked back and forth into him.

"You taste so good," he murmured in her mouth.

"Crystal Ice wine."

"No. It's you. The wine was good, yes, but tastes so much better on your lips."

She dropped the tiny package on the couch and grabbed ahold of his hair with both hands.

"Can you be naked now?" She sucked on his bottom lip and ground her ass into his lap.

"Grace," he gasped. "Your present."

"This is what I want." She searched for the bottom hem of his shirt and tugged it over his head, tossing it across the living room.

• • • •

"SEE? I ALWAYS LISTEN to your requests." Brady kissed her cheek and cradled her naked, sated body into his side. There wasn't a lot of room on the couch, so he had to pull her in tight.

Too bad.

The gift he gave her was somewhere. She didn't want to open it. It made her uncomfortable. The gesture. She'd never been with a man during the holidays or her birthday. Had never received a gift from anyone other than her family.

This was too... too personal. Too intimate.

"Aren't you glad you listened to me?" Grace draped her arm across his chest and swirled her finger around his belly button.

"So very glad. And you're going to be glad I got you a gift."

"Brady. I didn't want you too."

"Too late. It's nonrefundable."

Grace propped herself up on her elbow, which was hard to do on the narrow couch. "You didn't."

Mischief danced in his eyes. "Open it." Grace dropped her forehead to his chest and moaned. "If you're worried because you didn't get me anything, don't be. Not only do I not want you to waste your hard earned money on me, this is the best gift I could ever ask for."

"Sex?"

"Well, that's a side benefit. Being with you makes everything complete. I'm not a materialistic guy. I don't need anything else."

"But you think I'm a materialistic girl, which is why you defied me and got me something."

Brady chuckled.

"Okay. Fine. I am a materialistic girl in some ways. I'm not a snob. Yes, I love a good pair of heels, the higher the better, and I love clothes. Dressing up is fun. But I'm down to earth as well."

"You don't have to sell me on you. I like you just the way you are."

Damn. She couldn't do this. Not only was her heart going to be trampled on, but Brady's was as well. Her scandal wouldn't go over well with him. Neither would her news about moving.

She was going to hell for stringing him along. After the New Year, she'd end things with him once and for all.

Brady squirmed underneath her, reaching across with his arms. "Here," he said, placing the small box on his naked chest. "Open it."

"I'm sure there's a way for you to return it."

"Nope."

"Shit."

Brady laughed at her curse and propped himself up to sitting. He picked up Grace as if she weighed nothing and sat her next to him on the couch.

"You realize we're both naked. Opening a present. Shouldn't we get dressed first? Or at least find a blanket?"

"Nope. I like you naked. Think of it as another Christmas present to me. See? Now I have two and you haven't even opened your first one yet."

"Why can't *you* be *my* Christmas present?"

"I claimed that idea first. No copying."

"You're such a child. Fine. Give me the thing." She ripped the beautifully wrapped present from his hand and tore it open.

"Wow. I expected you to be the type who tried not to rip the paper."

"This is what happens when people don't listen to me. I get cranky."

"Good to know." He kissed her nose with another chuckle.

Grace bit her bottom lip as she tore away the last of the paper. A tiny white box glared back at her. It couldn't be jewelry. That would scream long-term commitment. She couldn't accept it.

But she wasn't ready to let Brady go yet. He'd tire of her in time. He had to. They all did. Maybe she could let it play out a little longer until he sent her to the curb.

She lifted the lid to the box and gasped.

"Brady?" With shaking fingers she picked up the end of a flash drive, letting the bomb dangle between them. Heat rushing through her veins like lava, she burned from shame. Fear. Mortification. It couldn't be the one...

"I loaded it with my grandmother's and mother's favorite recipes."

"You... what?" Relief washed over her, and she sunk back into the couch.

"I asked first, so it's not like they're Marshall secrets. Hope, Mia, and Jenna gave me some of their favorites as well. Lily gave me a takeout menu to scan. I guess she doesn't cook. Alexis gave me some of your mom's that she said you really like."

"Recipes?"

"Yeah. For your collection. You're always on your phone looking them up. I figured one place to hold them would be kind of handy."

"You collected recipes?"

He lowered his head, his anxious smile fading into disappointment. "It's not a lot, I know."

"Brady." Relief. Joy. Love. They all filled her heart. "This is the most thoughtful," she flipped a leg over his to straddle him, "wonderful." She kissed his lips. "Amazing." She kissed his cheeks. "Beautiful." She kissed his neck. "Perfect gift." She kissed his mouth again.

He cradled her face and moved her away from his mouth a fraction of an inch. "So you like it?"

"No. I love it."

And I love you.

CHAPTER TWENTY-TWO

AS THE DAYS GREW COLD and the nights grew colder, Grace and Brady's relationship grew stronger.

And hotter.

She'd stopped making dinners for the entire Marshall family and toned it down to dinners for two. Except for a handful of nights when Mrs. Marshall wasn't feeling well, or when there was a big storm and he had to plow until the wee hours of the morning, Brady spent every night in her bed.

When she woke, he was usually gone, but not without a sticky note on the counter and coffee in the pot.

This morning was one she cherished. He'd promised to stay with her until she had to leave for work. The hint of the morning sun peeked its way through her curtains, and Grace stretched and arched her body into his... pillow. Opening one eye, she peered out and saw his side of the bed was empty.

Straining, she listened for noises from her kitchen or bathroom.

Nothing.

The clock next to her bed told her it wasn't even time for her to wake up yet. Her eight o'clock alarm wasn't due to ring for another twenty minutes. Plenty of time for morning snuggles... or more.

If Brady was here.

A commotion from the living room had her sitting upright. Someone opened the door.

She heard the jingling of keys and the closing of the door. It had to be Brady. Clutching his pillow into her chest, she called out.

"Brady?"

"Are you expecting someone else?" He poked his head in the bedroom and gave out a low whistle. "Aren't you a sight for sore eyes."

"How long have you been gone?" she asked. It was getting easier to not blush at every compliment he dished out.

"I went down to the Sunrise Diner to get us breakfast." He held up a bag and a beverage tray. "Two lobsterman's specials. And two coffees."

"I can't eat all that."

"I know. I'll eat what you don't finish." He toed off his unlaced boots and shimmied out of his winter coat, all while balancing the bag in his hands. He plopped down on his side of the bed, making her body bounce up and down, and pulled the covers over his lap.

"What are you doing? I'll get up."

"Breakfast in bed." He took out one of the Styrofoam containers and placed it in her lap. "I didn't want to chance waking you by cooking. And we don't have a lot of food in the fridge."

We. She reminded herself not to get too swoony over Brady. "I know. I need to go to the store today."

"You have the shop. I'll go for you." He kissed her on the lips and settled into his seat, fluffing two pillows behind his back and placing the other Styrofoam container in his lap.

Grace watched him slice through his pancakes with his plastic fork and knife as if this was their normal routine.

"What is it?"

"You're too good to me."

"You deserve it." He placed another quick kiss, this time on her nose, and went back to work sawing into his stack of pancakes.

No. She really didn't. She didn't do anything to deserve a man as wonderful as Brady.

"First time I've been in the diner since I was in high school."

With his mom big on making hearty breakfasts every morning before the workday started, this made sense. Why would he want to go to a greasy spoon when he had his own farm fresh eggs and sausage made for him?

"Over the years, I've heard about Priscilla and her quirky aura readings," he'd said after wiping his mouth. "But I gotta tell you, she totally freaked me out this morning."

"She read my colors one night too. Red, I think she said. With a layer of green."

"Guess I'm yellow and pink. Kind of shrunk my manhood a little."

Grace peeked under the covers. "I think you're good."

"Thanks." He leaned over her pancake breakfast and gave her a maple syrup kiss. He did that a lot. Kissed her just for the sake of kissing her. "She said pink people are very romantic and once they found their soul mate they'll stay faithful, loving, and loyal for life."

Pancake lodged in her throat, and she had to beat her chest and down the rest of her hot coffee to break it up. Her plan was backfiring. Brady wasn't supposed to say stuff like this to her.

The more time they spent together the more he was supposed to realize Grace was absolutely *not* soul mate material.

"Tomorrow is Valentine's Day. Can I be honest with you?"

Yes! Tell me it's an overrated holiday and you want to break up.

No! What the hell was she thinking? She didn't want to break up with Brady. It would crush her. Kill her. She wouldn't be able to breathe if she didn't have him by her side every night, holding on to her, whispering encouraging words to her, no matter what the topic.

Whether it was her cooking or her store or her terrible singing in the shower, Brady had a way of making her feel confident, so sure of herself when in reality, she didn't have a freaking clue what she was doing.

"I'd say you're usually too honest with me."

Brady moved his empty tray to the nightstand and turned to her. "The last time I celebrated Valentine's Day was when I made a heart out of clay in fifth grade and gave it to my mom."

"That's sweet."

"My brother continued to give her stuff he made at school, and my dad would do something nice. Buy her flowers, whittle her something out of wood, or bring her shopping for material to make a quilt."

"Does she still like to sew?"

"She usually makes a quilt every winter and donates it to the school to raffle off at a fundraiser event."

"Has she been working on one?"

"She's starting to. I brought her into town the other day to pick out material."

And by "into town" he meant thirty minutes away to Rockland where there were a handful of stores to actually buy stuff.

"You're a good son."

"I try."

"And I know she appreciates all you do."

"You have me off track."

Yeah. Back to him breaking up or not breaking up with her. By the way one hand moved unconsciously along her leg and the other through her hair, she'd say she was pretty safe on the not breaking up end of things.

Her conscience, however, was anything but safe.

"I've never celebrated Valentine's Day with a girlfriend."

"I can't believe you've ignored your girlfriends on the most highly overrated, overpriced, commercialized holiday." She feigned a gasp.

"What I meant was." Brady took her half-eaten breakfast and set it on the mattress behind him and pulled her sideways across his lap. "I've never had a girlfriend to celebrate with."

"You've had girlfriends though." She'd heard about them when she was younger. There were flocks of girls who applied every spring and summer to work on the farm with Brady and Carter.

"Not long term. No one special." He ran his hands through her hair and draped it over one shoulder. "No one like you."

"You make it really hard to think when you say stuff like that."

"Is that so?" he asked with a wicked gleam in his eye.

"Can I be honest with you?" Somewhat honest. Not completely.

"I'd like that."

"I've had boyfriends, but I've never had one at Christmas." Sort of a lie. She was sleeping with Robert at the time. Mistress didn't exactly constitute her as girlfriend. And all he got her was a room at the Ritz and a night of sex. Just like every other time they hooked up.

Grace clenched her body, not wanting to think about him.

"You okay?" Brady stroked her back like a man who cared. A man who loved her.

"I've never had one on Valentine's Day either. I don't want you to get me anything." She put her palm over his mouth when he opened it to speak. "All I want tomorrow is to be with you. If your mom is sick, be with her. If we get a nor'easter, I'm riding shotgun with you in your plow truck. I'll take you any way I can, Brady Marshall."

"It's a date, Grace Le Blanc, but we're doing more than just hooking up."

Funny. It wasn't anything special when she just "hooked up" with Robert, but spending the night with Brady was the best gift he could give her.

"Being with you is fine enough." And she wholeheartedly meant it.

"Grace." He pushed her hair back, those gray eyes darkening. "I've been afraid to say this. Afraid you weren't ready to hear it, but I'm going to risk it." He stroked her cheeks with the pads of his thumbs and kissed her lips with his words. "I love you."

Unexpected shivers and warmth simultaneously rocketed through her body.

Grace gasped and laughed and choked at the same time. He loved her. This good, honest, amazing man loved her. She forgot about her leaving in a few months, about the secrets she held, and let herself love.

Let herself be loved. It was selfish, she knew. But she needed this.

"I love you too," she whispered across his lips.

She cherished every night he came to her door, sat at her table, and spooned her all night.

These nights would end. Too soon they'd be memories of her past. Good memories. The pain would come when he learned she was leaving. That she had no desire to stay, and there was no way he would leave.

Until then, she'd cherish all the time she had with Brady as if it were her last.

• • • •

MARCH FIRST. BRADY didn't think this day would ever come. He was sure his mother didn't either. Her last round of chemotherapy. Her specialists were pleased with the progress she'd made and were hopeful this would be it.

Opening the passenger door for his mom, he held her hand and helped her to the ground.

"How are you feeling?" He draped his arm around her shoulder and guided her into the hospital.

"The same as the last ten times you've asked me."

"Sorry. I'm nervous and anxious and excited for you."

"I know, honey." She reached up and patted his hand. "You've got spring around the corner and don't need the burden of—"

"Stop." He planted his feet and turned his mother to face him. "I don't want to hear one word about you being a burden to me or to Carter or to anyone. You'd do the same for us. Hell, you do more. A hell of a lot more. You're the strongest, bravest woman I know. You're a fighter. Your doctors say the same thing. We've got this, Ma. You're going to beat it."

"Now what did you do that for?" She sniffed and swiped at her eyes. "Who would've thought. Allergy season and it's barely March."

Unlike Brady, Dorothy Marshall did not like to show emotion. Her heart was nowhere near her sleeve. Only Carter and Brady, and their father, had access to it. Some have said she was cold, but that was because she didn't trust many. Never opened up or revealed much about herself.

The farm and her boys. That was Dorothy Marshall.

Brady stood back while she checked herself in. When the nurse called her name, he followed her to a private room, all too familiar with the drill.

"Oh, my book. I can't believe I left it at home," she said as the nurse prepped her sites for the chemo.

"I can run home and get it."

"No. By the time you get back, I'll be almost done." It would take forty minutes round trip, and her chemo treatment would be at least three hours. They both knew this, but he didn't argue.

"We've got a million magazines, Mrs. Marshall. Soon as I'm done I'll go get you some."

"Thanks, Leah."

Leah had been the nurse every time his mother had come in for treatments. All of them were wonderful, but Leah seemed to get his mom the most. She didn't want to make friends. Didn't want idle chatter.

Sometimes Brady and Carter came with her, other times they tag-teamed. Since Carter had an early morning consult with a new client, Brady brought his mom in for what they hoped to be the last round of chemo.

It wasn't like he had a fear of needles, but they sure weren't his thing. Carter got the willies from them and liked to take on second shift, arriving after everything was inserted and their mother was covered with a blanket.

The men and women who went through these treatments were brave as hell. And the kids. Damn. It broke his heart to see a cute little bald-headed kid with a smile and a "thank you" on his lips after treatment.

Brady didn't know if he could be so brave.

Leah came back with a stack of magazines and placed them on the tray next to his mother's side. "All the good ones are already taken. Some of these are more than a year old. I'll be back later to refresh the stack for you."

After she left the room, his mom picked one up and flipped through the pages. "Do people really read this gossip? I mean, who cares what Hollywood couple is getting married or who is cheating on who? It's not like we know these people."

It was better to have her annoyed at society than dwelling on her condition so Brady agreed as she skimmed the pages of the magazine.

She didn't read any of the articles as she flipped. And then she paused and picked up the magazine from her lap to bring it closer to her face. She forgot her reading glasses as well so that shouldn't have been a concern, but her mouth flopped open and her eyes grew wide.

"Mom?"

A loud gasp and an incoherent noise escaped her lips. Then, with a burst of energy he'd never seen during a treatment, she slammed the magazine—if a magazine could be slammed—shut and dropped it in her lap as if it had suddenly turned red hot.

Worry, fear, anger all etched in her tight face. She stared at the magazine in her lap as if it was about to jump up and claw at her throat.

"Mom?" he asked again. "What's wrong? Should I get Leah?"

Clenching her teeth and her shoulders, she nervously shook her head. "No," she said without moving her jaw.

Something in the magazine triggered this bizarre reaction from her. Brady reached for the magazine and she snatched it away.

"No," she said again.

"Mom?"

"Just leave. I need to rest." She closed her eyes and leaned back into the chair, her tense body doing anything but resting, still clutching the magazine.

Respecting her wishes—which was why they got along so well—he left her alone and went for a walk through the halls of the hospital.

Something spooked his mom. Spooked the hell out of her.

And he'd make sure he'd find out what it was.

CHAPTER TWENTY-THREE

"SHE WANTS WHAT?" GRACE balanced her cell phone between her shoulder and ear as she pushed the shopping cart down the cookie aisle. She may need to unload the shelves into her cart for this favor.

"Yesterday was rough for her. Maybe she wants another woman to talk to," Brady said on the other line.

His mom was in rough shape last night, so he'd stayed home to be close to her. While Grace missed his warmth in her bed, she also respected his love and devotion to his mom.

"Is she doing any better today?" She tossed a package of double stuffed Oreos in the cart.

"I don't know. She's acting strangely. Won't talk to Carter or me, but she wants you to come over."

Grace stopped, wheeled the cart backward, and tossed two more packages of Oreos in her cart. No need to hit up the wine aisle. Alexis brought over a case of wine the other day. Another one who'd been acting weird.

Since she watched Sophie last month, Alexis had been less snarky. Even laughed at a joke Grace had made at book club a few weeks ago and complimented her on her slutty brownies, a recipe Mia had found and begged Grace to make.

"As soon as I get home and unload the groceries I'll be there." Not with bells on. Hanging out with Dorothy Marshall was not guaranteed to be a good time.

"Thanks. I love you. See you soon."

Grace dropped her phone in her purse and checked out the liquor aisle. She'd need something stronger than Lobster Red after this.

Brady greeted her at the door with a kiss and a warm hug. "I missed you." It had only been two days since she'd seen him, but she missed him too.

"Absence makes the heart grow fonder." Listen to her, all romantic and gushy.

"Let's not test that theory too often. My bed isn't as comfy as yours."

"So you're using me for my comfy mattress?"

"That and other things." He kissed her again, his winter facial scruff tickling her lips, and then unbuttoned her coat.

"Now you're taking my clothes off in your kitchen?" she whispered, giggling when he gently poked at her ribs.

"Brady," his mother said from behind, instantly ruining the mood.

"Hi, Mrs. Marshall. How are you feeling today?" She wore jeans and a baggy sweatshirt, her bald head covered in a scarf. Years of working outside in harsh conditions had weathered her skin, yet she still looked young. Today, she even looked fierce.

Ignoring her completely, she handed Brady a piece of paper. "I need you to go to Fabric Barn and get me more batting and thread."

"Now?" He rubbed the back of his neck and wrinkled his nose.

"Yes."

That would mean he'd be gone for at least an hour. Maybe longer if he needed help finding items on her list.

"You sure you don't want me to stick around?"

Yes! Stick around! Grace wanted to scream.

"We will be fine."

"I can call Carter, see when he'll—"

"I don't need a babysitter twenty-four seven. Just go."

Brady opened his mouth, probably to argue, and wisely shut it. No one messed with Dorothy.

"Okay." He gave his mom a kiss on the cheek and did the same to Grace. "Call me if you need anything. Both of you."

As soon as Brady left, Mrs. Marshall turned and walked away. Figuring she was supposed to follow, Grace toed off her sneakers and joined her in the living room.

Sitting tall and strong in her usual chair, this time without the quilt wrapped tightly around her, Mrs. Marshall tapped on a magazine in her lap. Grace never would have pegged her as a reader of Hollywood gossip.

Taking a seat at the end of the sofa near her, Grace did her best not to show her nervousness. Nervous about what, she hadn't a clue. The woman hated her for no apparent reason.

"How long are you planning on stringing my son along?"

"Excuse me?"

Mrs. Marshall flipped open the magazine and with a force of aggression Grace wasn't expecting, handed it to her.

Reluctant, Grace took it from her. "What is it?" she asked, not looking at the magazine.

"You tell me." She sat ramrod straight, her eyes accusatory and fierce.

Grace glanced at the headline on the left. A Hollywood divorce announcement. Old news. The magazine must be from last summer. Then she saw the pictures on the other side. Gasping, she dropped it on the floor, her fingers singed.

Robert had insisted the pictures he took of her in bed would never see the light of day. They'd be damaging to his marriage and career, while she was a nobody and didn't have a reputation to worry about.

Oh, how wrong he'd been.

"I..." She couldn't form words, much less sounds.

"The article says you had an affair with a married man while his wife was pregnant."

Grace knew he was married, not that his wife was pregnant. She'd learned about that when Brielle Powers caught them in her bed, her baby bump evident in her tight dress.

The model was a fashion icon. Her husband a well-known British actor. It was in both their best interests to keep Grace a secret. When Brielle all but blackballed her from the fashion industry, Grace packed up and moved home.

Robert had never lived up to his promise of helping her make it big. When he'd been drinking and she'd asked for his help with getting her recognized, he'd laugh and tell her she was no good.

Grace blamed it on the alcohol and possibly his guilt of cheating on his wife. It wasn't like he had a solid reputation in that department anyway. He was a known philanderer, which was why she hadn't felt *too* guilty about having the affair.

He'd promised her big things. Not money or material possessions, those she didn't want. She wanted to own her own franchise, to be appreciated by the fashion industry, and he had connections through his wife.

It was sick. It was twisted. It was so, so wrong, but Grace had been at rock bottom. She had no pride and saw no value in herself.

She didn't succeed working at the vineyard in Italy. She struggled through fashion school, eventually earning her degree in liberal arts. But clothes were her thing. She had an eye for them.

Just not design. Which was why coming to Maine to hide out and process was the only choice she had left.

And she was broke.

Feeling the daggers from across the room, Grace lifted her chin, faking dignity and poise.

"I'm not the same woman I was back then. I made mistakes and have worked hard to be a better person."

"So this filth is true?"

She hadn't read the article and didn't want to. It didn't matter. Whatever it said couldn't be worse than the truth.

She was a dirty whore who had no right being with someone as good and pure as Brady Marshall.

"I'm not... her anymore."

"Does my son know about your scandalous past?"

Grace remained silent, refusing to discuss this with his mother, who hated her on pretense alone.

"For some reason, he thinks he's in love with you." Grace closed her eyes, forcing back her tears. "He has a big heart. One that will be crushed to pieces if he were to ever learn he was duped a fool."

Clenching her hands until her manicured nails bit into her palms, Grace forced herself to remain calm, eyes still closed.

"I pray to God he never finds out about this."

Her eyes flung open. So she would keep the secret?

"You'll end things with my son. Now. He'll think he has a broken heart, but it will heal when he finds the right woman for him." Mrs. Marshall stood, her body rigid. "Leave. I don't ever want to see your face again."

Grace prayed her shaking legs would hold her as she stepped past Mrs. Marshall and into the kitchen. She didn't bother trying to put her sneakers on all the way and shoved her toes into them, her heels sticking out in the back. Grabbing her coat without putting it on, she let herself out of the house and somehow made it into her car and back to her apartment before she had a full meltdown.

As soon as she closed the door behind her, she curled up into a ball in the middle of her bed and cried.

And cried. And cried. Her throat dry and hoarse, her body shook with convulsions and pain until she could no longer move.

Sometime later she woke to the ringing of her phone. Rubbing the dry grit from her eyes, she rose and found her purse under her coat on the floor in the living room.

Brady.

Two missed calls and six new texts. She couldn't read them or listen to his voice. Powering off her phone, she tossed it in her purse and went to her room to change into large sweatpants and a loose sweatshirt.

Somehow she needed to end things with Brady, to come up with a reason why they needed to break up.

The ugly truth was easiest. He'd want nothing to do with her once he found out. But his mother wanted to protect him from the nasty truth. Needing time and fearing he'd show up at her doorstep, she dug out her keys and left.

For hours she drove around aimlessly with no direction. No purpose. No hope. De`ja` vu back to Paris a year and a half ago.

And just like then, she had no friend to call. No sister to lean on.

If she told her new friends what she'd done, they'd disown her as quickly as Brady would. She'd never had close girlfriends before. Lots and lots of girls and guys to hang out with in her teens and early twenties, sure. No one she'd refer to as a best friend.

No one to share her secrets with. To go to for advice. To cry with.

Lily, Hope, Mia, and Jenna were Alexis' friends first, and Grace knew better than to come in between them. She'd done that in high school, intentionally sleeping with boys who were Alexis' friends.

Her sister got all the attention, and Grace wanted some too. It took years of traveling and living on her own to realize how self-destructive she'd been. It was her fault Alexis hated her. Her fault she didn't have a sister to confide in when she really, really needed one.

Getting caught in Robert's bed was embarrassing. She was mad he never made due on his promise of getting her into the fashion industry. She was ashamed his wife had been pregnant; a new low for her. She was mad and pissed off, yes.

Losing Brady was more. So much more. Her lungs constricted, making it hard to breathe. Her muscles weakened and trembled.

Knowing she wasn't safe on the road anymore and couldn't go home and risk Brady coming over, she went to the only place she thought would be safe.

Home.

CHAPTER TWENTY-FOUR

HER PARENTS WERE GETTING ready for bed when she knocked on the back door and entered the kitchen.

"Hey, beautiful daughter." Her dad kissed her nose and held up his mug. "Don't tell your mother I had a cup of hot chocolate before bed. She's been trying to get me to cut back on my sugar intake."

"Secret's safe, Daddy." She was good at keeping secrets. Grace melted into her father's embrace and inhaled his familiar scent. Wood shavings, grapes, and a hint of soap.

"What brings my favorite youngest daughter by at nine-thirty?"

The kitchen was dark, with only the light above the sink shining, which hopefully covered her red and splotchy face.

"Can I sleep in my old room tonight?"

"Oh, honey." He squeezed tighter. "Everything okay with you and Brady?"

Her stomach spasmed, and she broke down in tears again. Soon there was another set of arms around her.

"Sweetie." The warmth and love of her mom's voice and comfort was too much, and her legs gave out.

"I gotcha," her dad said and helped her to the couch.

He laid her down and covered her with a blanket. She curled on her side, tucking a throw pillow against her chest.

"Want to talk about it?" her mother asked, sitting next to her, rubbing her side.

"I... can't."

A few minutes later her father brought a mug of hot chocolate with extra whipped cream. "I know you've out-grown it, but this used to make you feel better when you were little."

Her throat tightened with pain. The guilt clawing at her. Her parents didn't do anything to deserve her behavior the last few years. Hell, two decades. Always supportive in her need to be free, to be adventurous, to not commit to any-thing, they loved her without question.

And she took advantage of it, squandering her college money and taking for granted they'd always be there for her.

Which they were.

"I love you guys," she croaked, her eyes too dry to cry anymore. "I'm sorry."

"Sweetheart, whatever it is, we'll always love you. Noth-ing will change that."

"I've been," she sniffed, "a shitty daughter. I know you don't like swearing, but that's the only word to describe me."

"You're a free spirit, Gracie." Her father took a seat in the rocker across from her, still holding her hot chocolate. "We love that about you and would never want you to change."

"Is that a nice way of saying I'm a screw-up?"

"Honey." Her mother sighed. "You've never been a screw-up. You take risks. You grab onto life and run with it. You make life happen. We've always admired that about you. Even Alexis does."

Grace snorted and shifted, sitting up and tucking her feet under her. "Alexis is your level-headed, responsible, reli-able, got-her-shit-together daughter."

"And you're our determined, liberated, strong-willed, fun-loving, big-hearted daughter," her father said, handing her the mug.

Grace sipped the whipped cream and then the cocoa. "And more fashionable."

"See? Hot cocoa does make you feel better."

"Thanks, Mom. Dad." Grace straightened her legs and wrapped her free arm around her mom. "I'm going upstairs. Don't um... don't tell anyone I'm here, okay?"

"We're here if you want to talk about it." Her mom hugged her and passed her off to her father for another hug.

Her legs were heavy, but she managed to climb the stairs to her old room and crawl under her covers.

Sleep, however, did not come.

The room was bright with the sun's rays when she heard her door open and felt the bed sink.

"What's going on?"

"Alexis?" Grace blinked open her eyes and pushed herself up with her elbows.

"My God. You look like shit."

"Thanks."

"I mean it. Your eyelashes are stuck to your cheek." Alexis peeled the false eyelashes off and flicked it onto the carpet. "What the hell is going on? Brady's been blowing up my phone all worried about you, and then I saw your car in the driveway."

She should have thought about that one, hiding her car.

"I just ... need some time alone."

"You live in an apartment by yourself. I'd say you're more alone there than at Mom and Dad's. It's you and Brady, huh? He wouldn't tell me what was up. Something is wrong."

"What gave it away?" She pushed her hair out of her face and rubbed her eyes.

"The fact you left your house in that ugly ass shirt."

Grace looked down at her chest. Brady had worn it to her apartment one night, coming straight from Ty's after helping him work on the lawnmower.

The gray Cabela's shirt had a rip in the armpit and a grease stain across the chest. She'd washed it a few times, and it wouldn't come out. She shrunk into the comfort of the worn material.

"What did he do? How did he hurt you?"

"What?" She was tired and not thinking straight, and couldn't have heard her sister correctly. "Why do you think it's his fault?"

"Because I've been there."

"Ben?"

"Yeah. When I found out he had a baby and had never told me the entire time we were dating that he had a pregnant ex-girlfriend back at home... yeah. Shit. Fan." Alexis scooted up on the bed and rested her back against the wall. "I was a moping mess. Looked a lot like you do right now. Minus the black river of makeup. I wished I had my sister here to talk to."

Grace hiccupped and tears flowed down her cheeks. "But you hate me," she practically whined.

Alexis sighed and handed Grace a box of tissues. Apparently, she'd come prepared. "I don't hate you."

"You don't like me."

"You sound like a spoiled teenager right now."

"See?" Grace sniffed, unsure where this was going. Having a heart to heart with her estranged sister the day after her boyfriend's mom told her to get the hell out of his life was not where she pictured herself.

"I don't not like you. We're different. You know I don't do this." Alexis waved her hand between them. "The emotions. The talking."

"We haven't talked in years."

"I know. A lot of that is my fault."

"What? Who are you and what have you done with my sister?"

"Funny. Honestly?" Oh, there goes that word again, slapping her in the face. "I've always been a bit jealous of you."

"Of *me*?"

"Again. The teenage dramatics. One of the reasons I never talked to you about... life."

"What was there to be jealous about? You were the one with all the friends. Miss popular. Everyone in town knew who you were. You were Grumpy's favorite. He practically willed the entire vineyard to you when you were in high school. Your future was mapped out for you all pretty, and I had no direction. No friends."

"Um, are we remembering the same Grace Le Blanc? How many boys climbed up the maple outside my window to sneak across into your room? Not until Ben did a guy climb that tree for me."

"Ben climbed the maple?" Grace crossed her palms over her heart. "That's so sweet."

"I know." Alexis blushed and lowered her head.

"Boys only climbed up because they wanted to get laid. They had no interest in me."

"Same thing."

"Is it?"

That caused Alexis to pause. Her face softened, and she curled her lips in as if thinking of an appropriate response. "You always seemed so... put together. Pretty. Nice clothes. Makeup always in place. You laughed a lot. Always had a party to go to while I stayed home and worked in the vineyard."

"The clothes, the makeup. They were a mask, Alexis. I lived the 'mind over matter' mantra. I thought if I looked the part, I'd be happy."

"You fooled me."

"And myself. For too damn long I fooled myself."

"You're not happy with Brady?"

Tears welled up in her throat. Grace brought her knees to her chest and hugged them tight. "I've never been happier. He's perfect in so many ways. In all the ways that matter. When I'm with him I feel... worthy."

"So what went wrong?"

"You don't," Grace shook her head, "you don't want to know."

"I may not want to, but will it help to have someone to talk to? Did you tell Mom and Dad?"

"No. I can't tell them. They'll never look at me the same way again."

"I doubt that. You're Dad's princess."

"More like the town whore."

"Please don't tell me you cheated on Brady."

"Oh my God! Never."

"Okay, so what is it?"

"My past. I did stuff I'm not proud of, and it's come back to remind me of what I am."

"Which is what?"

"I can't," Grace whispered.

Alexis slid up the bed and squeezed herself between the wall and Grace. They'd never done this before, sat in bed, or even on a couch, and talked. Shared secrets. Cried. So much of Grace wanted to believe she could tell her sister the sordid details and not lose the new connection they were building.

"One thing Ben has taught me, you always need someone to talk to. There's nothing wrong with leading a private life, but you need one person in your life you can tell the ugly truth to. Whether it be your best friend, your parents, your boyfriend." Alexis squeezed Grace's knee, the gesture new and awkward. "Your sister."

"So if I tell you my secrets, you'll tell me yours?" Grace attempted humor to lighten the moment.

"I've always wanted a sister I can share my ugly skeletons with."

"They better be good because mine's a doozy."

"We gonna do the one-up game?"

"I've got you beat, hands down. No matter what you tell me, my skeletons are worse."

Grace poured it all out. Every detail from her careless dating years to her attempt at fashion school, not even coming close to measuring up with the other men and women in the class. Her designs weren't original enough. They were pretty but had been done over and over again.

It was when she was at her lowest, broke and afraid to come home, that she'd met Robert and fell for his promises.

"Holy shit." Alexis let out a loud sigh. "Ho-ly. Shit."

"Yeah." Grace was quiet, letting her sister process. "So," she said after a few minutes, "did I one-up you?"

"Frick. You one-upped Ben with his secret baby." Alexis tapped her head against the wall. "I feel like I need a stiff drink. A shot of whiskey or something."

"I wouldn't say no to that. Or to Oreos. I have three packages of double stuffed in my apartment. Keys are on the floor. Maybe you could buy out all the magazines as well. Can't wait for the rest of the town to see the pictures. "

"I thought you said it was an old magazine from last summer. If anyone around here had seen it, you would've heard about it by now."

"Maybe." She sniffed.

"And Dorothy told you to keep this from Brady?"

"Yeah. Which is why I'm avoiding him."

"He could find out some other way."

"Maybe. I need to break it off with him, but he'll want to know why. Telling him I'm a dirty whore didn't work the first time. Or the second."

"You didn't."

"Maybe not in those exact words. I tried to stop things before they started, and he refused to listen to reason."

"He loves you."

"Better to have loved and lost..." Grace waved her hand through the air, unable to finish the statement, her heart too heavy with grief of what she was about to lose.

"I like Dorothy."

Grace snorted. "She's yet to show her nice side to me."

"She's jealous of you taking Brady from her."

"You think?"

"I know. Anyway, I like her, but this isn't her decision to make. You need to tell Brady. If he truly loves who you are now, he'll be able to look past your... past."

"I don't think so. You're still having a hard time processing. I know you're trying not to picture the scene. Brielle walking in on me and Robert."

"I don't know who they are, but I can only imagine. Scratch that. I don't want to imagine."

"You're better off."

"You know what I think?"

"Yeah."

"I think you need to tell him the truth."

"Not what I thought you were going to say." Grace climbed out of bed. "I have to pee." She padded across the hall and took care of business. While washing her hands she lifted her head and looked in the mirror. "Shit."

She hadn't looked in the mirror since she'd finished putting groceries away and prepped herself for hanging out with Mrs. Marshall for the day.

After nine hundred bouts of crying, Grace figured her makeup had to be completely wiped away. Well, it was. From her eyes.

Four coats of mascara blackened under her eyes and half her cheeks. Damn waterproof mascara holding up to its name. She peeled off the remaining false eyelashes. Taking a washcloth from the cabinet, she scrubbed her face and pulled her hair back into a ponytail.

"That's an improvement," her sister said from the bed. "You must be hungry. Mom and Dad went to Rockland for the day. Let's go raid their kitchen."

"They're avoiding me."

"No. Actually, they wanted to come upstairs with me. I told them I'd take care of you. Asked if they could give us some privacy."

Grace stopped midway on the stairs. "You did?"

Alexis shrugged. "When I found out about Ben's baby, the last people I wanted to face were Mom and Dad. No offense, rents," she called down the stairwell, even though they weren't home.

"No offense, but the last person I thought about talking to was you." Alexis barked out a laugh. "For real. I wanted to. Wanted to have a sister to talk to and wished you didn't hate me and judge me so I could talk to you."

"I've been a real bitch, haven't I?"

They were still in the middle of the stairwell, sharing the same step, facing each other.

"I've been calling it passive aggressive."

"You know what I really didn't like about you when you came home?"

"You're supposed to be making me feel better, remember?"

"I hated how sweet you were. How all my friends, whom I've just made in the past few years, all loved you. I hated how Ben thought you were cool and would tell me about The Closet and how proud he was of you. I hated how my daughter loved all the ugly girly things you got her. And I hated how you never responded to any of my one hundred percent intentional passive aggressive bitchy retorts."

"Wow."

"And I hated how Brady Marshall took one look at you and fell in love. And you were so innocent to it all. You didn't ask for the attention. I noticed how you declined some of the invitations from our friends."

She said *our* friends. Damn tears were coming back.

"I noticed how kind you were to everyone. How humble. How insecure. I wanted to be your friend as well and didn't know how."

"Alexis." New tears fell. Not from pain and hurt, but of a new kind of love. Grace opened her arms and squeezed her sister tight, holding on for dear life.

"My hair," her sister mumbled, sniffing from below. Grace towered over Alexis by a good five inches. "Your snot and tears are soaking my scalp."

Chuckling and wiping her nose with the back of her hand, Grace pulled away.

"Very ladylike. Go wash your hands. I'll make breakfast." Alexis marched down the stairs first, most likely wanting to hide her own tears.

There was still one more secret. Arianna had hooked her up with a lease in Boston. Grace's dream of opening The Closet in a big city would be coming true.

And she'd be leaving Crystal Cove.

Again.

Soon.

CHAPTER TWENTY-FIVE

"GRACE. HONEY. WHAT is going on?" Brady let himself into Grace's apartment with the key she'd given him last month and wrapped her in his arms, pressing her into his body. Relief had flooded him when he drove by and saw her car in the parking lot. "You've got me worried senseless. Where've you been?"

He pulled back, holding on to her shoulders with his hands, searching her face for clues, signs of where she'd been for the past two days. Her body was limp under his hands, not the strong Grace he knew and loved.

"What happened?"

She blinked rapidly and looked over his shoulder. "We need to talk."

His mouth grew dry, and the breakfast sandwich he had for breakfast grew hard as a rock in the pit of his stomach. "When you say it like that it sounds..." Not good.

He loosened his grip on her shoulders, and her body swayed away from him. "We should sit."

Her eyes remained downcast, and it wasn't until she moved herself to the couch and sat that he noticed her clothes.

Sweatpants and a wrinkled sweatshirt. They were at the point in their relationship where he'd seen her in everything from her *grannie panties,* as she liked to call them, to her sleepwear. And his favorite, her birthday suit.

But Grace didn't lounge around all day in her ratty old sweats. She took them out when she cleaned the apartment, and never wore them for long, and not because he enjoyed ripping them off her.

She was always put together. Her idea of "slumming it" was wearing leggings and a long shirt.

Today, hunched over like someone close to her had passed away, she looked like death herself.

"Honey." Brady kneeled on the floor at her feet and took her hands in his. "What is it?" If someone close to her had died he'd have heard about it by now. Alexis would have said something.

"No. Don't." She shook her hands away from his. "You need to sit. Over there." She pointed at the other end of the couch.

He moved and sat next to her, thigh to thigh. When she shifted away, he tried not to be offended.

"Honey, did I do something wrong?"

Her body flinched, and she made a snorting-sighing sound. "No. Never."

"Then what is it?" He reached for her hands, but she tucked them under her thighs.

"I told you from the beginning we weren't right for each other."

"No. You're not doing this again. I love you. You know that. And I know you love me. Whatever it is that's got you doubting yourself and me, we'll get through it." He rubbed her lower back, and she arched away from him.

Jumping to her feet, she turned to him, fists clenched. "Don't touch me. I can't... I can't do this if you touch me."

"Honey."

"And don't *honey* me. I can't." She clawed at her scalp and lifted her hair by its roots. "There's a lot about me you don't know. I'm not proud of the choices I've made. I did some... things I'd rather keep hidden forever."

"Grace, the past is the past. It's the now that matters."

"That's easy to say when you don't know how ... messed up I am. I was."

"I love you, Grace. Nothing you can say can change that."

"Really?" For the first time since he entered her apartment, she looked up at him. Her green eyes round and scared, the whites of her eyes red as if she'd been crying. "Even after seeing this?"

She took a piece of paper from the deep pocket of her sweats and unfolded it. Brady took it from her with confusion.

A sour, bitter tang coated his mouth. The pictures singed his eyes. The woman he loved, with only a black censored line covering up her breasts—breasts he knew too well—and a skimpy black thong lay sprawled out on a bed.

According to the article, the bed of a married man, his wife pregnant with their child at the time.

Brady violently rolled his shoulders, his skin tightening with unfamiliar rage under his shirt.

"What's this?" he croaked out. "Is this true?"

She nodded, her face void of expression.

Brady closed his eyes, a poor attempt to clear his head of the images in the magazine. The other one with her wearing a barely-there dress showed her clinging to a man twice her age.

"I slept with him in hopes of getting a job in the fashion industry. He had connections."

Wadding up the clipping, he tossed it aside. "Is he backing your shop?"

"No. I didn't get a dime from him."

"And you're angry about that."

Grace sneered. "Of course not. He's slime. I'm ashamed I ever stooped that low in order to build my career. I was an idiot."

"Had you not been caught..." Brady needed to know. Was this the life she wanted? Sleeping with famous men, rich men? Traveling the world and staying in fancy hotels? He couldn't give her this life.

"I don't even have the right to be insulted by that comment. Honestly?" She snorted and shook her head, an internal monologue happening that he'd like to be a part of. "Honesty. You deserve honesty."

"That would be nice." He needed her to talk because he didn't know what to say.

He listened quietly while she told him how she first met this Robert asshole. The empty promises. Her failure at making it big in Paris.

Brady's first reaction was shock. This was the love of his life sprawled out for another man. They both knew there were previous lovers, but they didn't dwell on it. That, unfortunately, was a part of their lives.

What he hadn't expected was to learn Grace had such low respect for her body that she'd sell it to the highest bidder. His love for her, knowing how broken she'd been, wanted to hold her close and kiss her wounds.

The manly pride in him was embarrassed to be with a woman who now graced gossip magazines. Who knowingly carried on with a married man in order to advance her career.

"I'm going to need time."

"I know. I can apologize until I'm old and gray, but it won't take back who I was."

"I'm going to need some space, but we'll work through it." He still couldn't touch her, afraid he'd forgive her secrets too quickly when he needed time to process.

"Work it out?" Grace jumped back. "We can't work it out."

"We agreed when we first started dating to keep the past in the past. I would have liked to know about this before the rest of the world, but you're right—this isn't who you are anymore. This isn't the Grace Le Blanc I fell in love with."

"No. You don't love me anymore."

"Unless you've changed who you are now, yeah, I still do."

"You can't." She backed away even further, fear across her face.

"Why?"

"You want honesty. I can't do this."

"Do what? Us?"

"Brady." She closed her eyes and bit her lip. This time it wasn't a flirtatious move, but one of pure pain. "I'm not staying in Crystal Cove. I'm moving at the end of the summer. That had always been my plan. I never meant to stay."

"You're ... leaving?"

Dealing with shady pasts, he could get through, but Grace moving...

"I wasn't meant to live in a small town. As soon as people learn about my past, I'll be blackballed, just as I was in Paris. One of my designers offered me a lease in Boston. I'll be opening another The Closet store there in a couple months."

"Your store here."

"I'll hire an assistant manager and run it from afar. I'll check in when I come home to visit my family."

"You've had this all planned. Leaving us. Leaving me."

She bit her lip again and slowly nodded.

"You never had any intention of making this, making us, last."

She closed her eyes, her chest heaving, and shook her head.

His heart, his trust, his pride shattered into a million pieces in his chest. Without saying another word, he went to the door and let himself out.

And mentally said goodbye to Grace for good.

· · · ·

GOING TO THURSDAY NIGHT book group was the last thing on her mind, but Alexis gave her no choice, showing up at her doorstep and pounding on her door until Grace opened up.

"Suck it up, buttercup. You're going."

"I worked all day. I have stuff to do tonight." Which was the truth. Arianna's wealthy favorite uncle was all about supporting her and investing his money in what he said was amazing talent.

He had his attorney draw up the paperwork, and Grace hired one online based out of Portland and had her read the fine print. Sean McGregor would earn thirty percent of the profits from the Boston location of The Closet, and Grace would have free rent, only having to pay utilities.

The lease off Newbury Street had to be ridiculously high. The offer was too good to be true, but Arianna swore her uncle was legit, and her attorney said it was sound on her end.

There was a lot to do before the July fifteenth grand opening. Now that she was single she had more time on her hands. She shopped around and found stores who were going out of business and selling their fixtures dirt cheap.

Her shipment of sleek wooden hangers with The Closet burned into the side came the day before. The boxes took over her living room, but since she wasn't entertaining any type of guests, it didn't matter.

Over the past few weeks, Lily had popped in the store when she had a lull in between clients to keep Grace company. Hope and Mia had invited her to dinner. Jenna asked if she wanted to see a movie.

Grace had declined all invitations. Alexis, however, didn't get the memo and barged into the apartment.

"If you're so confident you made the right move, dumping Brady and moving to Boston, then show your face with pride. Besides, Hope is making strawberry daiquiris, and Jenna has chips and salsa."

"My hips don't need any more calories. I buy out aisle four at the grocery store every week."

"Who hasn't bought out aisle four? It's the mothership of aisles. Cookies, crackers, and all things carbs should not be nicely packaged in one convenient place."

"And did you want to drag your ass out after cleaning it out?"

"Hell no. But I did. And I made friends for the first time in my life. Come on." Alexis tugged at her hand. "We can talk about the book, or we can Google pictures of Chris Hemsworth."

"How about Henry Cavill."

"Done."

Somehow while Grace had been moving like a zombie from her apartment down the stairs to The Closet and back up to her apartment again, March turned to April and the weather from cold to somewhat cold and rainy.

She covered her head with her hands as if saving her messy bun from getting messier, and ran down the stairs to Alexis' SUV.

"I didn't even change," she said, looking down at her wet leggings.

"It's just us. Your friends."

Her friends. And she had a sister now to kick her in the ass and even hug her now and then when Grace became a slobbering mess, which she'd been every day since the afternoon Brady walked out of her apartment.

After hours and hours of crying, she'd called Alexis and told her everything. Including her plans to move away. Alexis was hurt Grace was leaving again, but this time she swore they'd keep in touch.

"Wait." Grace put her hand on the steering wheel. "Isn't it my turn to be designated driver?" They rotated roles every month, including donning the DD. It wasn't often needed, but Celeste insisted they assign one if they used her bookstore to meet. Mia's mom was gracious that way and even stopped in from time to time to discuss their monthly read.

When talk turned to men and sex, she couldn't say good-bye fast enough.

"I've got you covered. Besides. I shouldn't be drinking in my condition."

"Okay. Thanks. Wait. What?" Grace spun in her seat and stared at Alexis' belly.

"Easy. I'm an exhausted mother of a toddler who hasn't slept for more than five straight hours in nearly two years."

"Ohmygawd. Could you be pregnant? I hear pregnant women are tired all the time too."

"Heck no. Ben's okay with me not wanting any more kids. I'd never really planned on having any, but I couldn't imagine our lives without Sophie."

"She is the cutest little thing."

"Truth. And some days I worry that I'm not good enough for her. I mean, isn't it wrong of me to not want more kids? Am I selfish for not giving her a brother or sister?"

"You have to do what feels right for you and your family. There are plenty of one-child homes, and those kids turn out fine."

"I guess. But what if I'm screwing up her life?"

"Are you kidding me? You and Ben are the best parents in the world. She's blessed to have you guys."

"Don't go all sappy on me or I'll stop telling you shit."

Grace *tskd*. "Such potty talk for a mommy."

"Shut it, bitch."

Grace laughed for the first time in weeks and continued to do so as she walked through the door to Books by the Ocean.

"That's a nice sound." Lily rushed up to her and hugged her tight. "We were worried you wouldn't come, but Alexis said she'd make sure you did."

Her heart squished with kindness.

"And if you didn't show, we'd be marching our asses over and crashing your place." Mia, always so direct, handed her a daiquiri.

"We've been worried about you." Jenna elbowed Lily aside and hugged Grace. She held out her drink so it wouldn't spill, and Hope took it from her. "You don't have to talk about it if you don't want to. We've got your back no matter what."

She always liked this one. Jenna didn't say much, often declined invitations to go out. More of a hermit and quiet in her sweet and adorable way, Grace recognized a bit of hiding in her as well.

Maybe she had skeletons. Doubtful they could one-up Grace's though.

"I don't really feel like talking about it."

No one but Alexis knew the true story. Unless Brady said something. Or her friends read gossip magazines.

"Give me a hug and then you can have your drink back." Hope squeezed her and handed her the daiquiri. "Let's go sit and pretend we've read."

Two daiquiris later, they all knew the entire story, including her plan to move by the end of May.

"You said you'd be here throughout the summer," Alexis said.

"That was the original plan, but Arianna's uncle signed the papers already. I can open for business on July 15th and start setting up in June."

"That's only two months away." Lily's lower lip turned down at the corners, and she wiped her eyes. "I really like having you next door. And living upstairs. Even though I figured eventually you and Brady—shoot. I'm such an idiot."

"No. It's okay. I knew the thing with Brady was only temporary."

"It was more than a *thing.* Ty spends a lot of time at the house working on the reno. He says Brady's miserable. He misses you."

"He'll move on."

"I don't think he wants to." Of course, Lily the romantic with the newest relationship still wore rose-colored glasses.

"It doesn't matter anyway. I'm moving to Boston, and we know Brady's not going to give up his family farm to live in a city. He wouldn't last a weekend."

She still had to find affordable housing. There were a few online roommate connection sites she'd been searching through and had some possible leads.

In a few weeks, she'd drive down and meet with possible roommates and check out the apartments. Surely there were women in Boston as wonderful and supportive as those sitting here with her tonight.

"You guys," Grace kicked back her third drink, her eyes suddenly growing fuzzy. "You're the best. Will you let me crash your book nights when I come home to visit?"

"I still can't believe you're leaving. We barely had time to get to know you." Jenna leaned her head on Grace's shoulder.

That was nice. Jenna was a sweet girl.

"Well," Grace slurred. Did her friends always look like funhouse mirrors? "You can always read about me on the Internet. I found more pictures that were too risqué for even those trashy magazines."

"Oh, honey." Jenna lifted her head and took Grace's glass from her.

"Hey. I was drinking that."

"It's your fourth in less than two hours."

"It's my third. Maybe second."

"Fourth."

Geesh. Was there a stereo on in the store?

"Tomato tomah—" Tears welled up in her eyes. Everything reminded her of Brady. She couldn't stay in Crystal Cove any longer. "I need to leave."

"I got her," Grace barely heard Alexis say behind her as she stumbled out the door.

CHAPTER TWENTY-SIX

THREE MONTHS. SOMEHOW Brady had survived without hearing Grace's laugh. Without touching her soft skin. Without kissing her lips.

Hell, when she confessed the details about her life before him, he saw red. Not so much at her for being foolish and naïve, but at the asshole who cheated on his pregnant wife and filled Grace with lies, then disgraced her by sharing private pictures of her.

It would have been a hard pill to swallow, but he would have worked it out with her. Their love was strong.

If she hadn't planned on moving away. She didn't ask him to come with her. Didn't even hint they could make a long-distance relationship work. All along her plan had been to dump him and work somewhere more her style.

He should have known from the beginning. Crystal Cove, and sure as hell Marshall Farm, was not for Grace Le Blanc. His mother had been right. Grace wasn't the girl for him.

If only he could make his heart believe it.

"All that's left is the backsplash," Ty said, snapping Brady from his wallowing.

"Hm? Yeah. Kitchen looks good."

"You're a good sidekick."

Brady knew next to nothing about installing floors and refinishing cabinets, but Ty was a good teacher, and Brady had plenty of time on his hands.

Now with spring underway and his seedlings sprouting, time was not on his side. Thankfully, Brady didn't need his help anymore.

"Listen, uh, Lily and I are having a barbecue for my dad for Father's Day. The more the merrier. Do you, your mom, and Carter want to come on by?"

Carter never turned down an invitation, and his mother needed to get out. With her cancer in remission, he would have thought her mood would be brighter. Only she'd seemed more aloof and depressed than when she first was diagnosed, even if she was gaining some of her strength back.

Brady had no desire to step off the farm, ever, but he'd do it for his mom. If she wanted to go.

"I'll check with them and get back to you."

Ty unbelted his tool belt and set it on the kitchen counter. "Mind if I stick my nose in your business for a sec?"

"Will it matter if I say yes?"

"I'm not one to offer unsolicited advice."

Brady opened the fridge and took out two beers. "I have a feeling I'm going to need this." He popped the tops off the bottles and handed one to Ty. "Let's go outside."

It was a little past eight and the June sun still hung low in the sky, casting streaks of pink and purple across the horizon. He led them through the blueberry bushes, the berries starting to form in their hard green shell. In another month they'd be ready for the picking.

Funny how last year at this time he'd been content with his life. His mom didn't have cancer. He didn't pay much attention to Alexis when she'd complain about her younger sister being home.

Work had been his life. His fun. He recreation. His pastime. His chore.

All he had to show for his life was his farm. Not much had changed in the year.

Except now he had a broken heart and crushed soul to go along with it.

He and Ty crossed through the Jersey berries and into the Blue crop. "When I first met Lily I knew she was way out my league," Ty said, sipping his beer as he kept in step with Brady.

"You two are perfect for each other."

"It took a while for me to figure that out. I don't know how much you know about her past, but Lily comes from ... money." Ty seemed to hesitate a little. "She's pretty much disowned her family. You don't know dysfunction until you hear her story. Which isn't mine to tell."

"Good thing she has you and your family in her life then."

"It is. It took me a while to look at it that way. I live a simple life. My parents aren't wealthy. I didn't go off to college, and I slid into my father's carpentry business."

"You served in the military. People respect that. It's honorable." Brady sipped from his beer, not sure where Ty was going. He was a quiet guy. Kept to himself, similar to Brady.

At least, that was how it felt. It stung.

"I pretty much pushed Lily away for keeping her heritage, her past, from me. I said some things I shouldn't have said and pushed her away. It didn't take long for me to realize my life was shit without her. She couldn't help her past, and it had nothing to do with what we had together."

Ding ding. Brady realized what Ty and everyone else thought. That he was an asshole for breaking up with her because she'd made poor choices in her past. Ironically, that wasn't what tore him to pieces.

The heart to heart wasn't doing anything to change his feelings toward Grace though. She'd never intended to have a lasting relationship with him, yet told him she loved him. Strung him along for all those months and was now laughing behind his back in her fancy Boston store.

"I'm a forgiving guy, Ty. Despite what you may believe, Grace's past is not what destroyed us. It's something ... something she did while we were together. Something that can't be fixed."

"Hell. I'm sorry, man. I should've minded my own business. I figured—"

"I know. I'm sure most people assume I'm the asshole here." Shit. He didn't mean to say that.

"Grace broke it off?"

Brady curled his lips in and cursed himself. Making Grace out to be the one at fault wasn't his plan.

They finished their beers and walked the perimeter of the field and made their way back to the driveway.

"Let's just say, we were never meant to be."

"That's what I said about Lily and me." Ty handed him the empty bottle. "Thanks for the beer. Sorry for being a dickhead and sticking my nose in where it doesn't belong. You'll still come on Father's Day?"

"No apology needed. And yeah. I'll come."

He waited until Ty's truck turned at the end of the driveway, then he went inside.

"You and Ty have a nice romantic stroll?" Carter asked, pouring himself a glass of water.

"Yup."

Carter chugged the water and set the glass down. "You okay?" He wiped his mouth and filled it up again.

"Yup."

"Shit." Carter dumped the water and opened the fridge, pulling out two beers. "I thought by now you'd come out of your funk."

Brady didn't respond, accepting the beer and taking a healthy swallow. Better to keep his mouth full of the cold ale than say words he didn't mean. Or didn't want people to hear.

"You know what you need?" his brother annoyingly continued. "You need to get laid."

"Not everything's about sex."

"Says the guy who's not getting laid."

"Thanks for the brotherly chat. I'm going to bed."

"Alone," Carter called to his back. "You know. Boston isn't that far. Quick road trip. Four hours maybe? If you miss her that much you should at least see what she left you for."

His words stung.

Carter was a dumbass, but smart enough to figure out the truth. Still dumb to think Brady could pick up in the middle of blueberry season and traipse off to Boston. If he didn't have a business to run. A family to care for.

He trudged up the stairs to his room and closed the door behind him. Sinking into his bed, he sipped from his beer and sighed.

Maybe Carter was right. Maybe he should at least make an attempt to see Grace in her new life.

Maybe seeing her in Boston surrounded by traffic and tall buildings and a world of fashion, he'd realize they truly didn't belong together.

Because his heart was a traitorous thing making him think they still did.

When morning rolled around he remembered his brother was a dumbass with dumb ideas. There was no way in hell Brady could drop everything and go to Boston. Not now. Not ever.

He got up like he did every day for the past eighteen years and started his morning routine. His mother was back to hers as well, making big breakfasts, working in the gardens. Planting seedlings and often working alongside Brady pruning the bushes.

June rolled into July, which rolled into picking season. Locals were eager to pick first. He kept them up-to-date by posting on the Farm's website and Facebook pages, announcing which blueberries were ready when.

The Northland and Patriot berries had come in full and large this season. There was still a lot of ripening that needed to happen, but he opened the farm for a few hours on Monday, Wednesday, and Friday for picking.

He and Carter took turns picking up customers and driving them out in either the golf cart or the tractor—hayride style—to the ripe berries. By the end of July, he'd extended the hours to six a.m. to four p.m., closing on Monday and Thursday for ripening. The weekends were their busiest days, and he wanted to be sure the berries were in their prime.

The customers and the long days helped him not think about Grace.

As much.

She still monopolized his thoughts morning, noon, and night, but there were brief windows when a little girl asked him a question about the fake birds he'd staged throughout the farm or the slivers of soap hanging from the apple trees.

"The soap keeps the deer away," he told a little boy.

"But deers are nice."

"They are, but if we let them eat all the buds off our new trees, they won't grow big and strong and make apples for you to pick in the fall."

"Oh."

He loved how kids could either accept an answer without question or, on the flipside, ask four thousand questions. Three thousand of which he had no clue how to answer.

Today was one of those days he both loved and dreaded.

Thursday. Closed.

Too much quiet time on the farm. Too much time for memories of Grace's kindness to slither its way into his heart.

Too much time to look back on all the wonderful, self-less, beautiful gestures she did for others.

Learning to cook. Cooking for him and his family even when his mother was difficult to be around. Watching her niece even when her sister chided her. Helping Ty find an engagement ring. Being humble when she was thanked and complimented.

Brady stooped to pick at a clump of weeds at the base of a Jersey bush. The sun shone bright and warm. The farm was just close enough to the ocean to have the benefits of a breeze.

It blew past him, and he could've sworn he smelled—even tasted—a hint of floral spice.

Grace. He swallowed. Hard. It had been nearly five months since he'd seen her.

The first weeks were the most painful. He could still smell traces of her on his clothes. Even on his pillow, though, she'd never slept at his house.

Five months later he shouldn't be smelling her. Not out in the middle of his blueberry bushes. Thank God they weren't together last summer or everything blueberry—his livelihood—would remind him of her.

Pink Converse sneakers appeared in his peripheral vision. Brady swallowed again and let his gaze travel up legs.

Long legs.

Legs he'd memorized a long time ago.

Legs that had been wrapped around him. Many times.

The fringe of denim kissed the tops of her thighs. He couldn't look any higher, scared what he saw would be a figment of his imagination.

"Hey."

Nope. It was real. She was real. The sweetness of her voice floated down to him. He wasn't ready for this. There was still too much built up anger. Built up hurt.

He took his time straightening his legs and coming to a full standing position. Brushing his hands off on his thighs, he skimmed the bill of his baseball cap with his fingertips and braced himself for the path his gaze was about to finish.

A bright pink shirt overlapped the top of her denim shorts by a few inches. He thanked her fashion sense for not showing any midriff.

Tickling, kissing, skimming his hands across her stomach and on her sides was one of his favorite places to touch.

Slowly, his gaze finished its slow walk up her torso, over the roundness of her breasts. Breasts she liked to cover with her arms. Breasts she said were too small but fit perfectly in the palm of his hands.

The pink shirt dipped, stopping an inch above her cleavage. Not an inch and a half. An inch. He knew because he'd spent a lot of time kissing her there as well. And along her neck, naked and long, covered only by the wisps of hair blowing in the breeze.

Her face was exactly as he remembered it. Except for the eyes. They weren't full of life. The green irises dark and worried. The smile on her lips forced.

Brady knew the difference. The "I'm okay" smile after his mother or Alexis had offended her was a far cry from the one that lit up her face when she was truly happy.

Like on Christmas Eve when he gave her that silly flash drive of recipes. It cost him less than fifteen dollars, and one would think he'd bought her a cruise around the world.

That was a genuine smile. She loved it. And she loved him. Or that was what she'd said.

"The blueberries look awesome."

"The Jersey berries aren't ready yet." Smooth.

"I sampled some along the way. I'm not sure what type those are," she pointed to her left, "but they're super sweet. I can't wait to pick them."

"We're closed today." Again. Way to make conversation.

As far as he knew, Grace hadn't been home since she moved to Boston in May. If she wanted to be a paying customer and pick berries while visiting her family, she'd have to do it during normal business hours.

When he wasn't alone. With her. In the bushes.

"I know. I came out here to find you."

If she said she wanted to stay friends, he'd have to turn her down. He couldn't pretend she hadn't hurt him, pretend he didn't know the curves of her body, pretend he didn't still love her.

"I'm busy." He adjusted his baseball cap again and turned, heading toward his tractor which was two rows over.

She followed.

Ignoring her, he started it up and was shocked when she jumped up, resting one of her gorgeous butt cheeks on his knee. "I've never been on a tractor before."

"Grace." He shut off the ignition and slipped out from under her, hopping down to the ground. The gentleman in him reached for her hand and helped her down.

Big mistake.

Her skin was satin against his. As soon as her bright pink sneakers hit the dirt, he let go.

"What are you doing?"

"Just thought I'd go for a ride."

"No." He took off his hat and wiped his forehead with the back of his hand. "Why are you here?"

"Honestly?"

"Please. Lie to me instead." He cringed. Sarcasm was never his strong suit, and he didn't think it sounded good on him now.

"You have every right to hate me." Grace sat on the dirty bumper of the tractor, her shoulders slumped over.

"I don't hate you."

"I hurt you. Not intentionally but selfishly."

"Why?"

"If I told you I was moving away, would you have wanted to start a relationship with me?"

He'd like to say yes, but he knew it wasn't true.

"I don't know."

"I do. I did. You're not the kind of guy who takes relationships lightly. If you knew there was no chance at us being forever, you wouldn't have been interested in me. Heck." Grace stood up and placed her hands haughtily on her hips. "Why were you interested in me?"

Going over the dozen ways she brought life and color to his gray world, or the hundreds of ways she'd made him smile, made him laugh, wouldn't help his cause any.

Hell, he didn't know what his cause was anymore.

Protecting his heart. That was all.

"You didn't come here to hear what first attracted me to you."

"Maybe I did." She brushed at a stray hair caught in her lashes. Real today, not the long false ones she liked to put on. "I want to know if it's enough."

"Enough?"

"Enough to make it work. I'd like..." she stepped closer, too close, and tipped her chin up to him. Those eyes, as green as the leaves on the Jersey bushes and round as the berries growing on top, focused on him. "I'd like a second shot at ... us." She placed her hands on his chest, and he did all he could not to drop his lips to hers.

He'd like nothing better. He'd love another shot. Another opportunity to hold her in his arms again.

But then she'd leave. She'd go back to Boston to her fancy life while he dug in the dirt and watched the weather and shoveled manure over his new plants.

Getting back together would only drag out the inevitable.

"Who says I haven't moved on?"

"Oh." Grace jumped back as if she'd been stung. "Oh," she said again. "I'm sorry. I didn't know. I don't want to be..."

The other woman. It was the only way to keep the band-aid on his wounds still intact.

"Okay." Grace pulled at the hem of her shirt straightening it, along with her shoulders, with a new determinedness, and a trace of sadness in her eyes. "Before I go, can I tell you something?"

Anything. Stay. Don't ever leave.

"If you hurry."

Grace nodded. "You're a good man, Brady. You're kind and thoughtful and loyal. You're funny and intelligent. And sexy." She gave him a half-assed smile. "I hope your new ... girlfriend appreciates all you have to offer. Don't settle for anything less than you're worth. And you're worth ... everything."

"Uh. Yeah." Guilt crept up his spine. She'd feel like a fool once she found out he was just as single as he was before he met her.

"That's not what I came to say though." Grace tucked her hands in her shorts, the white pockets peeking out from under the short hem. "After high school, I couldn't get out of here fast enough. I thought this town was too small for me. I thought if I experienced a fancy vineyard in Italy I'd fall in love with my family's business. Only I discovered I wasn't meant for the business. Drinking wine was my specialty."

"Mhm." Brady didn't know what he was supposed to do or say, so he copied her and tucked his hands in the front of his jeans as well. She was stalling and he didn't like that he didn't mind.

"I've always been a bit of a clothes whore. Okay, bad choice of words there." Grace lifted and dropped her shoulders. "So then I tried my hand at fashion school."

"Grace," he interrupted. "I know this already. What is it you're trying to say?"

"I went to Europe to find myself. To figure out what I wanted to do in life. I thought I knew and then ... I didn't. When I came back to Maine it was supposed to be temporarily. I didn't think I belonged here. That's why I wanted to leave."

"Again. I know."

"No." She took her hands out of her pockets and gripped on to his forearms. "You see, I did find myself. Here. In Maine. With you."

"In Boston." He warmed under her touch, still hating the visceral reaction he had to her.

"I don't regret going to Europe. Do I regret some of the choices I made? Yes. But if I didn't go, if I'd stayed in Maine, I wouldn't have been happy. We may have hooked up, but I doubt it. I'd have always been the obnoxious, trampy younger sister of Alexis. You want to know what I learned?"

"That you love fashion, and Boston is the city you were meant to live in."

Grace shook her head. "I discovered myself. I realized I wasn't running away from my life in Maine, I was trying to find myself. I learned it's okay to be different. It's okay not to fall into the family's footsteps. I also learned to love."

Brady balled his hands into fists in his pockets, forcing them to stay put.

"I learned what it's like to have real friends. And I learned how to be a sister. I couldn't have done that if I didn't leave and if I didn't come back."

But you still live in Boston.

"That's nice."

Grace licked her lips and stepped back.

"I like who I am now. I respect that you've moved on. I won't do anything to interfere with your life, but I want you to know you'll always hold a special place in my heart."

Unclenching his hands, he slipped them out of his pockets and ran them across his face. "You'll always be special to me too, Grace."

Tears filled her eyes, and she nodded. "Thank you," she whispered. "Thank you for saying that. I'll always regret how much I hurt you. More than any of the mistakes I've made, that has been my biggest."

"Grace."

"No. Don't say anything just to be nice." She held up a hand and walked backward. "I won't get between you and your new girlfriend. If I see you on the street, if she comes into The Closet, I'll be civil. I promise."

"You're not working at The Closet anymore."

"Oh. I guess I didn't mention that." Grace flashed him with another sad smile. "Boston isn't for me. The people I love and cherish are here. I moved back home."

Brady stood like an idiot with his mouth hanging open as Grace spun around and ran down the row of blueberry bushes.

CHAPTER TWENTY- SEVEN

SHE WAS SUCH A FOOL. Of course, Brady moved on. He was perfect boyfriend and husband material. Why he had been single in the first place was a shocker to Grace.

Wiping the tears and dirt from her eyes, she looked left then right at the end of the row. Seeing Brady again had her disoriented, not only physically but mentally as well. In her mind, she thought she'd talk to him, ask him for forgiveness, and then jump into his arms and kiss him senseless.

That was how it worked in the movies.

Only Brady hadn't reacted when she touched him, except to recoil. She felt the tenseness in his chest, then in his arms. She hadn't meant to make him wince, and it hurt knowing her touch did that.

With her track record as a slutty mistress, she couldn't blame him for thinking she'd try to take him away from another woman.

Her stomach shook from tears. She didn't want to picture Brady touching another woman. Of someone else being on the receiving end of his charming smile and soft kisses.

Tears blurred her vision, and the drumming of her heart lodged its way up to her ears so she couldn't even hear her own footsteps on the gravel pathway.

"You're such a fool," she said aloud.

"No. I am."

Grace gasped and whirled around. "Brady?" She wiped under her eyes with the back of her index finger, not caring how much black mascara came off.

"I'm sorry."

"I can't possibly imagine what you have to apologize for." She sniffed, wishing she had a tissue. Pretty soon her nose was going to run, and nothing but a queen-size blanket would be able to stop it.

"Plenty." He reached into his back pocket and handed her a handkerchief.

"Guys don't carry handkerchiefs around with them anymore."

"It's a rag. Sometimes I need one working out here."

"Why?" She didn't care why. She needed to get the hell out of dodge before her face turned into a total snot bucket.

"Do you really want to know why or are you going to take it?" He shook it at her and she swiped it, not even turning around to blow her nose.

"Thanks," her voice was nasally through the rag.

"I lied to you."

"What?" Again the annoying nasal voice.

"Maybe not lied, but let you assume. I sort of implied something that was never true."

"You never loved me." Her worst fear had come true. "I should've known." Even if she and Brady couldn't be together, she could hold on to the love they once shared. If it was a sham...

"Hell! Why would you ever think that? I haven't stopped loving you since the first time I kissed you."

"Stop." Surely her raccoon eyes and toddler nose was enough to keep him at bay. "I won't be the cause for another breakup. I appreciate you saying that—"

"Hell, Grace. I don't have a girlfriend. Do you really think I could move on so quickly after everything we shared?"

"What?" She needed to hear it again. Or was she having a heat stroke in the middle of his farm? Was he a mirage? His words all in her head?

"Honey." Those hands. Big, strong, warm, comforting. Those were real. Solid and strong as they cupped her cheeks. "There is no one else."

"Are you sure?"

"Very. Are you sure you're moving home?"

"I already did."

And no one told him? "When?"

"Last week. I wanted to get everything in order before seeing you. I know I don't deserve your trust or your love, but I promise I'm not leaving again. Well, I'll go to Boston from time to time to check in on The Closet, but my home is here."

"You'll fill me in on work later. First, tell me again. You're staying in Maine? For good."

"If this is where you'll be. Yes."

Brady crushed his mouth against hers, not taking her gently like he normally did. She clutched his shoulders and held on for dear life while he welcomed her home.

When they were both short on air, he released her lips. "We agreed to keep the past the past, but I do need to know one thing."

"Anything."

Brady rested his chin on top of her head. "That morning after your prom when I found you naked out here in the blueberry bushes..."

Grace giggled. "You thought I slept with your brother."

"I found him with his pants down too."

"I won't share his secrets, but I can tell you mine."

"I don't want secrets between us, Grace."

"Me either." She took off his baseball cap and turned it backward so she had better access to his face. "I was drunk."

"Most bad stories start this way."

"And agreed to a game of strip poker."

"With my brother?"

"And some others."

"I'm not going to like this."

Grace giggled again.

"It was down to me and Shep Gagnon."

"Shep? He could eat you in your sleep. He had to be at least four hundred pounds in high school, and I don't think he's dropped an ounce since."

"Shep was nice."

"Not if he forced you to take your clothes off."

"Anyway, I thought I had him beat. I was down to my underwear and bra and bet it all. He beat my straight with a straight flush."

"Let me guess. My dumbass brother thought it would be funny to take off with your clothes?"

"Yeah. He told me where they were. I got a little lost out here when I stumbled upon ... you." She pulled his head down and kissed his lips.

"I'll never forget the image of you staggering among my blueberry bushes stark naked and drunk."

"And I'll never forget you coming to my rescue. Then and now."

"Always."

"I like that."

"Me too." That mischievous gleam in his eye twinkled back at her. "So you've never made love in the middle of my blueberry farm?"

"I can't say I have."

Brady swooped her up and tossed her over his shoulder in a fireman's carry.

"Brady Marshall, you put me down." She pounded on his perfect ass, only making him chuckle. Then, because she couldn't resist, she grabbed on to both cheeks.

"I like it when you play rough," he teased. He stopped moving and slid her down his body, his eyes and mouth hungry. "I love you, Grace. I never stopped. Even when I thought I should."

"I love you too, Brady. Always."

"Always."

And then he gently laid her in a patch of grass and showed her just how much he loved her.

CHAPTER TWENTY-EIGHT

"I MISSED THIS," BRADY snuggled Grace from behind, his words kissing the back of her neck.

"Mm. Me too. More than you can possibly imagine."

"I can imagine."

Grace turned, resting her hands between her cheek and her pillow so she could take in Brady.

"I can still see traces of insecurity in your eyes." She ran her foot up and down his calf, waiting for him to respond. "I'm happy here. With you."

It had only been three days since they'd reunited and unless they were working, they were together. After making love in his field, Brady had carried her back to his tractor and driven her back to her car with promises he'd be by her apartment later that night.

Mrs. Marshall had been in the parking lot when Brady had dropped her off and the look of shock on her face could be seen clear across town.

She was not happy to see Grace.

"I trust you." They kissed until his stomach growled with hunger.

She giggled. "I'll get us a snack. You," she got on her knees and leaned over him, "don't move."

She made a quick trip to the bathroom and then found an apple and a granola bar in the kitchen. Now that they were back together, she really needed to go grocery shopping again.

When she went back to the bedroom Brady was placing his cell phone on the nightstand.

"Everything okay?"

"It was my mom."

She crawled into bed and offered him the granola bar. "She's upset we're back together."

"I told you not to worry about it." Brady pulled her until her back and bum spooned his core.

"I don't like that I'm causing friction between you and your mom."

"You're not." His words whispered across her neck. "She knows how much you mean to me."

"She's also mortified her son's girlfriend has nude pictures circling gossip magazines and the Internet."

"I'm sure Carter's dated some sketchy girls in the past as well," he teased.

Grace bumped her butt against him. "Not funny." She was glad he could tease about it. "I don't want to be your dirty secret."

"Honey." Brady turned her so their bodies faced each other and draped his leg over hers, scooting her closer. "I don't ever want to hear you talk like that. Okay? I love you. Whatever happened before us doesn't matter. I don't know how to make you believe me."

"I do believe you. It's your mother who needs convincing."

Brady traced her jaw with his thumb. "Funny you say that."

"Uh oh. I don't like the sound of your voice."

"My mom asked if you would come to dinner tomorrow night."

"Is she going to send you on an errand and threaten me if I don't leave you?"

"What? No. She would never..." Brady shot up pulling the sheet with him. "Did my mom threaten you?"

"Not exactly."

"The day of her last chemo. The magazine." Brady slapped his forehead with the palm of his hand and clutched onto his hair. "That's what had her freaked." He dropped his hands and scrubbed them across his face. "She invited you over and sent me to the Fabric Barn so she could, what? Blackmail you with the pictures?"

"No." She saw how Brady's shoulders slumped, how his lower lip pursed low as if someone sucked the air out of his body. "She didn't threaten me, Brady. Your mom loves you and was worried about your reputation. I chose to leave. It was my idea to move to Boston long before the pictures went viral."

She hated talking about this so soon after they were finally back together.

"My mother knew all along and didn't tell me. When we broke up she didn't ask why. Didn't comfort or even bad mouth me. It was as if..."

As if Grace never existed. Best to wipe her out of his life completely.

"I'm shocked. It's not like my mom."

"Brady." Grace stroked his bare shoulder and inched her fingers up his neck, turning his chin to face him. "Your mother loves you and never intended to hurt you. She wanted to protect you from embarrassment. Don't be mad at her."

"Even now." He shook his head in dismay. "Even now, after being scorned, you're protecting her. This is why I love you. This and nine thousand other reasons."

"Only nine thousand? Pssh. Guess who loves who more?"

"I'm going to work my ass off every day to show you how much I love you."

"You do have a fine ass. I look forward to watching it work." Grace squeed when Brady flipped her to her back.

"I know what you're trying to do, distracting me with sex."

"Farmboy, you're the one who pounced on me."

"And you're the one who stole my heart."

• • • •

"IT'S NICE TO SEE YOU again, Mrs. Marshall." Grace handed her a tray of brownies—already taste tested—and searched the room for backup.

Nope. They were totally alone.

She did her best to sound casual and mask the nerves buzzing around in her body.

"Hey, you." Brady came in behind her and dropped a kiss on her shoulder. "I'm going to take a quick shower. I'll be back in a minute." He looked from Grace to his mother and gave her a look as if to say *be nice.*

"Would you like some lemonade?" Mrs. Marshall asked. "And you can drop the Mrs. Marshall bit."

Not even five seconds alone and already the claws were coming out.

Mrs. Marshall handed her a glass and padded through the living room. "Call me Dorothy," she said, completely throwing Grace off guard. "Let's sit on the front porch."

She tugged at the ancient door and sat in the closest rocker. Grace settled into the one next to her and sipped her lemonade.

Wasn't this nice? Not. Brady had better hurry the hell up.

"I was only twenty-five when I met Doug."

Okay. A trip down Mrs. Marshall, er Dorothy's, memory lane was not where Grace expected this conversation to go.

"My parents didn't approve. I had my masters in accounting and was working with a big bank in Portland."

"Wow. I didn't know." And why would she? It wasn't like the woman ever initiated a conversation with her before.

"My girlfriend and I drove up the coast one summer on a girls' weekend trip. We stayed in Rockland, where my girlfriend met a guy and, well, she hung a sock on our motel door and I had nowhere to go."

Grace sipped her lemonade and pushed her foot off the floor sending her chair into a gentle rocking motion. This story could get good if Dorothy didn't hold back any details.

"So I went for a drive and ended up in Crystal Cove. I must have run over something and had to pull over. When I got out of my Dodge Charger I saw I had a flat. Believe it or not, I was a lot like you."

An unladylike snort escaped Grace, and she spilled her lemonade on her white shorts.

"I loved shoes and short skirts. When Douglas Marshall stopped to change my flat, he swept me off my feet with one swift glance, and I was a goner."

"That's a romantic story."

"I thought so at the time. My parents were not impressed."

"Are your parents still around? Brady's never mentioned them."

"Because he's never met them. My parents said they'd disown me if I married a poor farmer like Douglas Marshall."

"Seriously?" Grace leaned forward, her eyes focused in on Dorothy as she casually rocked in her chair and sipped her lemonade.

"Daddy thought I was wasting my college degree by living on a farm. Mamma agreed. Back then a woman always agreed with and supported her husband."

"And you married Mr. Marshall and never spoke to your parents again?"

Dorothy placed her glass on the nearby table and folded her hands in her lap. "It's a bit more complicated than that. There was a lot of fighting. When Doug found out how my parents felt, he packed my bags and kicked me out of this house. He didn't want any trouble between me and my folks."

"How did Mr. Marshall's parents feel about your relationship?"

For the first time in months, Dorothy smiled. "They were like second parents to me. Eventually becoming all I had in my life. I understood where my folks were coming from. They wanted what was best. Were afraid I was settling and would grow tiresome of the farm life. A girl with an accounting degree digging in the dirt all day? Not for their daughter."

"I didn't know you before, but I can't picture you behind a desk. You look good in the outdoors."

She studied Grace, her fingers still tightly intertwined in her lap. "Do you know why I didn't want you with my son?"

Way to be direct. "Because of my reputation. Brady's a good guy. You were afraid I'd ... taint him."

"Not exactly." Dorothy brushed her hands down her thighs. "You reminded me too much of myself when I was younger."

"Me?" She would have laughed if Dorothy hadn't looked so serious.

"I loved Doug from the first moment I met him, but it wasn't all sunshine and roses. It was hard. Farm life is hard. There were days I second guessed my decision to give up my guaranteed salary for this life. My parents expected me to come running back to them when things got rough."

"Did you?

"No. And they never came to visit. Never contacted me. I wrote them when I was pregnant with Brady, but they never responded."

"I'm sorry. That must have been hard. It must still hurt."

She rocked her chair and stared out into the fields. "The first few months were bliss." A shy smile crept over her lips. "And then I had second thoughts. My pregnancy was hard, as were the winters, and I wondered if I made the right decision to leave the comfort and safety of home. What if Doug couldn't provide for me and our baby? There were times I thought about leaving."

Grace blinked back her surprise. Dorothy made the perfect farmwife. While they'd never been especially close, she'd known her forever. She'd worked her land with a smile on her face and pride in her heart.

"Did you ... did you ever leave him?"

She smiled and shook her head. "There's no way I would have made it a day without Doug by my side. He was my everything. We worked through it all together. My love for him and our children smothered the fears and insecurities I had. But you see," she turned to face Grace, "I was made for this type of work. I was an athlete, rugged, tough. You're not like that. The farm life was never meant for you. Your parents noticed that before you hit high school, and they never tried to push it on you."

No, her parents hadn't. They'd always supported her and loved her no matter her decisions. Funny how Dorothy knew that as well.

"You're a free spirit. I don't want you regretting giving up your dreams to settle here. I don't regret it. Ever. If it's meant to be, it will all work out."

"That's what you don't understand, Dorothy. I haven't given up anything. My dream was never to live in Boston or New York. My dream was to find myself. To figure out what I wanted in life. I thought it was to make it big and rich in the fashion industry but want to know where I found true happiness?"

"I have an idea."

And for the first time, Grace thought she did. Dorothy may not have come out and said it, but she had a feeling she and Brady's mom had come to an understanding.

"It's not just Brady. He's a huge part of my happiness, but I also learned to accept my failures and take pride in my accomplishments. I've made true friends for the first time in my life. My sister and I are finally close. And your son. He's given me the biggest gift of all. It's like the perfect storm of happily ever after. I can't find that in Boston or New York or anywhere else. It's all right here. I'm here to stay, Dorothy. And I hope to have Brady by my side."

"No place I'd rather be," Brady said, stepping out onto the porch, the screen door slapping shut behind him. "Everything okay out here?"

"Grace and I were having a little chat."

'That so?" He perched himself on the arm of Grace's chair and stroked her hair. "Everything okay?"

"You're going to continue working in your store?" she asked of Grace.

They'd made progress this afternoon, and now she feared it would all come crashing down again.

"I am. I wouldn't want Brady to give up what he loves, and I appreciate that he supports me in my career. Like you said, as long as we're together it will all work out."

"Your girlfriend has a good head on her shoulders. She's spunky. Treat her well." Dorothy stood up and patted Brady on the arm before going inside.

"Did she just say what I think she said?"

"She thinks your spunky."

"And she called me your girlfriend. Like she accepted we're together."

"I had a long talk with her yesterday." Brady wedged himself between Grace and the arm of the chair, picking her up and placing her on his lap. "She apologized for being territorial. I don't think her issue had ever been with you personally."

"You sure about that."

"Actually, I am. While the pictures are a bit shocking, she wasn't the least surprised you'd moved away."

"Way to hold me in such high regards."

"I overheard what she said to you. I didn't know that about my mom. Her giving up a career to work on a farm. I get it now. She was afraid you were doing the same and would regret it."

"Brady, I'd never regret being with you."

"Easy to say now when we're happy and in love. What happens in ten years when I have a huge pot belly and am bald and missing my front teeth?"

"First, you better be seeing a dentist every six months. Second, you work too hard to ever be too fat. And third, I'll still love you if, and when, you go bald."

"Good to know and right back at ya."

"Funny."

"We should talk about our future together."

"I'm not going anywhere."

"I know. But you're not programmed to do what my mom did for my dad. I don't expect you to give up your career for me."

"Who says I have to give up my career to be a farmer's wife? Just because you drive a tractor to work doesn't mean I have to."

"I hadn't thought of that."

"You thought the only way for us to be together was for me to garden and stuff?"

"You don't want to garden?"

"I'd love to have a normal garden, sure. But I can still work at The Closet and be a farmer's wife."

"Wife, huh?" Brady looped her hair around his hand and draped it over one shoulder. "You keep saying that. You planning on becoming a farmer's wife one day."

"Maybe. If the right farmer came along."

"Is that so?"

"That's very so."

EPILOGUE

"ANOTHER ONE BITES THE dust. Can't believe you got suckered into a commitment. I was holding out that you'd be my forever sidekick." Mia sighed and dropped to the couch opposite Grace. "Looks like it's just me and Jenna left. Cheers, girlfriend." She lifted her plastic cup in a mock salute and took a sip of her long island iced tea.

Once again their Thursday night book club had turned into friendly gossip and talk of love lives. Grace knew Mia was only teasing. Actually, her joke warmed her. Another example of how her girlfriends—yes, *her* girlfriends as well as Alexis'—were amazing people.

"No worries there, Mia. I'm actually more single than you. You're the one with the wild social life," Jenna said.

"Grace was my only partner in crime."

"Um, no offense?" Jenna joked, scooping up guacamole on her chip.

"What she's trying to say," Hope took a seat next to Jenna, "is that you're relationship material where Mia doesn't think she is."

Funny. Grace didn't think herself to be relationship material either. Not until she got one look at Brady's kind eyes and had been on the receiving end of his sweet kisses. Her body warmed when she thought of him.

Granted, it could be the August humidity, but she'd bet her shop it was Brady's love. Lost in memories of last night's lovemaking, she jolted when she got an elbow to the ribs.

"Hey." She balanced her drink so it wouldn't spill on her lavender shorts and gave her sister the side eye. "Easy there."

"You're going to make me not like you again if you keep going off into la-la land. It's bad enough with those two." She angled her head toward Hope and Lily.

"Oh, you're no better." Hope laughed. "It's been three years and you and Ben still act like you're on your honeymoon."

"Do not." Alexis tipped her cup to her mouth, but Grace could still see the blush on her cheeks trail down her neck.

"Ugh. You're all blinded by lust. Jenna, what are you doing tomorrow night? Want to hit up some bars? I'll even drive. Or book us a hotel."

"I can't. Jerry." She sat back and hugged a pillow to her chest.

She'd been caring for the old man for five years. It was what brought her to Crystal Cove. Rarely did she come out with them unless it was planned way in advance. Caring for a geriatric man twenty-four seven put a huge damper on her social life.

Grace hadn't given it much thought until lately. Jenna had always been the sweetest one of the group, and that was saying a lot. Lately, they'd witnessed more spunk in Lily, but she was still incredibly selfless as well.

Once again her mind wandered to Brady. The sweetest, kindest, most selfless man she'd ever met. He changed her world, her view of the world, and she'd love him for the rest of her life.

"Oh god," Mia moaned. "She's at it again."

Alexis elbowed her again. "It's my duty as your sister to keep you focused on the group and not your sex life."

"We've all been through it." Lily laughed. "Being in love looks good on you, Grace. Welcome to the club."

The six of them stood and clinked their plastic cups together. She bit her lip and grinned as she looked at each of her friends who were genuinely happy for her. Mia pretended to gag, but the light in her eyes showed she was only teasing.

The spark wasn't as bright in Jenna's eyes this time. Unlike Mia, Grace felt Jenna really did want to find someone.

And Grace would make it her mission to make sure her friends were as truly happy as she was.

THE END

ACKNOWLEDGMENTS

ONCE AGAIN THIS BOOK wouldn't have come together without my sprinting buddies. Well, it would have eventually been written, but not as quickly as it did. I appreciate the support and challenges you continuously post in our writing groups.

Thank you, readers, for filling my Facebook page with ideas and suggestions when I come begging for help. For this book, I had asked you all for cooking disaster stories. And the winner was ... Meg M! I enjoyed making Brady and Carter suffer through the garlic bulb vs. garlic clove ordeal. I'm sure I'll be working more reader cooking disasters into future books.

To Silla. I swear I know how to spell and punctuate and write a story. Thank you for being so thorough and gracious in pointing out when I don't.

Finally, thank you to my family for leaving me alone when I'm writing, and for pretending to be excited for me when I share my excitement about typing The End. I love you all dearly!

If you enjoyed *Here With You,* please consider leaving a review wherever you purchased the book. If you were gifted the book, you can still leave a review on Amazon, BookBub, and Goodreads.
I love hearing from my readers. Tell me what you think of Grace's story and what you'd like to see from me in the future! You can email me at mariannericeauthor@gmail.com. I do my best to reply to every email within a reasonable amount of time.

Did you know I have a PERMA FREE book? Yup, *Sweet on You*, book one in the Wilde Sisters series, is always free, and *False Start*, book one in the McKay-Tucker Men series is only 99 pennies! I share these specials (and so much more!) with my newsletter subscribers. Sign up today and you'll receive a link for a FREE copy of *Smoke & Pearls*, and you'll be the first to know when I have sales, new releases, and giveaways.

Sign up here: http://www.mariannerice.com/connect.html

Check out all the Well Paired Novels:

At First Blush here: http://smarturl.it/s58mzq

Where There's Hope here: http://smarturl.it/
wherethereshope

What Makes Us Stronger: http://smarturl.it/WhatMake-
sUsStronger

You can find many more titles by Marianne Rice by going to her webpage: http://www.mariannerice.com/books.html

• • • •

<u>The McKay-Tucker Men Series</u>
<u>http://www.mariannerice.com/mckay-tucker-men.html</u>
False Start
False Hope
False Impressions
<u>The Wilde Sisters</u>
<u>http://www.mariannerice.com/wilde-sisters.html</u>
Sweet on You
Then Came You
Wilde For You
<u>Rocky Harbor Series</u>
<u>http://www.mariannerice.com/rocky-harbor-series.html</u>
Staying Grounded
Strawberry Kisses
Wounded Love
Playful Hearts
<u>Well Paired Series</u>
<u>http://www.mariannerice.com/well-paired-novels.html</u>
At First Blush
Where There's Hope
What Makes Us Stronger
Here With You
<u>Christmas Series</u>
<u>http://www.mariannerice.com/marshmallows—mistle-toe.html</u>[1]

---

1. http://www.mariannerice.com/marshmallows--mistletoe.html

Marshmallows & Mistletoe

Don't miss out!

Visit the website below and you can sign up to receive emails whenever Marianne Rice publishes a new book. There's no charge and no obligation.

https://books2read.com/r/B-A-LKSE-SPHX

BOOKS 2 READ

Connecting independent readers to independent writers.

About the Author

Marianne Rice writes contemporary romantic fiction set in small New England towns. She loves high heels, reading romance, scarfing down dark chocolate, gulping wine, and Chris Hemsworth. Oh, and her husband and three children. You can follow her all over social media, and keep up to tabs with her latest releases on her website: www.mariannerice.com

Read more at www.mariannerice.com.

Made in the USA
Lexington, KY
12 November 2019

56900392R10214